Merrychurch Mysteries by K.C. Wells

Truth Will Out

"…an enjoyable, feel good cozy mystery. Great for a trip, or a rainy fall afternoon where you can curl up with your furry four-legged buddy and a cuppa something hot. I'm looking forward to the next in the series."

—Gay Book Reviews

"I loved it and cannot wait for the next one, and I highly recommend it!"

—The Novel Approach

"*Truth Will Out* is a rather quintessential British mystery…. I look forward to more adventures in Merrychurch."

—Joyfully Jay

Roots of Evil

"It's a good mystery, but with fun, snark and sassiness that only K.C. can provide in her way."

—Love Bytes

"A good mystery, a murder, a list of potential killers, and Mike's and Jonathon's minds. It was captivating and funny."

—OptimuMM

A Novel Murder

"I found (book three) just as lovely and enjoyable as the first two books."

—Dear Author

"If you haven't had a chance to read this series, you are missing out. I hope K.C. plans to write more in the future."

—Love Bytes

By K.C. WELLS

Published by DREAMSPINNER PRESS
www.dreamspinnerpress.com

IN HIS SIGHTS

K.C. WELLS

DSP PUBLICATIONS

Published by

DSP PUBLICATIONS

5032 Capital Circle SW, Suite 2, PMB# 279, Tallahassee, FL 32305-7886 USA
www.dsppublications.com

In His Sights
© 2023 K.C. Wells

Cover Art
© 2023 L.C. Chase
http://www.lcchase.com
Cover content is for illustrative purposes only and any person depicted on the cover is a model.

Trade Paperback ISBN: 978-1-64108-480-2
Digital ISBN: 978-1-64108-479-6
Trade Paperback published May 2023
v. 1.0.0

Printed in the United States of America

Acknowledgments

My thanks to my beta team, as always.

Special thanks to Jack Parton for his knowledge of Boston.

EXTRA special thanks to Geoff Symon for his invaluable assistance and for putting up with countless messages. That went above and beyond. Thank you, Geoff.

IN HIS SIGHTS

K.C. WELLS

CHAPTER 1

Boston, MA. Tuesday May 15, 2018

DETECTIVE GARY Mitchell took one look at the naked dead man lying facedown on the bed and his day officially went to shit.

Aw Christ, not another one.

The bedroom was an eerie carbon copy of the previous crime scenes. A small bottle sat on the nightstand, and Gary didn't need to see the label to know it contained GHB. On the bed beside the body were a tangle of red rope and a pair of handcuffs. He glanced at the rug, and sure enough, there was the soiled condom. Gary returned his attention to the deceased, noting the marks on the wrists and ankles, just like the previous victims.

This one struggled too. At least until the drugs kicked in. It was all supposition until the autopsy, but Gary saw no reason why the killer would change his MO. It hadn't gotten him caught so far, right? Why change a winning formula? The thought made Gary's blood run cold.

But what made his heart sink was the bloodstain on the corner of the white sheet that covered the guy's lower back.

"We've already taken photos of the scene." Detective Riley Watson picked up the condom with his nitrile-covered hand and dropped it into an evidence bag, then sealed it. He scowled. "God, I wanna catch this bastard." He scribbled on the label, noting the time.

Gary didn't respond. There was no need. They all wanted that.

Detective Lewis Stevens stood next to Del Maddox, the medical examiner. Lewis stared at the sheet, then raised his gaze to meet Gary's. "Wonder what it's gonna be this time?"

"Maybe he's obliged us by signing his handiwork," Del muttered. He pulled back the sheet with care and sighed. "Here we go again."

A letter *X* was carved into the victim's lower back.

"Done before death occurred, like the others?" Gary inquired. The amount of blood pointed to that conclusion.

Del nodded. "Looks like he used the same implement too."

Lewis grimaced. "Jesus. I hoped we'd seen the last of this guy."

"You and me both." Riley peered at him. "I bet it's days like this that make you sorry you ever left Vice. Chelmsford PD get a lot of these kinda cases?"

Lewis shook his head. "Never saw anything like this."

"Give it time," Del observed. "You've only been in Homicide for what, four years? Wait till you've been at it for as long as I have." He gazed at the deceased, and Gary noted the compassionate glance. "He could be my age."

"Can we save the chat for later and concentrate on doing our jobs?" Gary's stomach roiled, and a rock had taken up residence in his chest.

Lewis was silent, but his scowl said plenty. Riley gave a respectful nod and withdrew to talk to the uniform boys.

Del glanced at the nightstand. "Thoughtful of the killer to leave the drug. Now I know what to look for in the tox screen. Except if he's anything like the previous victims, there'll be a whole cocktail of drugs inside him." He addressed Gary. "How many of these guys do we have so far?"

"He's number five." Another one to add to the board. *Any more and we'll need another board.* Gary couldn't suppress his shiver.

Del pursed his lips. "So, five letters now. Anyone succeeded in making a word from the previous four?"

"None that make any sense."

"The killer's probably a Scrabble player with a list of obscure words." Both Gary and Lewis gaped at him. Del pushed out another sigh. "Sorry, guys. I'm as gutted as you are, but humor is my default when I don't want to think about a maniac being out there." He gestured to the body. "Help me roll him so I can take a look at the front."

The three men gently rolled the body with a care that was almost reverential. The man's wide staring eyes threatened to unravel Gary's self-control, and he had to force himself to shut off his emotions and look at the body objectively. The victim was maybe in his mid to late forties, with a salt-and-pepper beard and dark brown hair tinged with silver at the temples. A handsome man who'd clearly kept himself in good shape.

I hope you didn't suffer. Except Gary knew it was a false hope. The knowledge that he'd been cut before death and the bruising on the guy's wrists and ankles were grim indicators to the contrary.

Del gestured to his assistants who were standing to one side, maintaining a respectful silence. "Okay, boys." They lifted the corpse and placed it in an open body bag. Gary watched as they zipped it closed, obliterating his view of that staring face. They hoisted the bag onto a stretcher before carrying it out of the apartment. Riley bagged up the cuffs, rope, and bottle and handed them to one of the assistants, along with the bag containing the condom, to accompany the body to the morgue.

Del stripped off his gloves. "I'll get onto this one first thing tomorrow morning." He peered at Gary. "I'll see you there?"

Gary nodded. He knew Lewis wouldn't attend. He'd barfed at his first autopsy, and that was the last time he'd visited the morgue.

Del followed his assistants to the front door. The police officer let them through before reattaching the yellow tape that barred entrance to those neighbors who tried to get a glimpse. The officer was polite but firm, and the rubberneckers soon gave up.

Gary's hackles rose. *Yeah, someone is dead. You can read all about it in the media tomorrow.* Christ, number four had made the headlines before the ink was dry on Gary's report. He breathed deeply. His energies were best directed to the case.

Riley came over. "The victim's name was Marius Eisler, age forty-five." Gary's stomach clenched, but he pushed down hard on the momentary flash of nausea that always accompanied a surge of grief.

Keep focused.

Riley continued. "The body was discovered at twenty-three-hundred hours by the guy from the apartment next door, one Billy Raymond. He had a key. He said Marius had a habit of working late and not eating properly, so Billy regularly dropped by with food. He didn't see anyone. Uniforms have questioned everyone on this floor, but no one saw our man."

"Too much to hope there are cameras?" Gary asked.

Riley snorted. "Sure, they have cameras in the hallway downstairs, but they don't work. The neighbors said there were always guys coming and going."

Lewis rolled his eyes. "Another queer? Now *there's* a surprise." Riley fired him a disgusted glance.

Gary didn't bother reining in his glare. "I'm going to pretend I didn't hear you say that. Now why don't you go speak with Sergeant Michaels? See what else you can learn about the victim, the building…."

Lewis's brow furrowed, but he went without a word.

Gary breathed a little easier. He didn't need Lewis's shit right then. He scanned the bedroom. "No sign of a cell phone?"

Riley shook his head. "Just like the others. We've searched the whole apartment." He gazed at the rumpled sheets on the bed. "I'll bag these too." Riley glanced toward the door with a distant stare. "This was one talented guy. Did you see his paintings?"

Gary hadn't seen a thing. He'd been in too much of a rush to prove that nagging feeling in his gut wrong.

One look at the blood on the sheet had confirmed his fears.

"Our killer's not in any hurry, is he? Five bodies in two years." Riley's shoulders slumped. "I really thought he was done. Nothing since December."

Gary had hoped the same thing. "What worries me is those letters. How many bodies are there going to be before whatever it is he's spelling out begins to make sense and we get a lead?" Because so far they'd had precious few of those.

He walked into the living room, leaving Riley to remove the sheets from the bed, and paused to get a feel for the place. The heavily varnished wooden floor and oak furniture gave the apartment an elegant appearance. It wasn't cluttered, and judging by the size of the windows, Gary imagined it would be a light, airy room in the daylight. Every inch of available wall space was taken up with paintings of men. Some of the models were clothed, but most were nude or seminude, and all of them were good-looking. An easel stood by the window, a table next to it on which sat an open box filled with squeezed tubes of oil paint. A glass jar filled with dirty liquid held three long thin paintbrushes, and there was a palette covered with blobs of paint, a layer of clear wrap laid over it. A couple of rags smeared with colors sat beside the palette, and the odor of turpentine lingered in the air.

Gary went closer to look at the canvas sitting on the easel. It was a detailed study of a middle-aged man, clothed, sitting in a wide armchair, the same chair that stood beside the comfy-looking couch. The artist had yet to work on the clothing; the model's shirt was blocked in solid colors, shades of dark and light.

And now he'll never get to finish it.

Riley joined him. "According to the neighbor, this is how the victim earned his living. I googled him. Pretty well-known artist. I'll see what else I can find out tomorrow." He inclined his head toward the door. "The CSIs are here to dust and document the scene."

Beside him, Sergeant Rob Michaels cleared his throat. "I'll secure the scene once all the evidence has been removed."

"Thanks, Rob."

Lewis came over to them. "I don't think there's anything else we can do here."

Gary had to agree. The day had almost ended, and he was in dire need of sleep. "I'll see you both in the morning. You can write your reports then." He bade a good-night to Rob, and once the officer at the door had let him out, he hurried along the hallway to the stairs, stripping off his gloves and stuffing them into the pocket of his jacket. Some doors were open, and residents peered out as he passed.

Gary paid them no mind. He was too busy thinking about their victim.

Please, God, let us catch him. Don't let there be a number six.

GARY LET himself into his apartment and bolted the door behind him. The silence that greeted him held none of its usual comfort.

He knew why. All the way home, his head had been filled with thoughts of Brad. No, even before that. Memories of his late brother had suffocated him all day, to the point where he'd struggled to maintain his focus.

He'd have been forty-five today. The same age as Marius Eisler. It had taken every ounce of effort not to react when Riley had revealed the victim's age.

Gary trudged into the kitchen and peered into the fridge, not that he wanted anything. The neatly stacked microwave meals, bottles of iced tea and water, and foil-wrapped lump of cheese made the fridge's interior appear as minimalist as his apartment.

Despite his fatigue he wasn't ready for bed yet. Gary filled the kettle, then opened a cabinet to remove the box of chamomile tea. Its fragrance always soothed him, and right then he was in need of soothing.

When are we going to get a break? He loathed the hollowed-out feeling that pervaded each time he confronted their lack of success. The killer was either blessed with unholy luck or phenomenal planning skills. *How can he slip by unnoticed? Surely* someone *must have seen him.*

If they had, they had yet to come forward.

Sure, the police had the guy's DNA, thanks to the condoms, but he wasn't in the files. He left no prints, a fiber here and there, and appeared to have chosen victims who had a steady stream of male visitors. Lieutenant

Travers had already intimated that the chief was making noises about bringing in more men. The shit had hit the fan after the discovery of victim number three, Geoff Berg, when some bright journalist had worked out all the victims were gay men.

Worked out, my ass. Someone leaked it.

The headlines had screamed Killer Targets Gay Men! for a couple of weeks, but as the months passed and no more bodies turned up, things quieted down. Thank God the letters had remained confidential. They had one tool left for weeding out the crank confessors. But that didn't relieve the resulting pressure Gary and his team found themselves under once news had gotten out.

The kettle whistled and he turned off the gas. As he poured water onto the tea bag, his phone pinged, and he glanced at the screen.

Still coming Sunday?

What the hell was his mom doing awake at this hour? Except he knew that was a stupid question. She'd been a poor sleeper for the past twenty-three years. As usual, cold fingers traced a path around his heart at the prospect of the monthly ritual of Sunday lunch. He hated himself for even thinking like that. Seeing his parents shouldn't be a burden, shouldn't fill him with apprehension.

But it did. And he knew he'd go, because not to would be unthinkable. Unforgivable.

He typed with his thumbs. *Sure*. There was no reply, but that was typical of his mom. Her texts were always succinct and infrequent.

Gary took his tea and went into his bedroom. He placed the cup on the nightstand. The closet door stood ajar, and Gary moved toward it without thinking. He stepped into the closet and headed for the built-in drawers. He paused, his hand on the knob, his heart racing.

Will it help?

He ignored the quiet inner voice. He opened the drawer and removed the folded sweater, inhaling as he held it close. Whatever scent it had possessed had long since disappeared.

Gary returned to his bed and sat in the center, pillows stuffed behind him. He buried his face in the soft yarn.

I'll find him, Brad. I promise. I haven't forgotten about you.

The reminder was etched onto Gary's skin.

CHAPTER 2

I PICKED UP the red pen and walked over to the wall. "Goodbye, Marius," I intoned as I crossed out his face. Where the two thick strokes met, they obliterated his mouth. "Pity I couldn't have done that when you were alive." Anything not to have to listen to him drone on about his painting.

The four photos to Marius's left bore the same red cross. I gazed at the image on the right, enjoying the tingle that started in my chest, then spread outward. My stomach fluttered. Waiting was murder.

I grinned at my own joke. I had time to enjoy the intoxication a while longer, to bask in the radiant, fierce joy that had accompanied each death.

Marius's departure had been particularly delicious.

Once he'd gotten over his initial surprise—like the rest of them—he clearly relished the prospect of getting me in his bed. He wasn't on his guard. Why would he be? He knew me, after all. So easy to slip the Rohypnol into his glass and watch as he drifted into unconsciousness. And when he awoke, bewildered to discover he was naked, bound, and gagged, he'd pulled against his bonds. The sharp scratch as I administered the ketamine only added to his befuddled state.

I saw him resign himself to the act that was to follow. It was almost a pity to disillusion him.

Almost.

I waited until I'd filled him to the hilt before leaning forward to whisper in his ear.

Enjoy it. This is your last fuck. Because when I come?
You die.

And there it was, the ultimate thrill. Not penetrating that tight hole, not driving myself deep into him—that was an act to be *suffered*, not enjoyed. Even carving into his flesh brought merely a trickle of expectation. No, the anticipation of taking his life, of knowing he was unable to struggle against his bonds… *that* aroused me to the point of ejaculation.

I shivered. There would be time enough to dwell on Marius. The elation was still overwhelming. Another one gone.

I was in no hurry. My days had taken on a familiar pattern.

Erase one of those sluts from the planet.

Watch the news.

Add more names to the list.

Cross off the names of those who'd eliminated themselves.

Lay the groundwork for the next one.

Wash, rinse, repeat….

Only seventeen more to go. Seventeen men, out of a field rich with possibilities. The world would be all the better for the loss of those twenty-two souls. I'd have preferred a total of twenty-six, but it wouldn't fit.

Then again….

I might change my mind when I reach twenty-two. There are plenty of men to choose from, after all. And why stop if I'm getting away with it?

I gazed at the photo that took center stage, framed with bare wall, the images of my victims—actual and potential—kept at a distance so as not to taint it with their presence. Men like them had tainted him enough.

They're going to pay for what they did. And I've got nothing but time.

My gaze alighted on the image I'd already picked out. A definite possibility. My only difficulty?

I'd waited five months between victims, and it had been torture. It didn't matter that it had been the shortest time span thus far. I didn't think I could wait that long again. Not while the heightened emotions of the kill lingered still. Not with all those faces staring at me from the wall.

Not with *his* face gazing at me. His voice in my head.

"I'm doing this for you," I whispered. "To avenge you."

I had another motive too, one that suffocated me, haunted me, but I knew of one way to assuage that emotion.

I smiled at the image I'd selected. A handsome face with bright eyes and a firm jaw.

"You're next."

CHAPTER 3

Wednesday, May 16

DEL ARCHED his eyebrows as Gary walked into the morgue. "I thought I'd have seen you earlier than this. You're three hours late." He gestured to the sewn-up Y-incision. "Or did you stop by to complement me on my needlework?"

"I'm here for the edited highlights."

Marius Eisler lay on his back, the Y-incision the only visible evidence of the autopsy. Gary had watched Del at work on a couple of occasions and knew the reinforced thick twine that closed Del's cuts concealed the heavy-duty, leak-proof plastic bag containing the organs, hidden from sight in the empty chest cavity.

"Body fluids have already gone to Toxicology, but we know what I'm looking for."

"Your initial findings?" Gary knew better than to ask for more than that: It would be a while before the full autopsy report was finalized.

"As you correctly surmised, the letter was carved into the skin prior to death." Del's gaze bored into him. "And we know this how?"

"By the wound. Prior to death, the heart is working and blood is sent there. It has a different color, and the wound is significantly bloodier. After death, it's paler, more… withered, and there's less blood."

Del smiled. "Full marks, Detective. Good to know you've been listening. Although I'd expect nothing less from one of Boston's finest homicide detectives."

"I know there was a condom, but—"

"But you assume nothing, which is how it should be," Del interjected. "And yes, penetrative sex took place prior to death."

"Can you tell if it was nonconsensual?" The bruising on Marius's wrists and ankles appeared darker against the pale skin.

"Hard to tell." Del frowned. "Who's to say rough sex isn't consensual? There's some abrasion, some internal bruising, but nonrough sex can create some injury. What *you* want to know is if there was an

overabundance of injury. There wasn't. As for the body fluids, I'll test for
GHB, Rohypnol, ketamine, and barbiturates, although we found no GHB
in the previous victims." His gaze flickered to the body on his table. "This
one likes his routines." He frowned again. "So why does he leave the
GHB at the scene? He doesn't leave any trace of the other drugs he uses.
Is it some kind of message?"

Gary glanced at the table before meeting Del's gaze. "I'll be sure to
ask him—once I catch the bastard."

"WHERE HAVE you been?" Lewis demanded as soon as Gary walked
into their office space.

Gary came to a halt. "One of us had to go talk to Del. Did *you* want
to do it?" As if he didn't know the answer to that one.

"Okay, so I had a weak stomach that one time," Lewis countered.
His mouth went down at the corners. "Travers wants to see us all, ASAP.
Riley's already in there."

Aw crap.

Gary had a feeling a ton of shit was about to roll downhill, aimed
right at him.

Without a word, he followed Lewis to the lieutenant's corner office.
Riley sat facing Travers's desk, its surface invisible to the eye, hidden
beneath an explosion of paper, folders, and coffee cups. Gary gave it a
cursory glance before meeting Travers's stern gaze.

"It may look like the aftermath of a robbery, but trust me, it's
organized chaos. I know where everything is, and I can lay my hand on
anything in seconds."

Gary held up his hands. "Hey, I didn't say a word." He knew better.

"Your expression said enough." Travers pointed to the empty chairs
next to Riley. "Sit." No sooner had Gary's ass touched the worn leather
seat than Travers launched into his controlled rant. "So now we've got
five bodies, and we're no closer to discovering who's trying to wipe out
Boston's entire gay population." As usual, Travers didn't raise his voice.
He didn't need to. His clipped tone was sharper than a razor, honed by
years of practice.

"Hey, we don't know—"

Travers cut Riley off. "He's killed five. Who knows when he'll stop?" He picked up the folded newspaper from the top of a pile of others and tossed it at Gary. "We made ink again. Only now it's worse. The press has gotten hold of the stuff about the bondage gear. Great. That's just great." He squeezed the words through his teeth.

"I know you're pissed," Gary said, "but—"

"Pissed?" Travers glared at Gary. "I'm not pissed. Trust me, when I reach pissed, you'll know about it. The only thing saving your asses right now is that it hasn't gotten out yet about his little calling card. We've already had three guys stroll in here to confess to the killings, and Lord knows, that's only the start."

He sounded as weary as Gary felt, and Gary was bone tired. He'd slept little the previous night. Every time he closed his eyes, two men's faces swam there: Marius, staring at him before they'd zipped him into the body bag, and Brad.

Except Brad was never far from Gary's mind. There were occasions when he'd realize with a hot flood of remorse that he hadn't thought about Brad for a couple of days.

That was when the sweater would come out of the closet.

"We're exploring every avenue," Gary ventured. "We've pulled all the records—"

"I know what you're doing. I've read the reports." Travers scraped his fingers through his graying hair. The lines around his eyes seemed deeper than usual. "You're in here because the chief feels we can be doing more."

"Hey, if the chief has any suggestions, let's hear 'em." Gary folded his arms, his jaw stiff, a dull pain pulsing through his temple.

Travers mimicked his stance. "Actually? He has one. There's a psychic who's worked with NYPD and Chicago PD."

What the fuck?

Gary gaped at him. "You're kidding."

"Nope, not even close. Chief says this guy's gotten results. So he thinks we should bring him on board. Guy by the name of Dan Porter."

Lewis snorted. "Hey, we could give my grandmother a call. She reads stuff in tea leaves. Or there's this woman who claims she can tell the future from dropping asparagus onto the floor and looking at the patterns it makes when it falls. Maybe *she* can find our killer. Want me to go to the store for a shit-ton of asparagus?"

Travers glared at him. "I'll try to remember not to repeat your suggestions the next time I get called into the chief's office." He sat in his chair, elbows on the desk, his fingers steepled, his gaze locked on Gary. "I know how it sounds." His low, earnest voice was clearly an attempt at mollification. "I was as incredulous as you, but I've done some checking. Dan Porter appears to be a genuine psychic."

"Is there such a thing?" Lewis retorted.

Travers ignored him. "His results aren't flukes, that's for damn sure. I don't claim to know how he does it, but he's helped cops solve crimes. And *that* came from the chief. He's been in contact with NYPD and Chicago to make sure the reports were accurate." Travers sagged in his chair. "All I'm saying is, maybe we should talk to the guy. It can't hurt, right?"

Gary struggled to breathe evenly, his stomach clenched. "No. We are *not* resorting to mumbo jumbo, voodoo, or any other new age happy crap."

Beside him, Lewis nodded. "The chief may go in for all that hogwash, but come *on*. We're the professionals here. We know how to catch this guy, and it's by good old-fashioned detecting."

Gary had to fight hard not to stare at Lewis. *Well fuck, we agree on something*.

Travers's face hardened. "Then get out there and detect. I don't want you coming in here and telling me victim number six has just shown up." He stood, reached for a coffee cup, and went over to the pot that sat in the corner.

Apparently they were done.

They trooped back to Homicide, and Riley perched on the edge of Gary's desk. "Okay, that was the last thing I expected."

"I know, right?" Lewis rolled his eyes. "You think the chief is smoking something that smells kinda funny? Because to come out with that horseshit…."

Gary huffed. "I'm not even going to give it headspace. Let's go look at the evidence from the apartment."

They headed for the tiny room they'd taken over after the discovery of body number three, Geoff Berg. It was nothing more than a closet with delusions of grandeur. One wall was obscured by the whiteboard covered in photos from the crime scenes.

"I'm getting some coffee. Want some?"

Gary gave Lewis an absent nod, his attention drawn to the photo of Marius Eisler. *Talk to me. Tell me what I need to know. Help me find this guy.*

"I'll have some too, thanks for asking," Riley hollered after him. "Asshole," he muttered once Lewis was out of sight.

Gary ignored him. Travers's suggestion had sent his mind in a direction he did *not* want to travel. He could still hear his parents' voices.

This one looks genuine. Why not give them a try?

What if they can tell us what really happened?

Don't you want *to know?*

Of course Gary had wanted to know. He'd ached to yell at his parents, to tell them they might as well pour their money down the drain for all the good it would accomplish. Those people were all fakers, charlatans, the whole damn lot of them.

"Where'd you go, boss?"

Gary blinked. Riley's eyes held amusement. Gary forced a smile. "For the millionth time…. Okay, I'm older than you, and I've been a detective longer than you, but that does *not* mean you have to call me boss. Hell, *you've* worked Homicide almost as long as I have."

Riley smirked. "Well, I'm not likely to call *Lewis* boss, now am I?" He clammed up as Lewis came back into the room, three cups held awkwardly.

Gary took one. "First step should be to get onto Grindr, Scruff, all the usuals. See if Marius was a subscriber." Except he knew getting access to records took time.

Riley made a note. "I'll do a search for his phone records too. I did check online when we were at the apartment. Marius didn't show up on either Grindr or Scruff."

"Which only means wherever his phone is—if it's still in one piece—the killer has removed the battery."

Lewis added, "And when we actually *get* the Grindr stuff—because it's an even bet this guy had it on his phone—I'll start the process of working through it, looking for any contacts with our list of crossover guys. God knows there's enough of them." He grimaced. "Can these guys not keep it in their pants? Seems like they're forever banging each other."

Whatever good opinion Lewis had engendered with his forthright remarks to Travers dissipated in a heartbeat.

Gary speared him with a hard stare. "Keep your opinions to yourself and keep looking. Anyone stand out so far? Someone we need to look at more closely?" He tapped the whiteboard. "Any luck on identifying our mystery guy?"

"Nothing so far. Still a dead end. But there *are* a couple of new guys who caught my attention."

"Great. We'll look at them." He sipped his coffee, his head still reeling from the chief's absurd suggestion. "A psychic. Now I've heard everything."

He stood in front of the whiteboard. Marius Eisler stared back at him, and Gary could almost hear his voice.

Find the monster who did this to me.

CHAPTER 4

DAN PORTER awoke with a jolt, hurling words into the darkness that surrounded him. "Don't go! Not yet!"

Useless words. The dream was over.

Except Dan knew deep down it was no dream, felt it all the way to his *soul*.

He flung back the damp sheet and sat up, tremors still rippling through him. *This is not fair.* The vision—because that was all it could be—was unchanged from its previous incarnations. Some higher cosmic force clearly thought it acceptable to send him the *same fucking vision* for *thirteen fucking years*.

At least he didn't get it every night. Sometimes Dan would go for months without it. What followed *those* stretched-out periods was nothing but stark fear.

What if I never get it again?

What if I never get to know why *I keep having it?*

What if I never learn who he is?

Those fears outweighed any feelings that some… thing was treating him unfairly. He'd rather have the vision than nothing, because he lived in hope that one day….

It always began the same way. Dan was on all fours on a bed, a rumpled sheet beneath him, and some unseen figure was behind him, sliding into him. The friction was exquisite, as was the scent that permeated the air around them, a hint of patchouli and a woody aroma he couldn't place. Now and again his mystery partner would move, covering Dan with his warm body, and it was then that Dan would see the man's forearm with its tattoo. No images, just two words: *Never Forget*.

Dan's heart pounded as it did during every such cryptic encounter. He longed to see the guy who alternated between fucking him with passion and making slow, lingering love to him, but there were no mirrors in the vision. Everything was distilled down to touch, smell, and sound.

The man's breath tickled his skin. His fingertips brushed against Dan's nipples, tweaked them, tearing groans from his lips. His lips grazed Dan's neck, his shoulders, his back. His grunts mingled with Dan's, and they were noises of pleasure, desire, lust....

And with each sensual encounter, Dan knew, from balls to bones, that he was safe. On awakening he yearned to sink back into the vision, but it never replayed more than once a night.

I want to meet him. I need to know if he's real.

Dan rubbed his chest, his fingers sliding through sweat. He traced the line of his scar.

Is he as real as this?

CHAPTER 5

Sunday, May 20

GARY SWITCHED off the car engine and sat, hands on the steering wheel, gazing at the house. Its cream exterior, sloping roof, red-brick chimney, and warm red roof tiles made it appear inviting, a home.

Which only goes to prove how deceptive appearances can be.

The external temperature had to be in the mid-to-high seventies, a beautiful day in Springfield, Mass., but Gary knew once he crossed that threshold, none of the day's warmth would make it inside. The sunlight would do battle with his mom's blinds and curtains, and the blinds and curtains would emerge victorious.

He gave himself a swift mental kick. *I'm not being fair.* Then the front door opened, and Gary's procrastination was at an end. His dad stood in the doorway, arms by his side, no hint of a welcome in either his expression or his body language.

Get in there and do your duty. Because that was all this was, pure and simple. A duty visit. Every time Sunday lunch rolled around, he'd drive an hour and a half—if he was lucky—hoping that in the intervening days since his previous visit, something had changed. He'd sit there in his car, staring at his childhood home, the same thought as always in the forefront of his mind: *This time it will be different.*

He'd learned to live with disappointment.

Gary got out of the car, locked it, and walked along the path that led to the gable-ended front porch with its gleaming red front door, its curved stone steps, and its two stumpy pillars, on top of which sat terracotta pots containing manicured shrubs. The house was asymmetrical, but the front yard was not. Trimmed bushes squatted in front, small and rounded on either side of the steps, larger and more oval toward the corners of the house. Gardening had become his dad's only pursuit since retirement, but it wasn't a passion with him. Gary knew better. It was merely a means of keeping his mind occupied.

I'm just the same, though. Work kept the pain at bay. And when work ended....

He raised his hand in greeting, and his dad's nod lightened his heart a little.

"Hey." Gary smiled. Then he remembered, and turned on his heel to return to the passenger seat for the flowers he'd chosen.

"You didn't have to do that." Dad's flat tone drifted across the front lawn as the bouquet came into view.

"I wanted to. As soon as I saw the lilacs, I knew Mom would love them." Their delicate color stood out against the cream roses and pink carnations.

Dad's smile was a welcome sight. "Yeah, she will." He stood aside to let Gary enter, then closed the door behind them, barring both sunlight and warmth from entering. "Your mom's in the kitchen."

Gary sniffed. "Is that roast chicken?"

Dad's wry chuckle evaporated yet more of the tension that had been building inside Gary since he'd left his apartment. "Is it Sunday?"

It was an old joke. The menu hadn't changed since he was a kid, when he and Brad would—

He swallowed, trying to dislodge the lump in his throat.

Mom stepped into the hallway, her eyes brightening momentarily at the sight of the flowers. "How pretty. Thank you." She accepted his kiss on her cheek and took them from him. "I'll put them in water." As she retreated into the kitchen, she called out, "Shoes."

Gary fought the urge to roll his eyes. Telling her he was thirty-eight and capable of remembering such ingrained routines would have cut no ice.

"I was out back, cleaning up." Dad inclined his head toward the rear. "Come see what I've been doing."

He followed his dad through the dining room to the french doors, their path flanked by the sideboard and the piano, both surfaces covered with framed photos. Gary didn't glance at them, not even once, because he knew each by heart, the same as he knew once a week, his mom would take out a soft cloth, pick up each and every one of those frames, and wipe them with care and love.

They are *pleased to see me.* He knew that too, but he was also aware theirs was a perfunctory reception. He wanted to yell at them, to break through the seemingly impenetrable wall of sorrow they'd erected around themselves. He wanted to shake them, to look them in the eye and shout that they still had him.

In the end, he'd do none of those things. He'd share his news, they'd talk about current affairs, what was happening in the neighborhood, his dad's numerous and constantly evolving plans for the garden, but they were going through the motions.

Nothing got through.

They died when he did.

GARY PUSHED his plate away, conscious of his mom's gaze on his half-eaten meal. He'd been hungry enough when they sat at the table, but the sight of that empty chair killed his appetite. Mom hadn't set places for four, but she might as well have done; an unseen figure had joined them, one who didn't eat, didn't speak, but whose chill presence could not be ignored.

One day. I'll break through one day. Because I'll find that bastard, and then *you'll see me.* Then *you'll know me again. And Brad will be at peace.*

It was Gary's mantra, one he believed with every fiber of his being. He loved his parents, and *dammit*, he wanted them back, the laughing, smiling couple who'd lit up his childhood.

The couple seated with him had died twenty-three years ago but somehow were still functioning, still shuffling through life, not living but existing.

My parents, the zombies. Except the thought contained no trace of humor.

"So are you any nearer to catching this guy?" Dad asked when Mom went into the kitchen to fetch the coffee.

Gary blinked. They *never* asked about his job. "We're working on it."

"That doesn't sound positive. He's killed five now, hasn't he? There was another one a few days ago."

"Yes."

Dad frowned. "Well, judging by what I've read in the papers, he's running rings around you all."

Then it must *be true, if it's in the news.* Gary knew better than to say such words out loud.

Dad wasn't done. "The Boston Strangler managed to kill thirteen women before they caught him. You're not going to let this maniac get *that* far, are you?"

"Dad… I can't talk about this, okay?"

Dad ignored him. "So who's in charge? Who's leading the investigation?"

Gary counted to three before answering. "That would be my squad."

It was Dad's turn to blink. "Oh."

Gary's ribs felt too tight, his stomach too heavy. That hollowed-out feeling was back with a vengeance. *The first time he wants to talk about my job, and why? To tell me I'm not doing enough. I'm not good enough.*

And just like that, he knew that when he left them, he wouldn't go home. He had to do something to end the day on a better note.

I need Cory.

He'd stick it out for a couple of hours; then he'd make his excuses and leave.

Gary didn't imagine for one minute they'd be begging him to stay longer.

HE SCANNED Cathedral Station's patrons, those at the bar or seated at tables, but there was no sign of Cory. Music pulsed through the floor, and voices rose to be heard above it. The happy scene felt incongruous after the frostbitten hours he'd spent with his parents.

That's why I'm here. He wanted to smile, laugh, chat….

He wanted to feel normal again.

Gary pulled his phone from his pocket and composed a quick text. *I give up. Where are you?*

Seconds later a reply pinged back. *The patio. I've got you a drink.*

Bless him. Gary pushed his way politely through the crowd and stepped out into the early evening air. Cory waved from a table next to the trellis festooned with a huge Pride flag, ivy curling its way upward and outward through the wooden structure. Black parasols covered the tables, and a railing separated them from the street. When Gary reached the table, Cory got to his feet and gave him an exuberant hug.

"What was that for? Not that I'm complaining," Gary added as Cory released him. Gary feigned pain. "On second thought, I think you cracked one of my ribs." He sank onto one of the metal patio chairs, and before he could stretch out a hand for the frosty glass of beer waiting for him, Cory placed it in his grasp.

"You look like you need that. The hug too." Cory cocked his head. "I don't have to ask how the parental visit went, do I?"

"No, you do not." Cory knew the score. Gary took a long drink. He glanced at their surroundings. "Don't look now, but I think you brought us to a gay bar."

Cory snorted. "You bet your fur it's a gay bar. And don't give me that. You knew exactly what kind of bar it was. You're a cop in this city— you know *every* bar. Besides, I didn't get a text from you saying no, no, no when I suggested it."

Of course he'd known.

"Why go to a dull and boring bar? The eye candy is *way* superior here." Cory gave a nod to someone over Gary's shoulder, his eyes gleaming.

Gary speared him with a look. "Down boy. We are *not* here to find you someone to go home with."

Cory pouted. "Spoilsport. If I'd known that, I wouldn't have worn this little ensemble." He gestured to his tight jeans and even tighter tee. "This is my best hookup gear."

"Do you spray those on?" Gary coughed. "You got your nipples pierced, I see." The sight unfurled something deep in his belly, a sudden rush of heat he couldn't explain. Then Cory's words sank in. "I can't believe you're still saying that."

"Saying what?"

"You bet your fur. You were coming out with that in tenth grade. Stephen King has a lot to answer for." Cory's obsession with *It* had lasted beyond high school.

Cory glared. "Don't you diss my hero. I treasure that book, especially after the movie came out."

"Surely that paperback has died by now. The back cover was already hanging off by the time we graduated."

"God bless stationery tape." He sipped from the tall glass filled with greenery.

"What *is* that you're drinking? A mojito?"

Cory rolled his eyes. "You just sit there and drink your nice but boring heterosexual beer, and I'll drink my *fabulous* cocktail." His eyes twinkled. "Except we both know the beer is a smokescreen, and the only reason we've stayed friends for so long is because you're a closeted gay man who has the hots for me, but who's never found the nerve to come right out and reveal your true feelings." He grinned. "Pun most definitely intended."

Gary laughed. "Yeah, that must be it. You see right through me." Cory's laughter mingled with his.

Sarcasm aside, Cory would never know how close he'd skated to the truth.

In the years since high school, Gary had come to accept that his attraction to Cory must have been a fluke—he was straight, after all—although it had felt only too real at the time.

And sometimes, he wasn't sure that attraction had entirely gone away.

Cory narrowed his gaze. "And for the record? There is nothing wrong with gay bars. Some of my more memorable hookups have been the result of a couple of hours in a gay bar." Another tilt of his head, those blue eyes locked on Gary's. "But you didn't ask me to meet you for a drink so we could discuss my awesome sex life. What's up?" His gaze grew warm. "Or is it because you saw them today?" When Gary didn't reply, Cory sighed. "It was bad, wasn't it?"

"No worse than usual. In fact, for one moment I thought it was better—until my dad basically asked me why I wasn't doing my job."

Cory choked, and wiped his lips with his napkin. "What the fuck?"

"You heard me."

"That really pisses me off."

"Hey, forget it, okay?"

"Why? *You're* not gonna forget it, are you?"

Gary shook his head. "No, but none of these good-looking guys are going to want to take you back to their place if your pretty face is all screwed up."

Cory gave a smug smile. "I'm pretty, am I?"

"Prettiest personal trainer in Massachusetts."

He preened. "Damn, you know how to make a girl feel good." Cory took another long drink. "I'm not stupid, you know," he murmured as he set his glass down on the table.

"Huh?" Gary frowned. "What are you talking about?"

"I know why you really wanted us to meet."

"Please, do tell. Because I didn't realize I had an ulterior motive." Except that was a lie. He'd needed a dose of Cory, and it had been too long since their last meetup.

He grounds me. He always had, even when they were teenagers. Gary had clung to him when his world blew up, and Cory had been there for him ever since.

"I read the papers, Gary. I see the local news. A guy out there is targeting gay men. And then you just *happen* to ask me to meet you for a drink?" He froze. "Did you want to warn me? Do you know who we should be looking out for?"

Aw shit.

Gary took a deep breath. "No. I can't tell you that because we don't know. Yet." But maybe Cory had nailed it. Maybe deep down, Gary had wanted to know his first crush was safe, that he wasn't taking risks.

Cory regarded him in silence for a moment, and with each passing second, Gary's stomach knotted. *Don't see too much. Please.*

Finally Cory leaned back in his chair. "I work damn hard, and yes, I play hard too. But... I don't date strangers. Even if I find a guy on Grindr, I'll check him out, see if anyone I know has been with him. And if someone I know has passed him my name and number, that's a safe bet too. We all look out for each other."

"Then I guess the gay network failed the five dead guys, because someone obviously wasn't looking out for them." The knot in his belly loosened a little. *He's being safe.* Safe was good. He gave Cory a speculative glance. "Did you know any of them? Had you dated any of them?"

Cory bit his lip. "*Dated*? How sweet. I hardly think my nocturnal activity could be called dating." His Adam's apple bobbed. "But since you're asking... yeah, I hooked up with a couple of them. Trey Hopkins. He was the first victim, wasn't he, two years ago?" Gary nodded. "And I hooked up with Vic Zerbe too. We actually came here last Christmas. We danced our feet off, then fucked till the wee small hours." Another swallow. "Three days later he was dead."

"How come you never told me?"

Cory blinked. "Because it's your job. Because when the news broke that all the victims had been gay men, I thought you'd only worry. But like I said... I'm a careful kinda guy. I don't even proposition my clients, and believe me, that takes some strength of will because some of them are fucking *gorgeous*." He drained the last of his mojito. "And also, because it's been a while since we did this." He leveled an accusatory glance at Gary. "You haven't even been to look at my new apartment, and I've invited you three times."

"Well, I'm here, aren't I?"

"And I bet you couldn't even tell me where I'm living now."

Gary put his hand on his chest. "Okay, you got me. I'll visit soon, all right? Now, what other news do I need to catch up on?"

"Nina's engaged."

Gary grinned. "That's awesome. Who's the lucky guy? Have they set a date yet?" Cory's little sister had been a royal pain in the ass when they were in high school, but she'd blossomed into an intelligent, beautiful woman Gary didn't get to see enough of.

"He's called David, he's an engineer, and he's crazy about her. And no, no wedding plans yet."

"What about you?"

"What about me?"

"You still young, free, and single?" Gary snorted. "Oops. Scratch the young part."

Cory gave him the finger. "Bitch. I'm thirty-eight, same as you. Way too young to settle down." His eyes held amusement. "We talked about this, remember? I'm busy looking for the next guy to play with." He folded his arms. "And what about you?" Before Gary could respond, Cory placed his hand on his heart and heaved an exaggerated sigh. "Oh, I forgot. You're single because you're already hopelessly in love—with me."

"That must be it." Gary smiled. "Do you know how rare we are?"

Cory arched his perfectly sculpted eyebrows. "A gay man and his closeted cop friend?"

"Jerk. I mean, we were best friends in high school, and we still are." Cory glanced over Gary's shoulder again with a clearly coquettish expression, and Gary gave him a mock glare. "Hey, I'm right here."

"And I'm flirting, so hold your water." He chuckled. "I think my luck is in."

"Another potential notch for your bedpost?"

"Honey, please." Cory had his eye roll down to an art. "Nothing so crude. We're digital these days."

"You're careful, aren't you? I might be straight, but I know there are nasties lurking out there. And if you're seeing a lot of guys…."

Cory laughed, a bright sound that turned heads and gained him a lot of appreciative glances. "Aw, I'm touched. You care." He patted Gary on the knee. "Well, you don't need to worry. Every three months I get to pee in a cup, have a legalized vampire draw blood, and I get swabbed at both ends." He grimaced. "Joy. Only I don't get the finger poke anymore, not now they take blood." He pouted. "Pity." Cory picked up his empty glass and made loud coughing noises. "I'd hate to cross a desert with you."

Gary laughed. He stood. "Same again?"

Cory beamed. "Please. And when you get back, I can tell you all about the hunky guys I get to work with."

"To quote you—joy." Not that Gary minded. He could sit and listen to Cory talk for hours. He'd walked into the bar with a load on his shoulders, and Cory had taken all that weight and drop-kicked it out of sight. Monday morning was only a matter of hours away, but he wasn't going to think about work.

When Monday arrived, he'd walk into that room, five faces would stare back at him, and Gary would pull out all the stops to ensure another face didn't join them.

For this hour or so, he'd do his damnedest to blot out their silent entreaties.

CHAPTER 6

Monday, May 21

GARY SCOWLED at the evidence board. "Why do I get the feeling that right now our guy is laughing his ass off? We've got his DNA from four of the crime scenes. He could've taken the condoms with him, but he didn't. So why leave them unless it's to taunt us?"

"He knows he's not in the files, that's why," Riley remarked. "It's weird. He leaves his spunk but not his prints."

A *clacking* sound followed. Gary twisted to look at him and blinked. Riley had a bag of Scrabble tiles on the desk and had five of them lined up in front of him. "What's your best word score so far?"

Riley snorted. "Looking better by the minute. *X* is worth eight points." He shuffled the tiles, then pushed his glasses higher on the bridge of his nose. "I'm gonna make a prediction, though. I think his next letter will be *T*."

Gary peered at the tiles. E-X-P-E-R. "Which is probably how he sees himself. And *we're* just the jerks who can't find him." He locked gazes with Riley. "Except there isn't going to be a next, is there? Because we're going to catch him before then."

Riley gave a solemn nod. "From your lips to God's ears, boss." He got up from his chair and wandered over to join Gary. "I've been looking at the intervals between deaths." He pointed to the first photo. "March 2016, Trey Hopkins. Then nothing until December that year." He rubbed his stubbled chin. "Why did he wait eight months? Did he only intend killing once and then changed his mind?

"We won't know the answer to that until we catch him."

Riley stabbed a finger at the next photo. "He waits six months and then does it again. Another six months. And then goes to five." He glanced at Gary. "You spoken to Kathy Wainwright about that?"

Gary nodded. "I know what you're thinking. Does this mean he's gotten tired of waiting so long between victims? I asked Kathy the same question."

"And what was our hot police psychologist's opinion?"

He gaped. "Excuse me? One, you shouldn't talk about her like that, and—"

Riley grinned. "Hey, she already *knows* I think she's hot. I asked her out."

"When was this?"

"Last month. She turned me down, in case you're interested. So what did she say?"

"She couldn't give me a definite answer." He cocked his head. "Why'd she turn you down? You're a good-looking dude."

"She said something about not being a cougar." Riley pushed out an exaggerated sigh. "And there you have it. My hopes of being the boy toy of a sexy older woman, dashed."

Lewis strolled into the evidence room. "I finished going through all the statements from the residents in Marius Eisler's building. I'm beginning to think this guy has Harry Potter's invisibility cloak." He flopped into a chair.

Gary's stomach gave a slow roil. "Let me guess. No one saw anything."

"Yup. They all said the same thing. Always a stream of different guys in and out of there. Some had to be models, of course. But maybe some were hookups too. He might've painted 'em then fucked 'em. Or it could have been the other way around." Lewis's eyes glinted. "Maybe sex got his creative juices flowing." He pulled his phone from his pocket and peered at the screen. "One woman did report seeing a guy in a hoodie the night Eisler died. She can't describe him, though. She said what they all said: 'Just another one.'"

Riley headed for the door. "I need caffeine." He waved his hand as he left the room. "Yeah, I'll bring you some too."

Lewis snickered. "You've got him well trained."

Gary stared at the board. "He's a good cop." The three of them had worked together as a homicide squad for the past two years.

"I called you last night."

"I saw that when I got home. Had my phone switched off as I wasn't on call. I figured if it was urgent, you'd have called again." The last thing he'd wanted to do was talk to Lewis.

"Since when do you switch your phone off?"

Gary raised his eyebrows. "Not that it's any of your business, but I went out for a drink with a friend."

"That gay guy again? The personal trainer?"

Gary narrowed his gaze. "Okay, a couple things I want to say here. Do you label *everyone*? Are we all reduced to gay, fat, skinny, pretty, ugly…? Do you ever refer to someone as *that straight guy*?"

Lewis shrugged. "I look for the distinguishing characteristic. You got a problem with that?"

He had more than a few issues with Lewis, but none he was about to share. As a cop he got the job done, but with no flashes of inspiration. Lewis plodded through his cases, dotting the i's and crossing the t's.

I don't have a problem with the way he works. I have a problem with the way his mind *works.* Now and then what came from that mouth had a tinge of ugliness to it—nothing too overt but enough to leave a sour taste. Certainly not enough to be worth reporting. And while Gary and Riley might have gone out on the weekend a couple of times, Lewis had never received a similar invitation and never would.

"Next question. How do *you* know who I was drinking with?"

"I heard you talking with Riley one time. He wanted to change gyms, and you recommended this place where a friend worked. Cory something or other? You were talking about him, where you met, stuff like that."

Gary took in Lewis's pinched expression, his pursed lips, the flush in his cheeks, and realization slammed into him. *He's jealous. Pissed that he didn't get an invite when Riley and I went out.* But Lewis came out with all the guys when they went bowling or drinking. *We're not joined at the hip, right?*

He regarded Lewis with wry amusement. "So you figured I had to have gone for a drink with Cory because I only have one friend?" Gary was done talking about this. "Let's get back to work. We need to find this guy."

"Except finding him is like looking for a proverbial needle in a haystack." Lewis gazed at the photos on the board. "We still going with the theory that he's using Grindr to choose his victims?"

"It fits the facts. He picks men who have a steady stream of sexual partners, where a guy going into the victim's place is an everyday occurrence so no one bothers to look at them. All our victims were on Grindr—well, we assume Marius was. We'll know more when they send us the records."

"He's trying to slow us down by taking their phones, isn't he?"

"Possibly. There's another possibility, though. What if he contacted them *outside* of the app? WhatsApp maybe? Conversations are encrypted, so we wouldn't see those—unless we had their phone."

Lewis scowled. "Do you know how many guys there are so far on our crossover list? Two hundred, and they all hooked up with each victim. Two hundred profiles to go through, interviews, alibis to check...."

"And one mystery guy who could be our man." Gary pointed to the slip of paper Riley had printed and stuck on the board. Kris Lee Arill. His name had shown up in the Grindr records for all the first four victims—only as messages expressing interest, no requests to meet—and they wanted to find the guy, if only to eliminate him from their inquiries, but there was a problem with that.

Kris Lee Arill didn't exist.

No phone records in that name, no address, no social security, nothing. He was on Grindr, but the account was fake, and the photos on his profile were images from the internet. Fake accounts were nothing new—especially if an individual was trying to track down some Grindr troll—but Grindr was obliged to comply if the police or FBI wanted to know what email address was associated with the account in order to trace it back to the originator.

Kris Lee Arill's email was fake.

Gary and Riley had come up with a workable theory. Grindr usually asked for an email or a phone number for verification when setting up the account. The fake email would have been jettisoned as soon as the account was verified, and if need be a phone number added that would not need verification. The jettisoned and deleted email could still be used as the login. The phone number could be a burner phone account, prepaid in cash and signed for with a fake name and ID.

"If our victims got together with this Kris, he was careful not to set up meetings in the app. So he had to have found another way to contact them."

Riley came back into the room with three steaming cups. "So far we've assumed there could be a legitimate reason why our Mr. Arill is hiding his true identity," he mused. "He could be a married man with a family, and he doesn't want his secret life getting out. If his wife or partner checks his phone.... A lot of gay guys come out late in life. Maybe he *can't* come out. Maybe he's in the public eye, and he thinks this could harm his rep."

Gary nodded. "That makes sense."

"And I've been thinking."

Lewis chuckled. "Did it hurt?"

Riley ignored him. "Our guy's setting us a puzzle, and this one's got a few pieces. Firstly, the same items have been found at every crime scene—the GHB, rope, and cuffs. We all agree they're important."

"Maybe Del Maddox is correct, and they're a message," Gary suggested.

"But then there are the letters. So what if his name is another puzzle?"

Lewis frowned. "What do you mean?"

He sat at the desk, grabbed the Scrabble bag, and tipped more tiles onto the wooden surface with a *clack*. Riley spelled out Kris Lee Arill, then proceeded to move the tiles around. "The *K* makes it a little easier. I mean, how many twelve-letter words contain the letter *K*?"

Lewis got onto his phone. He snorted. "About ninety-nine."

Gary stared at the tiles. "Who's to say it's one word? It could be two, three, four...."

Riley nodded. He pushed four tiles out on their own, spelling K-I-L-L. "There's the most obvious four-letter word. Except he's not gonna be *that* obvious, right?" He went back to shuffling the tiles.

"Why haven't we done this before?" Lewis demanded.

Gary knew the answer to that one. With each new victim, they'd identified men who had been in contact with them, but there was no evidence to point to them meeting their mystery man, so that was what he had remained—a mystery. They'd exhausted all the genuine leads, and there was nothing to go on with Arill.

A dead end.

"You're right, you know," Riley murmured. He raised his head and stared at Gary. "He *is* laughing at us." He shivered.

Goose bumps broke out on Gary's arms. "What is it?"

"I take it back. He *is* that obvious. And it's two words."

Gary frowned and walked around the desk to stand behind him. He peered at the tiles, and his stomach heaved. There was a sour taste in his mouth. "He's not planning on stopping anytime soon, is he?"

Riley shook his head. "You're not getting it. His name is linked to *all* the victims." His eyes were wide. "Don't you see? He knew what he was going to do, right from the start."

The black letters were stark against the white plastic.

S-E-R-I-A-L K-I-L-L-E-R

CHAPTER 7

Thursday, May 24

"NICE PLACE you've got here." The latex gloves were in my pocket, and I fought the urge to slip my hand into it, to brush them with my fingertips.

The guy beamed. "Thanks. I like it."

I glanced at the bookcases. "I'm guessing you're an avid reader." The spines revealed our tastes were nothing alike, but I wasn't there to talk books. I was simply biding my time until the perfect opportunity arose.

"I wanna talk about you." He looked me up and down in obvious approval. "This is a different look for you." His eyes gleamed. "Not complaining."

I managed a shrug. "I prefer casual." It was an effort to sit still, and my heart hammered. *Not yet. Wait.* I'd already decided when I was going to make my move, but the anticipation made my blood zing and my body tingle. Maybe it was because so little time had elapsed since the last one.

Is it too soon?

I guessed not. I'd anticipated wariness—that would have been understandable in the circumstances, given that it was only nine days since my latest victim had been discovered—but I watched him relax visibly as soon as he saw me at the door. *We're one big happy family, aren't we?* It had been so easy to slip names into my text, names I knew he'd recognize and trust.

Foreknowledge was a wonderful thing.

You think you're safe. You think you can trust me.

He was about to find out how wrong he was, on both counts.

He cocked his head. "You know, you were the last person I expected to see." He grinned. "Especially as you look nothing like the pic you sent."

"Yeah, well… I had my reasons for that."

"I didn't even know you were gay. You're not out, are you?"

I matched his grin. "Like I said… reasons. Was I a good surprise or a bad one?"

That gleam was back. "Oh, definitely a good one. In fact, can I make a confession?"

"They say it's good for the soul, don't they?" *And your soul is going to need all the help it can get.*

He leaned forward in a conspiratorial fashion. "Every time we meet? I can't help fantasizing about you."

"Me?"

He nodded. "Never believed I'd get my wish, though."

I could see him getting more comfortable, bolder…. *He feels in control.*

Perfect.

I leaned forward until my mouth was inches from his. "And what did you wish for?" I whispered. I could flirt too.

His direct stare locked onto my face. "You in my bed." His hand was on my knee, drifting higher. "Your dick up my ass."

I grinned. "Well, you know what they say. Be careful what you wish for." *Because you're going to get it, just not the way you expect.* My blood thrummed, my senses heightened. *Stick to the plan.* I pointed to the empty bowl on the coffee table. "Did we eat *all* of them?"

He laughed. "I guess you like sour cream and chive pretzels. Well, there's plenty more where they came from." He gave my thigh a squeeze. "I'll be right back." He got up and walked into the kitchen, his firm ass swaying.

I waited till I heard the cabinet door open, then added Rohypnol to his glass. I gave it a quick swirl, then stuffed the bottle into my pocket, my heart surging into overdrive.

"Hey," he called out from the kitchen, and I froze. "About that dick pic you sent… please, tell me that was yours."

I relaxed. "You're about to find out."

"Tease."

When he returned, the bowl refilled, I speared him with my most seductive smile. "And speaking of getting in your ass… is it gonna be tight?"

His eyes sparkled. "You bet your fur."

CHAPTER 8

Friday, May 25

RILEY STUCK his head around the door, and one glance at his face was enough.

Gary's heart plummeted. "He didn't wait five months this time, did he?"

His pained expression was answer enough. "I spoke with Rob Michaels. He's already at the scene, and the medical examiner is en route. An apartment in Jamaica Plain. And yeah, it looks like our guy's handiwork."

Gary grabbed his jacket. "Where's Lewis?"

"He's at the car."

They hurried through the building, neither of them speaking. Gary's mind raced, however. *Ten days. Ten freaking days since the last one. Jesus.*

Lewis was already behind the wheel and didn't waste time talking once they'd clambered in. The oppressive silence in the car wound itself around Gary's chest, tightening like a boa constrictor, gripping him until he fought to breathe.

"Why?" he murmured at last. "Why so little time between killings?"

"The last one made it into the media before we could blink. Maybe he gets off on seeing his work in print, in the news." Riley stared out of the window as they hit Riverway. "I thought we had more time."

"So did I." One thought occurred to Gary, and he was reluctant to give voice to it for fear the act would somehow talk it into existence.

"What's on your mind?" Riley's quietly uttered question was yet another indication that more often than not they were on the same wavelength.

"What if he's got a taste for it?"

Lewis snorted. "I think five bodies already told us the answer to that question."

"Yes, but five murders spaced far apart. Now this."

The low evening sun glinted on the calm waters of Jamaica Pond on their right, and it felt wrong that what promised to be a beautiful evening was about to be ruined with an unlawful death. Lewis turned left onto Pond Street, then a couple more lefts, until they pulled up outside two square red brick buildings, a path between them leading to a white portico. Two squad cars and the medical examiner's car were already parked on the street, together with an ambulance. A police officer hovered by the entrance, and they strode over to him.

"Third floor, Detectives. We've sealed off access, and we're interviewing the residents."

Gary glanced at his badge. "Thanks, Dietrich." He led the way into the building. They took the stairs in a hurry, and when they reached the third floor, yellow tape barred their way.

Officer Knox let them through. "On the right, guys." Beyond the door was another officer, talking quietly with a man seated on a chair, dressed in shorts and a tee, his head in his hands. "He found the body," Knox told them. "He works with the deceased. Guy didn't show up for work this morning, didn't call to say he wasn't coming in. His boss tried to call but got no reply. That was totally out of character, so the boss got worried and sent this guy to check. When there was no answer at the door, he called the building supervisor, who let him in." The officer's face was pale. "He said his boss wouldn't usually do something like that, but with another murder last week and knowing this guy was gay…."

"He thought he'd make sure everything was okay," Gary surmised. They walked to the door, which was ajar, more tape across it.

"Evening, guys." Rob Michaels met them as they entered the apartment's narrow hallway. "The body's through here." He indicated the door directly in front of them.

As soon as Gary stepped into the living room, he froze. "Oh God."

"What is it?" Riley was at his side.

Gary couldn't breathe. Facing them was a bookcase, its shelves filled with books, framed photos, and ornaments. *No. No. It can't be.* He walked over to the shelves, unable to take his eyes off the photo in its brightly colored frame.

"The deceased's name is Cory—" Rob started.

"Peterson," Gary croaked. Numbness stole over him, and pain speared through his chest.

"How did you know that?" Rob asked.

"Oh dear Lord," Riley whispered. He peered at the photo. "That's… that's you."

"Disney. Florida. 2001. We went there to celebrate my birthday." Fuck, he was cold. He turned to face Rob, who swallowed, his eyes filled with compassion. "I want to see him."

"That's not a good idea," Lewis muttered.

Gary gaped at him. "I want to see him."

Riley touched his arm. "Okay, okay." His voice was soothing.

"Didn't you recognize the address?" Lewis asked.

Gary shook his head. "He'd recently changed apartments." It felt as if a razor blade had lodged in his throat. "Last Sunday he was complaining I hadn't visited him yet." *Well, I finally got here, only, I was a little too late.*

Rob pointed to a door. "He's in there," he uttered in a hushed, respectful tone.

Moving as if in a dream, Gary followed Riley into the bedroom. Del stood beside the bed, gazing at the figure lying facedown, his face to one side, naked but for the pale blue sheet covering his ass and lower back.

The blood stood out against the pastel shade.

Dull eyes stared at nothing.

"He's been dead at least eighteen hours, but less than twenty-four at a guess," Del observed. "The muscles haven't released yet from rigor. I'd say he died last night."

"Del, for Christ's sake, hush," Riley ground out. Del blinked, his eyebrows arched, and Riley indicated Gary with a slight tilt of his head. "He's Gary's friend."

"Jesus." Del paled. "Gary, I'm so sorry." Then he frowned. "Should you be in here?"

"No, he shouldn't," Lewis gritted out. "And he's leaving right now."

Gary ignored him. "Another letter?" When Del didn't respond, Gary shuddered out a breath. "Was there another letter?"

Del nodded. "A *P* this time."

"There goes my theory," Riley murmured.

"Any signs of forced entry?" Gary demanded. He strove to put a lid on his emotions. His stomach clenched, and he fought the nausea that threatened.

"Gary…." Lewis's voice was uncharacteristically soft. "Dude, you can't be here."

He wasn't looking at Lewis or Riley or the nightstand or anything else. All he could see was Cory's face.

Riley tugged on his arm. "Come on."

Gary allowed himself to be led from the room, Lewis following them. Lewis grabbed one of the police officers. "Take Detective Mitchell home."

His words pierced the fog. "I'm not going home."

"Then back to the precinct. Anywhere but here. Riley and I will stay. Okay?"

Riley's eyes were kind. "He's right."

"I'm not leaving." Gary's jaw was tight.

"Yes, you are." Lewis locked gazes with him. "You have a personal connection to the victim. And you're not thinking straight." He addressed the officer. "Lomax, take him back to the precinct. I'll inform Lieutenant Travers of what's going on."

There was nothing to do but leave.

Gary walked out of the apartment, not hearing a word Lomax was saying. His foot slipped on a step and he stumbled, but Lomax grabbed his arm and held on to him. By the time they were outside, he couldn't fight the nausea a second longer. His stomach heaved, and he threw up onto the grass, retching, bent over until all he could taste was bile. His stomach muscles ached.

"Detective?"

Gary straightened, and Lomax held out a paper tissue. He took it without a word and wiped his lips. "Thank you," he croaked.

"I've got a bottle of water in the squad car."

Gary followed him to the car and waited as the officer opened the passenger door for him. He got in, still so fucking *numb*. Lomax handed him a bottle, and he drank a few mouthfuls.

"You keep that." The officer waited, and when they didn't move, Gary glanced at him. He pointed to Gary's waist. "Your seat belt."

The ache in Gary's throat hadn't eased. He fastened the belt with a click, and the car engine burst into life. They pulled away from the curb.

Gary leaned against the headrest and closed his eyes, grateful for the silence that fell. *Cory. Cory. You told me you played safe.*

Not safe enough.

His body and mind wanted to shut down, but he fought them, fought the emotional numbness that settled on him, a stifling blanket he wanted to throw off but lacked the energy for.

Did he know his killer?

Did he trust *his killer?*

Then such questions were shoved aside, and all he could think of was Cory standing beside him at Brad's graveside, Cory's hand wrapped around his, Cory at the prom, looking fucking *edible* in a tux, so breathtakingly handsome that the sight of him robbed Gary of speech. Cory and him bowling. Cory and him in college, drinking long into the night, putting the world to rights.

Cory flirting with every cute guy who crossed his path. Cory flexing. Cory swimming.

Cory—dead.

He wanted to cry, but he'd be damned if he was going to do that in a squad car with an officer he'd just met.

A hand nudged his arm. "We're here."

Gary thanked him, got out of the car, and headed for the elevator that led up to Homicide. The doors slid open, and Lieutenant Travers stood there, arms by his side, his face grave.

"Let's go to my office," he said in a low voice.

Gary knew better than to argue. He followed Travers to his corner office and waited while Travers closed the door. He pointed to a chair, and Gary sank into it. Travers went over to the filing cabinet. "You like bourbon, I recall."

Gary managed a nod.

Travers reached into the top drawer and removed a bottle and two glasses. He poured about two fingers into each glass, then walked around the desk to hold one out to Gary.

"Drinking on duty?" Gary murmured.

"You're not on duty, not anymore. When we've finished talking, you're going straight home."

Gary didn't argue. He'd expected as much.

Travers sat in his big chair, his glass in his hand. "I'm so sorry, Gary."

"Not as sorry as I am."

"Tell me about him."

He gazed at Travers with widened eyes. "Really?"

Travers nodded. "Bottling it up doesn't help, so let it out. How long had you and Cory been friends?"

"Since high school."

"Lewis said he was your best friend."

That one word in the past tense nearly broke him. "He was. Cory knew me inside and out. He was there for me when I needed someone." He took a mouthful of bourbon, wincing when it hit the back of his throat. "You know what I told him the last time I saw him? Which was Sunday, by the way." Six days ago. *Christ....* Gary inhaled deeply. "I asked if he had any idea how rare we were. I had a ton of friends in high school. Dated a few of them. And once I graduated, I never saw them again. Cory? That's a different story. We stayed friends. We were roommates in college when I attended Northeastern."

"And you stayed friends all this time?"

Gary shook his head. "We lost touch when we graduated. Not sure what happened there." That wasn't true. He'd thought Cory had gotten into a relationship with a guy who turned out to be very possessive. "We got out of the habit of meeting up. Then when I left the police academy, I looked him up." Mr. Possessive had dumped him, the bastard, and they'd regrouped.

"What did Cory do for a living?"

"He was a personal trainer. He worked in a gym in Brookline. He even got me to take out a membership, and we'd work out together." Despite his aching heart, Gary smiled. "That didn't last long."

Travers sighed. "Been there, done that, lost money. I could never keep up the effort either."

Gary took another mouthful. "You were right."

"About what?"

He sagged into the chair. "Talking helps." Except he knew when he got home, the glue presently holding him together would dissolve and he'd be a mess.

"Why did you meet him on Sunday?"

Travers was an okay guy, but that didn't mean Gary was going to share stuff about his folks. "It had been a while, that's all."

"You sure that was it?" Travers gave him an inquiring glance. "You don't think maybe you were checking up on him?"

"There might have been an element of that, sure. He asked if I wanted to warn him." Gary's throat tightened again. "I think I wanted to be certain he was being safe."

Travers's eyes were warm.

Gary had had enough of feeling like crap. He had to do something.

He drained half his glass and coughed. "That psychic…. The one the chief told you about. What's his name? Dan Porter?"

Travers frowned. "Yeah, that's him."

Gary looked him in the eye. "Call him."

"This can wait a while. You've just had a—"

"Call him."

Travers held up his hands. "Fine. I'll call him. But… I'm taking you off the case."

Cold trickled down his back, dizziness in its wake. "No. You can't do that. I'm part of the lead squad on this case, for God's sake."

"Not anymore." Travers's voice was kind but firm. "I'm making Stevens the lead."

"You're letting Lewis run this? No. You've gotta be kidding."

Travers's gaze narrowed. "Are you saying Stevens isn't up to the task? Is there something I need to know?"

"No, nothing like that," Gary remonstrated. "But please… don't do this. Don't take me off the case." He straightened in his chair. "You've told me God knows how many times the last six years that I'm one of your best detectives. So please, *use* me. I'll liaise with this psychic, I'll work on the previous victims, but don't shut me out."

If begging was what it would take, he'd beg. On his knees if he had to.

Travers studied him in silence. "Fine. But I have some conditions."

Relief swamped him. "Thank you—"

Travers held up one hand. "Wait. Hear me out. I'm letting you stay only because I need you on this. And if anyone finds out about this, it'll be my ass in the can. So here's the deal. You don't interview *anyone* connected with this death, okay? You can look at the evidence, but that's all. Work with what you have on the previous victims."

"Then you *will* contact this Porter guy?"

Travers nodded. "And now you're going home. I don't want to see you till Monday."

"But—"

"No buts. Go home. Don't call Stevens, Watson, Del Maddox…. In fact, don't call anyone. Do whatever you need to so that when you walk in here Monday morning for roll call, you're ready to work. Because I need you at the top of your game. You got that?"

Gary expelled a breath. "Thank you. And yes, I've got it." *Whatever it takes. For Cory.* He finished his bourbon.

"How did you get here this morning?"

"Riley gave me a ride."

"I'll have someone run you home."

Gary thanked him again, and Travers walked him to the door. Before he opened it, Travers squeezed Gary's shoulder. "My condolences on your loss."

"Thank you." And then he was out of there, walking on autopilot, not sure where he was heading, lost in a sea of voices and activity.

His stomach muscles still ached, and his throat was tight. All he could think about was Cory's face.

I became a cop with the idea that one day I'd find Brad's killer.

He'd always known that was a long shot—Brad had been gone twenty-three years now—but it had fueled Gary's resolve through college, the academy, his detective training…. After eight years of being a detective, he knew the chances of finding Brad's killer were pretty fucking slim.

But I'll find the guy who killed Cory if it's the last thing I do.

That could wait until Monday. What he'd like to do was go home, destroy a bottle of bourbon, and mourn a friend's untimely death.

Yeah, right. There was a ton of stuff he'd do before he reached for the bottle. He had people to call, and Cory's parents were at the top of the list, followed by his and Cory's mutual friends. Travers could tell him to stay away till he ran out of breath. That wouldn't stop Gary from trying to get into Cory's apps. *Cory wouldn't mind. Why else would he have given me the passwords?*

More importantly, he was going to replay every second of that last conversation with Cory because it had to contain clues.

His tears could wait. They'd come when the killer was behind bars.

CHAPTER 9

Sunday, May 27

DESPITE BRUSHING his teeth, Gary's tongue still felt as if it were made of suede, and he knew a couple of Tylenol would be needed sometime soon. The alcohol of the previous night might have dulled his senses for a while, but even before he'd opened his eyes at whatever godforsaken hour he'd awoken, grief slammed into him.

He's really gone.

That one thought had been enough to have Gary tugging the comforter over his head as if the act would shut out the memories that washed over him, but instead it had brought on a fresh tide of tears that soaked into his pillow, and he'd fallen into a fitful sleep. Three hours later, he figured it was time to rejoin the land of the living. He'd done enough wallowing.

Once he'd hauled himself to the bathroom, he realized Cory had been full of shit about one thing: There was no such thing as a no-hangover tequila. His body ached, his head ached, and he was nauseous. The shower promised relief, and God, he needed some of that.

Gary stood under the stream of hot water, letting it sluice away some of the muscle aches. *No more booze.* This wasn't him. He wasn't a big drinker. Christ, his bottle of bourbon had to be a couple of years old. He'd avoided alcohol Friday night, but on Saturday, a search through his cabinets had revealed the bottle of tequila Cory had given him for his birthday. Gary had been saving it for the next time Cory stayed over. They were overdue for a boys' night—

Except there won't be any more of those, will there?

Grief buckled his knees, and he let out a loud sob, bracing his arms, his hands flat to the white-tiled wall as a wave of anger and despair threatened to crush him, pulverize him. He slammed his fist against the tiles, wincing at the impact. "Fuck this!" He was not going to let it get the better of him.

A muffled ringing came from the other side of the door.

Phone.

He pulled himself together, flipped off the water, and grabbed a towel, which he hastily wrapped around his hips. He went into the bedroom, dripping over the carpet as he searched for his phone, finally finding it under a heap of clothing. When he saw Riley's name, he stabbed at the screen. "Here."

There was silence for a moment. "I was about to hang up. I couldn't decide if I should call you."

"I'm glad you did." His head was still complaining. "Bear with me a sec? I need to grab a couple of Tylenol." He retreated to the bathroom to drip over the tiled floor.

"I'm not gonna ask why, but I can guess." There was a moment's hesitation. "Fuck it, I'm asking. What juice were you on?"

"I sound hungover, is that what you're telling me? The poison was tequila, and for your information, I didn't drink all that much." Just enough to take the edge off a frustrating day.

"Okay. Drink plenty of water to rehydrate. Tylenol is our friend. Oh, and get yourself some ginger ale if you feel nauseous."

Gary smiled to himself as he opened the bathroom cabinet and reached for the bottle. "Could this be the voice of experience talking?"

"Tequila slammers. Never again. And avoid coffee. It doesn't help a hangover. It only gives you the jitters." A pause. "How you doing?"

Gary ran water into a glass, shook out two pills, and chased them down his throat. "I've been better." He was dying to ask about the case, but he had a feeling he'd be wasting his breath. Riley was a pal as well as a coworker, but that didn't mean he'd go against Travers.

"You gonna be at the precinct tomorrow?"

He frowned. "Of course. Why wouldn't I be?"

"I thought you might want to take some time—"

"I'll be there, okay?"

Another pause. "Travers said you've got to stay in the background when it comes to… to Cory."

"I know. He said the same to me Friday."

"Okay. Just checking. Hey, boss?"

"Hm?"

"Don't drink any more, okay? It cures nothing. Trust me on that."

"And there's that voice of experience again." Gary knew next to nothing about Riley's personal life, but then again, he didn't share about his either.

"Let's just say I've had my heart stomped on a couple of times. Tequila slammers, remember? They sound like a great idea—until the next morning."

"Not another cop who's been unlucky in love."

Riley chuckled. "Gee, I wonder why that is. And when you've had your water and ginger ale, get some rest. Best cure ever."

It was no surprise Riley had been the first to make contact. He was one of the good guys. "I hear ya."

"I'm really sorry, Gary."

His throat seized. "Okay, I need to go now."

"Gotcha. I'll see you tomorrow at roll call." He disconnected.

Gary turned the ringer off, placed the phone on the glass shelf above the bathroom sink, then gripped the cool porcelain sides, his gaze locked on the haggard man in the mirror.

I'm sorry too. He knew if Cory were there, he'd kick Gary's ass. *He'd be telling me to get out there and find the bastard who did this.*

Gary straightened, raised his chin, and looked himself in the eye. "And that's what I'm going to do." His phone vibrated against the glass, and he half thought it was Riley again until he glanced at the screen.

Oh dear Lord. Nina.

He didn't pick it up, hoping she'd stop, *praying* she'd stop, because he didn't think he could handle talking to her, not right then, not when his emotions were raw and frayed.

And if this is how you *feel, what state do you think* she's *in?* Nina's grief trumped his.

Gary expelled a breath, shoved down hard on his self-pity, and clicked Answer. "Hey."

"Can we meet?" Gary could hear the tears in her voice.

He stilled at the abrupt request. "When?"

"Now? Okay, not right this second. I have to get out of here. I need caffeine, although I'd prefer alcohol, but I think if I went down that route, I wouldn't stop, so let's stick with a coffee shop."

"Got one in mind?"

"The Thinking Cup, on Tremont, overlooking the Common. It can get noisy, but there's a view of the bandstand. Meet you there in an hour?"

Cory's little sister needs me. It was enough to bring him to a decision. "Sure."

"Great. See you then." She disconnected.

Gary toweled his hair. Anything was better than hanging around his apartment. He needed focus, but there was also a tiny part of him that wanted to be with someone who shared his grief, his emotions… his feelings for Cory.

"TWO LATTES, two Boston cream pies." The server placed the cups and plates on their table and withdrew.

Nina eyed the dessert. "He'd have a fit if he could see me eating this."

"And then he'd be telling you to go for a run to burn it all off."

They smiled, but Gary's stomach tightened.

Nina had looked okay at first glance, but once she'd stopped hugging him, it didn't take long for Gary to spot the shaky hands, the trembling lips, the bowed shoulders…. Her long brown hair was tied back, her face devoid of makeup, her expression a little vacant. Traces of the little girl who'd plagued him when he was a teenager were all but gone, submerged in the thirty-year-old woman she'd become.

She looks as if she's aged overnight.

Gary had thought the same thing that morning, gazing at his reflection.

Nina picked up her fork and cut through the ganache with its edge, revealing the cream filling but making no effort to bring it to her lips. Then she raised her chin and shrugged. "I think I've lost my appetite." She put her fork on the plate and pushed it away.

"All I've eaten since Friday is soup. Only thing I could keep down." His own dessert sat untouched.

She reached for the latte. "This smells good."

Around them were the sights, sounds, and aromas of the coffee shop: The gleam of the chrome espresso machine and bean grinder; customers working on laptops or tablets, reading newspapers. The murmur of voices; the clatter of dishes; coins clinking into a tip jar; a radio station playing music in the background; ice grating in the blender. The aromatic scent of freshly brewed coffee, warm caramel, and chocolate; the tingle of spices; and the enticing smell of fresh-baked cookies and muffins.

It was surreal. Life went on as normal, and yet so many differing emotions could lurk there, hidden from view. Anger, grief, frustration, defeat, resentment….

Cory's killer could be sitting a few feet away from us and we would never know.

Gary gave himself a mental shake and shifted his imagination into Park. "Where's your fiancé?"

Nina blinked. "You know about David?"

He nodded. "Cory told me. Your parents mentioned him too when I called." Not that he wanted to recall the conversation punctuated by sobs and labored breathing. It was Brad all over again.

I hope they're nothing like my parents. He wouldn't want Cory's mom and dad to join the ranks of the walking dead.

A brief spasm contorted her face, but she recovered quickly. "Yeah. Thanks for that, by the way. David's with them right now. I told him I wanted to meet you on my own. Besides, he's doing his bit to hold them together. I had to get out of there before I fell apart."

"It feels as if I've done nothing *but* fall apart the last two days." When she gazed at him with obvious concern, he sighed. "You're right to avoid the alcohol route. It sucks." At least he'd gotten stuff done before he hit the tequila, not that it had helped. None of their friends had heard from Cory, and looking at his apps proved fruitless.

"Ah. Thanks for the advice." She tilted her head. "But you didn't mind meeting me?"

"Mind? Why would I mind?" he lied. After a moment's hesitation, he took a careful step. "When was the last time you spoke with Cory?"

Beats of silence.

Nina leaned back in her chair. "Is that an official question? You're on this case? I didn't think the police department would allow that."

He swallowed. "I'm not asking as a cop—I'm asking as Cory's best friend. And you're right, by the way. I'm not allowed to work this case— at least not the parts of it that concern Cory. I saw him a week ago. We met at a bar."

She took a drink from her cup. "I know. He called me Sunday night when he got home. That was the last time we spoke." Her lips twitched. "He says you still have the hots for him." That spasm was back, but this time she didn't school her features. "Jesus. I keep thinking of him in the present tense, and then it hits me again, a sharp fucking knife lancing into my gut." She shuddered. "My parents are talking about funeral homes, the service, the freaking *music*, and while I know they're only doing that because they need to be doing *something*, I want to scream at them that none of that shit matters. None of it will bring him back." Her eyes glistened. "Who would want to kill Cory? He's—he *was*—the sweetest guy ever." Nina's face hardened. "It was him, wasn't it? That guy who's been killing gay men."

Gary couldn't speak. He handed her a paper napkin from the stand, and she wiped her eyes.

Nina inhaled deeply, then drank half her coffee. "I'm sorry. You can't talk about this. But I had to talk to someone, and he… he loved you like a brother."

"I felt the same." Well, not at first, but that had been a long time ago, and whatever feelings Gary had had for Cory back in high school had morphed into something better, something solid. *He could never be Brad, but he was the next best thing.*

When the thought occurred to him, he knew he should keep it to himself, but the words poured out before he could rein them in. "Did Cory mention dating anyone new?" He could hear Cory's voice, clear as a bell.

Dating? How sweet.

Nina shook her head. "No." Her eyes widened. "Wait—yes. He said some guy had sent him a dick pic, and when Cory asked to see the rest of him, he sent a photo." She fanned herself. "Gorgeous guy. *I'd* have dated him. Talk about movie-star looks."

Gary froze. "You *saw* the photo?"

"Yeah. Cory forwarded it to me." A hint of a twinkle in her eyes. "He didn't send the dick pic, though," she added with a pout that was so like Cory's it was uncanny.

He smiled. "He'd think of that as corrupting the innocent."

Nina stared at him, her mouth open, then guffawed, tears trickling down her face as she hugged her middle. At nearby tables, customers stared in their direction, then returned to whatever activity occupied them. When she finally had herself under control, she sagged in her chair. "Oh God. Thank you. That's the first laugh I've had since I heard." She chuckled. "Innocent? Honey, I haven't been that since tenth grade. Bless him. He *would've* thought that too."

Gary couldn't get his mind off the photo. "Can I see it?"

Nina gave him a speculative glance. "That's the detective talking. Sure." She pulled her phone from her purse, scrolled, then handed it to him.

Gary gazed at the screen. "I see what you mean about movie-star looks." The man was in his thirties, maybe, with a firm jaw, piercing blue eyes, and perfectly coiffed hair.

And nothing like Kris Lee Arill. If it *was* their man, the photo would lead them nowhere, just like the others he'd used.

He handed the phone back.

Nina snorted. "I told Cory this guy was out of his league."

"Maybe you should send it to the police."

She frowned. "But I already did. I showed it to that detective who visited. Stevens? Is that his name?"

There was a fluttering in his stomach. "When was this?"

"Friday night. David and I went straight to my parents when they called me with the news. There were two detectives. Stevens and...."

"Detective Watson?"

She nodded. "That was it. I can barely remember the conversation—I was that numb. But they asked the same questions you did, so I showed the detective the photo, and he gave me a number to forward it to." That tilt of her head again. "I thought you said you're not involved."

"I'm not. The fact that neither of my coworkers informed me of their visit should tell you that." Not even Riley. *I guess he's a cop first and a friend second.* "You said your parents are arranging the funeral. Any idea when it will be?"

"Next week sometime. Detective Riley said the bod—said Cory would be released to us pretty much right away, once they've done the... you know." There was no humor left in her sweet face. It had been replaced by the glisten of tears, a voice that cracked, a wandering gaze....

Gary reached across the table and took her hand in his. "Let me know, okay? I'll be there."

Nina's gaze alighted on their joined hands. "Thanks, Gary," she whispered. Then she looked him in the eye as she swiped at her wet cheeks. "Now find the bastard who did this."

Gary said nothing, but squeezed her hand tight.

I will. At some unearthly hour Saturday morning, he'd surfaced briefly from his disturbed sleep and made a promise to Cory.

He intended keeping it.

CHAPTER 10

Monday, May 28

ROLL CALL drew to a close, but Gary knew there was more to come when Travers entered the room and took over from Rob at the lectern. The rumbles of conversation from the assembled detectives continued. Travers rapped the lectern with his knuckles, then cleared his throat, and a hush fell.

"Okay, one last point. You all know we're now at six murders. I don't have to say how badly we want to catch this guy, do I?" Murmurs rippled through the rows of seated officers like a wave. "The chief...." Travers raised his voice, and silence ensued. "The chief feels we need a little outside... specialized help on this one, so we're bringing in a kind of consultant."

"What does 'kind of' mean, Lieutenant?" That came from Will Freeman.

"As of today, we've invited Dan Porter to work with the lead squad on this case. He's a psychic who's worked—" Loud muttering broke out, and Travers glared at them. "When you're done?" Silence. "Okay. If any of you skeptics out there would care to look, you'll discover Mr. Porter has helped both the NYPD *and* Chicago PD with a few well-documented cases. I've read statements from detectives in both those departments, and they all say the same thing. This guy gets results. And seeing as our killer just made a leap from five months to ten days between murders, I think we're in no position to turn down help if it's offered." Another glare. "Let me make it perfectly clear. I want full cooperation on this. From everyone. You're to provide any and all assistance required. However...."

Gary's skin prickled.

"Let me reiterate. We approached Mr. Porter, not the other way round, and he's agreed to work with us on one condition. *No one* outside of this department is to know of his involvement. That means the press, social media.... *No one*. You got that?" Travers scowled. "There's been enough ink and screen time wasted on this bastard already. We know the media will be falling all over themselves to get more information on this killer—nothing spells high ratings like a serial killer, right?—but I want them to be met with complete radio silence."

"So he's not doing this for publicity?" Lewis rolled his eyes. "Yeah, like we believe that."

"I don't care *what* you believe, Stevens." Travers's voice was cool.

"But you said his previous cases are well documented. So suddenly he wants to keep out of the limelight? Why now?"

"I have no idea. Maybe you should ask him. He obviously has his reasons, but whatever they are, letting the media in on this is a dealbreaker." Travers gazed around the room. "Have we all got that? Good. Have a great day, folks." And with that he marched out of the room.

The rumblings erupted immediately.

"As if anyone in here would let the media know," Will said with a sneer. "What message would that send? 'Hey, the police can't do diddly squat, so we're enlisting a psychic.'" Murmurs of agreement followed.

Riley glanced at the men and women surrounding them, his face glum. "*Any and all assistance required*? Yeah, right. No one's gonna talk to this guy on principle."

"Then *we'll* talk to him, all right?" Gary wasn't about to share his part in the proceedings. He'd gone out on a limb. His own experience of psychics didn't matter. If there was the slightest chance this guy Porter could succeed where they'd failed—so far—then Gary was prepared to accept what help Porter could offer.

"Sure, we'll talk to him," Lewis muttered. "But it's gonna be a waste of time, okay? And when this guy doesn't produce, remember, you heard it here first."

They filed back to the large office, but instead of heading for his desk, Gary went to their base. The sight of Cory's photo taped to the board sent a brief pang through him, but he took a couple of deep breaths.

You're a goddamn professional. Be what he needs.

Without looking, he knew Lewis had entered: That cologne he wore was a dead giveaway.

"I *am* sorry about your friend."

Compassion was the last thing Gary had expected. "Thank you." Maybe Lewis was human after all. He peered at the board. "No phone, like the others?"

"Yeah."

"Is Del doing the autopsy today?"

"He's already done it."

Gary turned. "When?" As a rule, Del didn't work weekends, although there was usually one forensic pathologist working Saturdays.

"He came in Saturday morning. Riley attended. We were here doing stuff for Travers."

A wave of gratitude crashed over him. "You all went to a lot of trouble. I do appreciate that."

"We didn't want you to have to confront all the prelim work. You didn't need that."

Gary sighed. "Sometimes you can be a real pain in the ass, you know that, right? And then you go do something like this."

Lewis shrugged. "You'd do the same for me if the roles were reversed."

"Is that why you haven't mentioned that you saw Nina Peterson?"

Lewis arched his eyebrows. "Travers said I was to keep you away from this one. So in my book, you didn't need to know." Another shrug. "If you've got a problem with that, take it up with Travers."

"That's why I didn't mention it either," Riley said from the doorway. Gary knew Riley's softer tone was meant to placate him.

"What about the photo Cory sent her? Did you get a result?" Gary glared at them. "You can share that much, surely."

Lewis took a moment before replying. "No luck. It was another stock photo."

Well, fuck.

"We're gonna get a break on this, you know that, right?" Riley's voice rang with confidence. "Who knows? This Porter guy might be it."

Gary ignored Lewis's barely stifled snort.

A taped box sat on the corner of the desk. Gary pointed to it. "That looks like evidence," he remarked, noting the seals.

"That's because it is. Travers had me and Riley go down there—on Saturday morning too—and pick out stuff that had belonged to all the victims. Mostly jewelry, watches… I guess it's for Mr. Psychic." Lewis made a spooky noise and waggled his fingers. "Get your tickets here for the first performance."

"Just can it, will you?" The phone burst into life, and Gary grabbed the handset. "Okay. We'll be right there." He replaced it. "Travers wants us in his office."

"Now what?" Lewis muttered as they headed in that direction.

Gary ignored him. As they entered Travers's office, the man seated in front of his desk rose, rubbing his hand down the leg of his pants as he did so. He was about Gary's height, maybe a little shorter, with warm brown hair styled in an expensively cut quiff sweeping up from his forehead. His shirt was deep purple, as was his tie, and his waistcoat and pants were dark blue. A jacket hung over the back of the chair. He stood still as they approached the desk and met Gary's gaze with an unblinking stare.

It wasn't a face that would have stood out in a crowd. A nondescript kind of face. Hazel eyes appraised Gary, the corners of his mouth turned slightly upward but not smiling. A square jaw with only the faintest hint of stubble. The guy exuded a calm that Gary envied.

"I'd like to introduce Dan Porter." Travers gestured to them. "Mr. Porter, these are Detectives Gary Mitchell, Lewis Stevens, and Riley Watson."

Mr. Porter gave a polite nod, which Gary returned. Riley took a step forward. "Hey." Lewis hung back by the door, silent.

"This is the lead squad on this case," Travers continued, "so you'll be working with them. We'll be interested to see what you can come up with."

Lewis folded his arms. "We don't need to tell you anything, do we? All we have to do is hand you something that belonged to the victim and *you* can tell *us*." His smug smile made Gary's hackles rise.

Mr. Porter's polite expression didn't alter. "You've been checking up on me."

Lewis scowled. "No."

"Yet you know I work by touch a lot of the time?" Mr. Porter's tone was even.

"I'm not stupid. I watch TV."

For God's sake…. The guy was there to help them, and Lewis was being a dick.

Travers studied Lewis for a moment, his gaze glacial, before addressing all of them in a low voice. Gary admired his restraint. "I want you to acquaint Mr. Porter with the case. Give him access to anything he asks for." Another glance at Lewis. "Did you arrange for items to be brought up from Evidence like I asked?" Lewis nodded. "Then I expect you to make those available to Mr. Porter." He raised his eyebrows. "Seeing as you already know how he works."

Gary bit back a smile. *Score one to Travers.*

"Anything?" Lewis's voice held ill-concealed incredulity.

Travers regarded him with mild surprise. "That comes from the chief. Got something to say, Stevens?"

Lewis stuck out his chin. "No, sir."

"Good, because at the risk of repeating myself, I want full cooperation." He glanced at Mr. Porter. "Thank you again for agreeing to this."

"Thank me when I've given you something solid to work on."

Gary led him out of the office and through the noisy hallway to the squad room. He was aware of eyes following them as they passed coworkers, but thankfully there were no comments. *Lewis has already made us look bad enough.*

When they reached the desks, Mr. Porter scanned their surroundings. "Is there any coffee? I haven't hit my caffeine level this morning."

"I'll get some," Riley said with a smile. "How do you take it?"

"Black, please. No sugar."

Riley headed out in search of caffeine.

Lewis leaned against Gary's desk. "So this is what you do for a living?"

"I wouldn't call it a living, exactly. It doesn't pay well, but then again I don't do it for the money. I do it to help people." His voice was deeper than Gary had expected.

"You got another job, then?"

"No."

Gary was no expert on body language, but even he knew what hands almost curling into fists meant. Mr. Porter pressed his lips together, his face contorted in a pained expression.

Is Lewis that blind? Porter does not want to talk about this.

"Even psychics have to buy groceries and pay rent," Lewis said with a shrug. "Not to mention buy clothes." He did a slow up and down glance.

"I don't do it for the money, because I don't *need* the money, okay?" Mr. Porter clenched his jaw.

If Lewis had tried to hide his sneer, he'd failed miserably. "Rich kid, huh? Mommy and Daddy have lots of cash?" He lowered his gaze to Mr. Porter's hands. "I bet you've never done a hard day's work in your life."

Mr. Porter gave a wry chuckle. "Oh my God, I feel as if I'm in a scene from *Jaws.*" His eyes held amusement. "You'd be perfect as Quint."

"Okay, that's enough." Gary glared at Lewis. "What is your problem? We're supposed to be working with Mr. Porter, not alienating him right from the start."

"Call me Dan." He smiled, his bland expression gone, and in its place, dimples and sparkling eyes. With that smile? It was a handsome face. Then the light in his eyes faded as he regarded Lewis. He folded his arms. "I don't have to be psychic to see you have an issue with wealth."

Lewis's eyes bulged. "I don't have an *issue*. But some of us got where we are because of hard work. No one ever handed *me* anything on a silver platter."

Dan's lips twitched. "Can't say I've ever seen a silver platter." He glanced at the desks. "Is this where you work from?" he asked Gary.

"We're using a closet as our base for this case."

Dan's eyes twinkled. "Closet? Kinda apt, given the victims are all gay."

"How do you know that?" Lewis demanded. "Did your spidey sense tell you?"

Gary knew Lewis could be an asshole sometimes, but his behavior since Dan's arrival had reached new levels of assholery. *What the fuck is he playing at?*

Dan hadn't unfolded his arms. "No—I read it in the paper this morning, like everyone else in Boston."

Yeah, he was pissed too.

Gary decided to take control of the situation. "Okay, it's a little bigger than a closet, but not by much. We've got a board set up with photos from the crime scenes." He peered at Dan. "Will you want a place to work?"

Dan nodded. "I'll need an office with really good light and no ugly furniture. And a computer. My friend Ed will be my assistant. He'll want to paint the office walls," he added, deadpan.

Lewis gaped. "What the fuck?"

Gary laughed out loud. "I *love* that movie." Warmth spread through his chest, and the tightness across his shoulders eased. He couldn't hold back his smile.

"What movie?" Lewis appeared bewildered.

"*The January Man*. Kevin Kline, Alan Rickman."

Dan gazed at him in obvious approval, his own smile reaching his eyes. Then he cleared his throat. "We can talk about movies later. Let's get started. Take me to your closet."

Gary led the way. What impressed him most about Dan was the fact that he was nothing like the psychics his parents had contacted. They'd seemed theatrical in comparison with Dan's forthright manner.

I like him so far. Their shared common interest had seen to that. It didn't mean Gary was going to believe everything Dan came out with. *I'm as skeptical as Lewis.*

The only difference was, Lewis didn't have Gary's incentive. Lewis made no attempt to hide his disbelief—Gary wanted to believe with all his heart, especially if it brought them closer to finding Cory's killer.

CHAPTER 11

DAN STOOD in front of the board, his head moving slowly as he took it all in. Gary watched him, aware of a tingling at the base of his neck.

What do I expect to happen? He goes into a trance and yells out the name of our killer?

So far, Dan appeared to be an ordinary guy—with great taste in movies. As soon as they'd entered the small room, Dan had come to a halt at the sight of the photos. Each victim was displayed with a central head shot, surrounded by crime scene photos showing the position of the body, marks, and of course, the letter carved into the skin above the buttocks. Gary left him to his own devices, not wanting to distract him. Riley was keeping quiet too. He sat in a chair, leaning forward as if he were mesmerized by the proceedings. Lewis stood apart from them, his back to the wall, silent, watchful, his expression neutral.

Gary was thankful for that. So far it looked as if Lewis had taken every opportunity to irritate Dan.

At last Dan took a step back, went over to the table, and picked up his cup of coffee. "I see the marks on their wrists and ankles. Anything I'm *not* seeing that's important?"

Gary joined him. "The killer had penetrative sex with each victim, and we don't know if it was consensual or not." Dan half-turned his head toward him, sniffing. He blinked, then went back to studying the photos.

Gary resisted the urge to sniff as well. *What's wrong with the way I smell?*

"Maybe *you* can tell us if it was consensual," Lewis muttered. "That *is* the idea, isn't it?"

If Dan heard him, he gave no sign. "Is this the order they died in?"

Gary nodded. He pointed to the first photo. "Trey Hopkins. March eighteenth, 2016. He was thirty-two." He moved his finger. "Denver Wedel. December second, 2016. Forty-seven."

"They both appear well-built. Did they work out?"

Another nod. "We'd hoped they were members of the same gym, but no such luck. Didn't stop us from checking out all the members and interviewing them. No leads. They were both popular guys." He indicated the third photo. "Geoff Berg. June sixteenth, 2017."

"And the waiting period between murders shortened," Dan mused.

"Yeah. Geoff was the youngest victim—so far. Twenty-nine. By all accounts, he was a fireball. He was also the victim with the most contacts to sift through." Gary pointed to the fourth image. "Vic Zerbe. December twenty-third, same year. Thirty-five."

Dan moved closer to the board and stared at the photo of Marius Eisler. "I saw this one when it happened. A little under two weeks ago, right? Another mature guy." Then he shifted to the farthest edge of the board. Gary's chest tightened as Dan peered at Cory's face, breathing a little easier when no comments were forthcoming.

Dan turned to face him. "How does he kill them?"

"We found ketamine and Rohypnol. The former appears to have been a fatal dose. Our medical examiner thinks the ketamine was used to sedate them. They'd have been awake but controllable before the ketamine killed them."

Dan shivered. "The killer doesn't appear to have a type, does he? They differ in age, size…."

Gary twisted his neck to stare at Lewis. "Don't you have something to say, seeing as you're now the lead on this?"

Lewis shrugged. "Why bother? You're doing fine without me. I'm just waiting for Dan here to announce who the killer is."

Dan focused on Lewis's face, his nose wrinkling as he grimaced. "Wow. And *this* is your interpretation of full cooperation?"

"I'm sorry—" Gary started.

Dan cut off Gary's apology with a raised hand. "It's okay." His tone was even, calm. "I'm used to this reaction." He studied Lewis in silence for a moment, and Gary noted how Lewis stuffed his hands into his pockets, his mouth pressed into a straight line. He didn't meet Dan's unbroken stare but glanced away.

Dan put down his cup and took a step toward Lewis, who flinched. "I've met plenty of skeptics in the police. Join the line." Dan folded his arms. "You want a demonstration, is that it? Okay, then. Give me something. I'm not making any promises because it's not something I can turn on and off like a faucet. And it helps if I'm in a mindful state, where I've concentrated on clearing my mind."

"And there we have it. The get-out clause if you don't come up with anything." Lewis gave a triumphant smile. "I knew there'd be one."

Dan took another step, until there was barely a foot between them, and Lewis seemed to curl up, shrivel.

What is he so scared of? Dan didn't appear to be the kind of guy who'd react physically, but Lewis looked as if he was ready to bolt from the room.

Dan clearly had the same thought. He backed off, his gaze still locked on Lewis. "Why don't you give me something personal of yours, Detective, and let's see what I can come up with about you?"

Lewis's Adam's apple bobbed violently. "Why don't we stick to the case?"

Dan said nothing but took a farther step away from him, and Lewis relaxed visibly.

Gary went over to the box on the desk. "This is the stuff Lieutenant Travers had us bring up from Evidence for you."

"Okay, about that." Dan joined him, peering into the box. "I meant what I said a moment ago. I can't turn it on and off. I've been dealing with this my whole life, and I still have no clue how it works."

"What happens when it does work?" Riley's eyes were bright. "This is fascinating."

Dan smiled. "I take it you don't think psychics are all fakers and charlatans?"

Jesus. It was as if he'd reached into Gary's mind and plucked the phrase from his memory. He had to suppress a shudder.

Riley chuckled. "Hell no. My grandmother was into spiritualism in a big way, and it was eerie, some of the things she knew. I guess I have an open mind when it comes to this kinda thing."

"How does the saying go? The mind is like a parachute. It only functions when it's open."

Lewis snorted. "Where did you get that? A fortune cookie?"

"My great-grandfather told it to me." Dan grinned. "Said he got it from a Charlie Chan movie." He returned his attention to Riley. "Sometimes I get images. Other times, visions. Those can be quite uncomfortable."

"Do you have to interpret the visions? Or are they pretty straightforward?"

"Both? It's not an exact science."

Lewis huffed. "I think *science* might be pushing it a little."

Dan ignored him. "The simplest explanation is…." He gave a shrug. "Sometimes I know stuff." Riley laughed, and Dan joined in. Then the laughter faded. "But being serious for a moment? There *have* been occasions when I desperately wanted to come up with something, and… zilch. Like I said…."

Riley nodded. "You can't turn it on and off."

Dan looked at Gary. "You choose something. Don't tell me anything about it."

Gary sorted through the evidence bags, scanning the labels. He chose a watch that had belonged to Vic Zerbe. "Do I need to take it out of the bag? The only prints on it were the victim's."

Dan nodded. "If that's okay."

Riley lurched to his feet. "Here. Sit."

Dan gave him a grateful glance. "Thank you." Gary opened the bag and placed the watch with its leather strap into Dan's hand.

"Do we need to hold hands? Put on creepy music?"

Gary glared at Lewis. "It's not a séance, you jerk." Lewis arched his eyebrows, but Gary was past being polite. Lewis's attitude to Dan was pissing him off severely.

Dan closed his eyes, his breathing slowing until there was little movement in his chest. No one spoke, not even Lewis. Gary took the opportunity to study Dan. He was about Gary's age, of average build, but slim across the hips. In fact, he was lean all over, judging by the way his clothes hugged his body. His air of concentration was impressive; it was as if he'd blotted them out.

After a moment of silence, Dan opened his eyes. "I'm sorry. I'm not getting anything."

Gary dropped his shoulders. "It's all right." His ribs grew tight, his breathing hitched.

"I'm probably jamming his frequencies," Lewis muttered.

Dan snorted. "I am *not* Tangina Barrons." His gaze met Gary's. "She was way cooler than me." That twinkle was attractive.

"Tangi—who the hell is that?" Lewis gave Dan a blank look.

Gary didn't hesitate. "The psychic in *Poltergeist*." He glared at Lewis. "If you're going to stay, you'll be quiet, okay?"

Lewis took a step back, gazing at him with wide eyes. "Okay."

Will Freeman stuck his head around the door. "Riley, there's a call for you."

Riley walked out, closing the door behind him.

Gary took the watch from Dan and replaced it in the box. "Let's try something else." He searched the bags, his pulse quickening when he saw Cory's name. *Do it.* Gary reached into the bag and removed Cory's pinky ring. His mouth dry, he placed it on Dan's upturned palm. As he withdrew his hand, their fingers brushed, and Dan jerked his head up, staring at him.

"Something wrong?" Gary hadn't gotten a shock when they touched.

"No, nothing."

Gary was no psychic, but even he knew that was a lie. Something had rattled Dan for a second.

Dan covered the ring with his hand and closed his eyes once more.

I was with Cory when he bought that. Cory had saved up all his money from mowing lawns one summer to buy it. When it grew tight, he'd transferred it to his pinky, and there it had stayed.

Dan was as motionless as a statue, and once again Gary felt sure he wasn't aware of anything but the object between his palms. Dan's breathing hitched, then hitched again, and goose bumps erupted over Gary's arms.

Something was coming, as tangible as an icy hand on Gary's nape.

Dan opened his eyes to stare at Gary. "Oh my God."

The tightness around Gary's ribs increased until drawing breath became a chore. Cold trickled through him at the sight of tears spilling onto Dan's cheeks.

Oh fuck. Gary couldn't move, was rooted to the spot. His throat seized.

Dan sagged into the chair, still clutching the ring. "I am so, so sorry. This must be killing you." He wiped his eyes with his fingers.

Understatement of the fucking century.

"*What's* killing him?" Lewis demanded.

Dan got up from the chair. He held out the ring, and Gary's hands trembled as he took it. Then he realized Dan's hands were shaking too. Dan shivered. "He's the reason you agreed to me coming on board with this case, isn't he? You want to find the man who did this to your best friend." Dan went over to the board, stopping in front of Cory's image. "It was his ring." It wasn't a question.

Oh God.

"Okay, who told you that?" Lewis asked.

Dan pointed to the ring in Gary's hand. "*That* did." He indicated Cory's photo. "And so did he."

"Wait—you see dead people too?" Lewis paled. "Fuck. I'm sorry, Gary. I didn't think—"

"I didn't mean it like that," Dan retorted. "And I'm not going to waste my breath explaining myself, not to someone who clearly thinks I shouldn't be here."

Lewis opened his mouth, then snapped it shut.

Gary's skin tingled. Pain lanced through his chest. "Did… did you learn anything about… how he died? Anything that can help us?"

Dan's hazel eyes held nothing but warmth and compassion. "I'm sorry. All I got was feelings about you. He… he cared deeply for you." He swallowed. "My apologies for the display of emotion. It happens sometimes, when the… signal, for want of a better word, is strong."

Gary fought hard to stay upright, not to deflate into a quivering mess. Dan laid his hand on Gary's shoulder, and there it was again, a visible tremor that rippled through Dan. He jerked his hand back, and it took every ounce of effort Gary possessed not to yell *What? What is it you feel that you're not telling me?*

Dan had taken Gary's disbelief and doubt, crushed them in his slim fingers, and cast them aside in a heartbeat.

He doesn't have inside knowledge.

He knows. *He fucking* knows.

How he knew, Gary had no idea, but that didn't matter. All that concerned him was Dan was the genuine article. He replaced the ring in its bag and resealed it.

Dan turned to Lewis. "Do you need another demonstration?" There was no animosity in his voice. If anything, he sounded as drained as Gary felt.

Lewis studied him in silence before responding. "No, that's okay. I think I've heard enough."

Riley came back into the room. "Lewis, you got a minute?"

"Sure. Unless Dan here is going to go through every piece of evidence."

Gary gestured toward the door. "Go see what Riley wants."

When Lewis left, Dan expelled a breath. "He's kind of… intense. What is his problem?" He sighed. "Stupid question. *I'm* the problem, obviously." He glanced at Gary. "Are you okay? I didn't mean to upset you, but…." He seemed to have regained his self-control.

Gary took a deep breath. "I'm okay. It's still pretty raw." Cory had only been dead four days, after all. *Is that all?* He glanced at Dan. "Are *you* okay? You sound kind of exhausted." Shock seeped from him, and with each breath he regained his equilibrium.

Dan nodded. "One thing I didn't mention when Riley was asking questions. The visions wear me out. I'll be okay if I sit quietly for a while. I need to recoup my energy."

"How far did you travel to be here?"

"Not that far, really. I live in New Hampshire. We're practically neighbors."

"Where are you staying?"

"I booked into the Fairmont Copley Plaza last night." He sniffed.

Gary frowned. "Do I have BO or something?"

"God, no, it's just…." Dan leaned in and inhaled. "What's that scent you're wearing? It seems familiar."

Mystery solved. "It's a throwback to when I was a teenager. My brother loved patchouli and sandalwood. My dad used to tell him he was an old man in a young guy's body." *Except he never made old bones.* "I found a cologne that reminded me of it. It's more cedar than sandalwood, but I like it."

It was more than that, but Gary wasn't about to share.

"Me too." There was a pause. "So… once I've recharged my batteries, I'll be ravenous. Can you recommend good places to eat around here? I looked at the hotel menu last night, and I have to admit, while it's pretty swanky, nothing leaped out at me."

"What do you like? Chinese? Indian? Thai? Mexican? Sushi? There are a ton of good restaurants."

"Sounds as if I'll be spoiled for choice." He bit his lip. "I don't suppose you know a good Vietnamese restaurant?"

Gary gaped. "You're kidding. Yeah, I do. It's one of my favorite places to eat. The Noodle Barn, Jamaica Plain. Not a fancy place, but the food is awesome."

Dan smiled. "Great. I'll try it this evening."

Gary couldn't help himself. "I'm overdue for a meal there. Can I join you?" He held up both hands. "I promise not to ask for demonstrations or ask lots of questions, but I know it's no fun eating alone. At least that's how I feel. You might be different." Except that first part was a lie. He had a shit-ton of questions.

Dan's smile reached his eyes this time. "I'd like that. I'd be grateful for the company, to be honest. And yeah, I'll pass on the demonstrations. I wouldn't mind answering questions, though." He cocked his head. "After what happened just now, I have a few of my own."

Gary had a feeling that meant talking about Cory. He wasn't sure he was up to that.

Before he could reply, Lewis hurried into the room, his eyes sparkling. "We got a break." He gave Dan a smug smile. "Looks like you've had a wasted trip, Mr. Porter. Someone's confessed to the murders." He glanced at Gary. "If you can tear yourself away, he's in an interview room. Work time." He strode out without a backward glance.

Dan expelled a long breath. "Wow. Talk about a short engagement."

"I wouldn't leave just yet. We've had at least five confessions so far." But something had clearly put a burr up Lewis's ass, and Gary wanted to know more. He paused at the door. "Still want to eat out?"

Dan's eyes twinkled. "Before Detective Stevens puts my bags in the trunk of my car for me and waves me off as I drive back to New Hampshire? Sure."

"Then wait here. When I come back, we'll exchange phone numbers."

Dan pointed to the box. "Can I take a look at what you've got in there? You never know…."

"Be my guest, but don't wear yourself out, okay?" He smiled. "In case this guy turns out to be another wacko who wants attention. And don't worry. Lewis won't be packing any bags." He left the room, his head in a spin.

Lewis wants to believe we've got our killer because that would mean the end of Dan's involvement on this case.

Gary's senses told him otherwise. Their man had a lot left in him.

Unfortunately.

DAN WAITED till the door closed, then flopped into the chair, his legs trembling.

It can't be. It just can't be.

Nothing in Gary's appearance had struck a chord, not even the fact that he was a redhead. His beard hugged his jawline, thick but not overabundant, a warm rich color that somehow complemented his blue eyes. The kind of man Dan would definitely look twice at, but that meant nothing. It certainly didn't mean Gary was the unseen lover from his visions, no matter how much Dan might want that.

But that scent....

It had to be a coincidence.

But you don't want it to be a coincidence, do you?

No, he didn't.

He found himself staring at the door, waiting for Gary's return. Talk about torn. As much as he hoped the killer had suffered an attack of conscience and decided to end his grim spree, Dan didn't want it to be true. Not yet.

I need to know more about you, Gary Mitchell.

If dinner was to be his only chance to discover more, Dan was going to learn as much as he could.

CHAPTER 12

WHEN GARY reached the interview room, Riley was standing outside.

He frowned. "You didn't need to wait for me."

"Lewis is in there with him." Riley was vibrating. "Things might be looking up, boss."

Gary arched his eyebrows. "Do you know how many voluntary confessions turn out to be people chasing fame or the result of mental illness? What makes you think this one is for real?"

"I don't. I've heard enough of these guys to know when something doesn't ring true. And we know how to deal with them. But you remember that painting Marius Eisler was working on? The one on the easel?" Gary nodded, and Riley inclined his head toward the door. "It's the guy in the painting."

Gary finally got why Riley was buzzing. "He knew the victim. He might know something that could help us." Riley nodded slowly. "What has he said so far?"

Riley consulted his notes. "He gave his name as John Reynolds at the desk. I'm running a background check. I just wanted to prepare you before you walked in there."

Gary patted his arm, opened the door, and walked in.

John Reynolds sat at the table, Lewis facing him, and a police officer stood with his back to the wall. The first thought to slip into Gary's mind was that Marius Eisler had been a truly gifted painter; he'd captured his model to perfection. An average-looking man of middle age, the kind of man you wouldn't look twice at.

John pointed to the camera high in the corner above the door. "Are you recording all this? Because I wouldn't want you to miss anything." He leaned back, his arms folded.

Gary took the empty chair next to Lewis, then gave a nod. Lewis glanced at the sheet in front of him. "This is Detective Mitchell, and I'm Detective Stevens. Your name is John Reynolds, is that correct?"

"Yes."

"You're forty-nine years old, and you live on Park Street in Dorchester."

"Yeah, yeah, that's me."

"What do you do for a living?"

"I'm an accountant." John stared at Lewis. "How come I'm not under arrest? Don't you need to read me my rights or something?"

Lewis flicked a glance in Gary's direction, then returned his attention to John. "So far we have nothing to arrest you for. You walked into the precinct and told the desk sergeant you're responsible for the deaths of six men." He leaned back, mimicking John's body language. "So we'd like to hear more."

Gary had a feeling the only thing they might possibly charge him with was wasting police time. It could be the only tool available to get him involved in mental health treatment if he needed it. He trusted his instincts. This wasn't their man.

And now to prove that supposition.

"Fine. You want details?" John counted off on his fingers. "March 2016, I killed Trey Hopkins. December same year, Denver Wedel. June 2017, Geoff Berg. December, Vic Zerbe. May this year, Marius Eisler. And last week, Cory Peterson." He smiled, as if he was expecting praise.

"Marius Eisler was painting your portrait." Gary focused on John's face. "You killed him before he finished it. Why was that?"

A shrug. "I didn't like the way it was turning out. I don't think he captured the real me."

"On the contrary. I think he nailed you," Gary remarked.

"Did you have sex with him before or after one of the sittings?" Lewis asked.

John flushed. "No."

"Then it was purely business? Your sole purpose in going to his apartment was to be painted?"

He swallowed. "Yeah."

Lewis smiled. "Ah. You went hoping for more, and he turned you down. Is that it?" When John didn't respond, Lewis leaned forward. "So why'd you kill the others?"

"Isn't it obvious? They were gay."

"And that was enough motive to kill them?"

John glared at Lewis. "That was all the motive I needed. They have to be wiped off the face of the earth."

"How did you kill them?" Gary didn't break eye contact.

John yawned, covering his mouth with his hand. "You already know how."

"Humor us. Tell us how it went down from your perspective."

He rolled his eyes. "If you insist. I tied them up, using cuffs. Happy now?"

"Not really," Lewis commented. "You could've read that in the papers. You still haven't told us how you killed them."

"I strangled them, okay? That's what the rope was for."

Gary nodded. "Oh, I see. And what did you do with the nail clippings you took?"

John blinked. "The… nail clippings?"

"We know you cut their nails—all the victims had a nail clipper beside the bed," Gary lied, "but no clippings could be found. So we figured the killer had taken them. What we couldn't work out was why."

"Mementos," John blurted.

"But what did you do with them?" Lewis demanded. "Stick 'em in a drawer? Encase 'em in plastic and make a coaster out of it? Of course, you might be more imaginative than me, but I gotta be honest here, I'm struggling."

He glared at Lewis. "What I did with them is my business."

"Let's go back to why you killed them." Lewis peered at his sheet where he'd scribbled a note. "They have to be wiped off the face of the earth, you said. Then why stop at six? Surely there are plenty more guys out there that need wiping off too."

Riley came into the room and handed Gary a sheet, then withdrew.

Gary glanced at it, suppressing his sigh. He showed it to Lewis.

An Internet search for John Reynolds comes up with nothing. This guy is a nobody.

John's voice rose. "Hey, I made a start, right? Someone else will follow my example and keep going. You wait and see. Bernhard Goetz had the right idea."

Aha. And now we have it. Gary arched his eyebrows. "The vigilante? He claimed he'd done a public service by killing four men."

John nodded, his eyes wide and bright. "See? That's what *I* was doing. I'll be a hero for making a stand."

Gary had heard enough.

"No, you won't," he said quietly. "You modeled for Marius Eisler, but that's all. How many times did you sit for him?"

"Twice."

Another nod. "Did he offer to paint your portrait, or did you commission him?"

"I asked him." John aimed a fierce look at Lewis. "And no, I *didn't* go there for sex. I'm straight. I didn't even know he was gay until I saw all those paintings." He grimaced. "I only went to him because I'd seen one of his portraits in a gallery. No one's ever painted me before."

Gary studied him. "It's obvious you know nothing of the circumstances in which these men died. You may be homophobic, but you're not a vigilante, a hero. You've never amounted to anything your whole life, have you? You're no one, Mr. Reynolds, but I think you badly want to be *someone*. How far did you think this would go? Your arrest? A trial? Not even close. But it *will* get you a charge of wasting police time. And maybe some help too."

John's eyes bulged. "I don't *need* any help, you hear? Now I want you to arrest me for murder. I killed those guys, and I want everyone to know about it."

Gary shook his head. "Sorry. I'm afraid I can't do that."

John regarded them in stunned silence, and as Gary watched, he crumpled, his chest heaving, his chin trembling.

Gary glanced at Lewis. "Book him." He stood and walked out of the room. Riley was waiting outside. Gary grimaced. "Lord, what a sad little man."

"Why do people do this?"

"For the attention? I'm not going to waste time speculating on his motives. We've got work to do."

When they walked into the case room, Dan was still sitting in the chair, staring at the photos. He turned to look at them. "I guess I'm not leaving, then?" He sighed. "You know, part of me hoped he was the genuine article. I'm sorry."

"Don't be," Gary told him. "It happens more than you'd realize. And if it gets him the help he needs, I guess it's almost worth it." He gestured to the evidence box. "Were you able to learn anything?"

"Nothing of any use, I think." He shuddered.

"What's wrong?" Gary and Riley asked simultaneously.

"I didn't pick up anything from the killer, but…." He shivered. "So much fear. These guys knew they were going to die."

"You couldn't see what they saw?" Riley's face fell. "Does that ever happen? You know, as if you're looking out through their eyes?"

"If you're asking me for a physical description of the bad guy, I'm sorry, no, I can't give you that." Dan picked up one of the evidence bags.

"The best way I can describe it is… it's as if their belongings soaked up all the raw, strong emotions they were experiencing. I'm not saying it doesn't *ever* happen the way you suggest—because now and again, it does—but it's rare." He stared at the board. "What interests me are these letters the killer carves into their skin, especially *where* he cuts them."

Riley walked over to the board. "What about them?"

"What do they call it when you get a tattoo there? A tramp stamp? Maybe that's a comment on his victims."

"He appears to choose guys who are on Grindr, Scruff, and other such apps. All the victims were very sexually active, and witness statements indicate a high volume of 'visitors' to their homes. So your theory could be right. Maybe he saw them as promiscuous."

"We think that's how he's targeting them," Gary added.

Dan pointed to the heap of Scrabble tiles on the desk. "Good idea. Has it helped?"

Riley huffed. "If you're asking what the letters mean, we haven't worked that out yet. But it did help us solve a puzzle." Gary listened as Riley brought Dan up to speed on their theories about mystery man Kris.

Dan shivered when Riley got to the part about the anagram. "Okay, that just gave me chills." He glanced at the board once more. "Do you think the letters are in a specific order, or is the killer giving you a puzzle to solve once you have them all?"

"We've tried multiple combinations, but so far they make no sense. And now we know he's in this for the long haul, I think your puzzle idea is the correct one."

"There *is* something I'd like to try," Dan murmured. "But I'd need you to do something for me."

"What is it you need?" Gary asked. "And when do you want it done?"

"Not today—I need to recharge my batteries first—but tomorrow, possibly." Dan touched the photos of the ropes and cuffs. "These might be more use than the jewelry, especially as the killer will have handled them."

"I'll have them sent up first thing tomorrow," Gary confirmed.

Dan studied the images. "Maybe he's into BDSM. Then again, maybe it's a red herring, but he's used them with all the victims." He turned to look at Gary. "Were any of the victims into BDSM? Was there any evidence of that at the crime scenes?"

Gary shook his head. "What would you look for as evidence?"

"Leather, bondage gear, toys, slings, photos…. Maybe you should look at the Grindr and Scruff accounts again," Dan suggested. "Cross-reference any guys who hooked up with all the victims and who are into leather, etc. But you'll already have done this."

Riley nodded. "The list is growing. We need to interview more of them. Maybe we need to *re*interview some of them."

"Cory wasn't into all that. At least, he never mentioned it." Gary didn't think the topic had ever come up in conversation.

"How long were you two in a relationship?"

Gary froze. "What?" *He thinks we were lovers? Dear Lord. How much does he know? How much does he see?* He felt naked, under scrutiny, his secrets laid bare for all to see.

A flush crept across Dan's cheeks. "Sorry. That's none of my business."

Gary struggled to claw back some semblance of calm. "No, you… you took me by surprise, that's all. Cory and I, we were just friends," he said as Lewis strolled into the room.

"Besides, Gary is straight," Lewis interjected.

What the actual fuck?

Before he could get a single word past the lump in his throat, Lewis scowled. "Well, you are. What's wrong with that?"

"Even if I *wasn't* straight, that's nothing to do with you." Gary's face grew hot. "And it's certainly not something you should be commenting on."

Dan cleared his throat. "If it's okay with you, I'll go back to the hotel. I need a rest."

"You do that," Lewis murmured.

Gary fired him a glance. "I'll walk you out," he told Dan. He waited while Dan picked up the jacket he'd hung over the back of the chair, then led him out of the case room and through the hallway. When they reached the main entrance, he paused. "If you're tired, we don't have to meet up later."

Dan smiled. "I still need to eat, don't I? And besides, you said the food was good." He removed his wallet from his pocket and pulled out a business card. "That's my cell. Text me with the address of the restaurant. What time are we eating?"

"Seven?" Gary took the card.

Dan nodded. "That gives me time to have a couple hours sleep. I got very little last night." He cocked his head. "Good luck with whatever you're doing now."

"Reading reports, writing reports, reading statements—the dull parts the TV shows leave out."

"But those are the parts that get the job done." He locked gazes with Gary. "You'll get him. I can feel it."

"As Riley says so often, from your lips to God's ears." Gary watched as Dan walked away from the building, a slim, elegant figure who moved with grace.

You just rocked my world to its foundations, Mr. Porter.

In less than twenty-four hours, Gary had gone from being a total skeptic to someone who believed.

More than that—someone who had hope.

CHAPTER 13

DAN STEPPED out of the shower and reached for a towel from the handrail. The nap had done him a world of good, and he was hungry. He ignored the temptation to call room service: He didn't want to spoil his appetite. A glance at the Noodle Barn's photos online had him salivating, and he was looking forward to the experience.

He wasn't sure if he felt the same way about spending an evening with Gary Mitchell.

He'd made a great first impression, recognizing quotes from Dan's favorite movies, thus establishing common ground. He'd been courteous—a damn sight more courteous than Lewis—and accommodating. All indications were that he was a fine detective and a thoroughly nice guy, but.…

Dan knew what was fouling up his antenna—it was that scent. He was still clinging to the idea that it was coincidental, but his resolve was waning.

I want it to be him.

He'd waited long enough, hadn't he? And if it *was* Gary then some greater power really liked Dan, because *holy hell*, he was freaking perfect.

I always did have a thing for redheads.

Except *having a thing* was as far as it had ever gotten. Once bitten and all that.

He's my reward for all the crap I've endured for the last ten years or so. Although the concept made him smile, sending warmth curling through him, Dan doubted its veracity. The universe didn't work like that, at least not where Dan had been concerned. In *his* universe he kept his distance from men he found attractive. Experience had taught him well.

His phone buzzed, and he walked over to the nightstand to pick it up. He peered at the screen and warmth became heat, spreading through his chest, up his neck, and reaching his face.

Gary here. Can I give you a ride? Parking can be a nightmare in Jamaica Plain, plus I know the area.

Dan's thumbs got busy. *Sounds good. When will you get here?*

Seconds later, a reply pinged back. *Six thirty?*

Sure. See you then. He tossed the phone onto the bed, then sat.

An hour to wait.

An hour of trying *not* to think about Gary.

It was more than that familiar scent, and Dan knew it. Their fingers had touched, and… he couldn't quantify the sensation. He'd never felt anything like it. He hadn't lied when he'd told Gary he'd like company while he ate, but he was honest enough to admit if Gary hadn't made the suggestion, Dan would have invited him.

This is not good.

He needed to remember he was there to do a job, to help the police find a killer. That had to be his focus.

Except that focus had already become blurred.

What is it about you, Gary Mitchell, that turns me inside out?

IT WASN'T a large restaurant, and Gary had nailed it when he said it wasn't fancy, but the atmosphere felt right. One wall was plain brick with the words Noodle Barn stenciled on it in white paint, and the opposite wall was a deep shade of red. Bare bulbs in metal cages hung from cables descending from a ceiling track. A red padded bench ran the length of the brick wall, and dotted along it were wooden tables to seat two or four customers. The rest of the floor space was taken up with tables arranged to leave enough walking space around them, surrounded by black-painted chairs.

The food was a blend of Vietnamese and Thai, and one mouthful of the dumplings had been all Dan had needed. "You weren't lying." His taste buds were in heaven. "This is awesome."

"Wait till you try the mango rice. I know I suggested it, but—"

"You had me at mango. Then you went and mentioned shrimp, and that was it, I was drooling." *And the fact you're looking edible in a casual brown sport coat that picks out the color in your hair has nothing to do with it.* Dan had removed his own coat not long after they'd arrived.

Gary took a long drink of water. He hadn't suggested alcohol, which was a relief. Dan wanted to keep a clear head, and he was having enough of a problem achieving that with Gary facing him. "There's something I've been meaning to ask."

Dan steeled himself for the usual questions.

How long have you known you were psychic?
Tell me about some of your experiences.
Can you read minds?

"Ask. If I can answer, I will."

Gary pushed away his empty plate and wiped his lips on a napkin. "Lieutenant Travers told us you'd requested that your involvement be kept secret. Surely publicity means more work?"

He relaxed. "Do you recall Lewis asking if I did this for a living?"

Gary huffed. "Not a conversation I'm likely to forget. Is this where I apologize again?"

Dan smiled. "There's no need. And Lewis's behavior only reflects badly on him. I told him it didn't pay well, but that I didn't do it for the money. That was partly true."

"Which part?"

He sighed. "I don't charge for my services. And I like to keep things private. I prefer to work in the background, helping where I can."

Gary arched his eyebrows. "A man of independent means?"

"You could say that. Lewis's barb about me being a rich kid? Guilty as charged. But that has meant I have the time and the finances to go where I'm needed. I don't need publicity because believe me, word of mouth is more than enough."

Dan's brush with unasked-for publicity had left him wary and scarred, and he didn't intend repeating the experience.

Their entrées arrived, and he was grateful for the welcome interruption. He wasn't about to reveal his history, and he hoped to God Gary wouldn't press him further. Thankfully the food occupied them for a while, but the knot in Dan's stomach prevented total enjoyment. He couldn't finish it, so he contented himself with eating all the chicken, the fat shrimps, and the succulent pieces of mango.

Gary seemed to be suffering from a similar affliction. Then Dan remembered he wasn't the only one who'd had a stressful day.

He put his fork down. "I think I'm the one who should be apologizing."

Gary's brow furrowed. "For what?"

"I put you through the wringer today. You should've told me." His and Cory's relationship must have been pretty special. Dan envied him. He'd never been that close to anyone his entire life.

"That was sort of the point of the exercise."

Dan froze. "You gave me that ring on purpose?" Gary dipped his chin to his chest. "Why?" Then he saw the light. "It was a test, wasn't it? You're as skeptical as Lewis—you're just not as vocal about it." An iron band tightened around his chest, and his appetite deserted him. God, the only one who'd been honest with him was Riley.

Gary jerked his head up, his cheeks flushed. "Look, I'm not proud of what I did, but I had my reasons, okay? I don't have a clue what Lewis has against… people like you, but believe me when I say you're not the first psychic to cross my path. My experience has taught me to have no faith in stuff like this."

"We're all fakers and charlatans, is that it?"

Gary held up his hands. "Hey, I'll admit it, I thought that. When Travers first mentioned bringing you in on this, I shot him down without a second's hesitation."

Dan reined in his bitterness. "And now? What about now?"

"Lewis probably thinks you had inside help, that someone told you about Cory, but I don't believe that." A shiver rippled through him. "I watched you. I saw how deeply you were affected by… by whatever you felt. You're no fake."

Gary's words rang with sincerity, and Dan experienced an unexpected release of tension, leaving him weak and giddy. "Thank you. I meet so many people who think I'm a fraud. And even when I give them the answers they're looking for, some of them still doubt."

"When did you first know you could do this?"

Dan wiped his lips, then dropped the napkin onto his plate. "When I was nine or ten. I was always the one who could 'find' things," he said, air-quoting. "Mom was forever misplacing her scissors, her reading glasses, her keys, and I'd tell her where she'd left them. I think my parents found it amusing… until the day they discovered it was more than guesswork."

"What happened?"

"I walked into the kitchen one morning, and Mom was standing at the sink, staring out the window. I went over to her and hugged her, because it seemed like that was what she needed. That wasn't what caused the upset that followed—it was when I told her it was okay, Aunt Jane would be fine. She gazed at me with a frown and asked me what I meant. I said Aunt Jane and Uncle Frank could always try again, and that she wasn't to be sad about the baby."

"Oh God. Had she miscarried?"

Dan nodded. "But what spooked my parents was that they hadn't told me about it. Mom had only heard it from my grandmother less than ten minutes before I walked into the kitchen. There was no way I could've known."

"What happened then?"

Dan could still see the kitchen, his parents on one side of the table and him on the other. They'd sent his older brother and two sisters outside to rake up the autumn leaves that covered the backyard. "They sat me down and asked questions. How had I known? Were there other things that I knew that no one had told me? I didn't understand myself what was going on—how could I hope to explain it to them?"

"Did it affect your relationship with your parents?"

Another nod. "They don't talk about it. When I was working with NYPD and Chicago PD, I didn't tell them. My sisters think I'm weird. My brother? He's much more laid back about it. When I moved to Litchfield, he asked if I'd gone there to get a job with Spooky World's Nightmare New England." Gary frowned, and Dan gave him an inquiring glance. "Your parents never took you there when you were a kid? It's a commercial haunted park."

Something flitted across Gary's face, and then it was gone. "No, they never did. It wasn't their kind of thing." He gave a half smile. "Your brother sounds okay."

"One Christmas he gave me a DVD of *The Dead Zone*, that movie with Christopher Walken about the guy who knows things?" Dan chuckled. "He said I'd like it because it was about people like me."

"You live on your own?"

Dan cocked his head. "What you really mean is, am I single, married...." He held up his left hand. "Look, no ring. I don't do relationships. I don't even do *friends* all that well. High school was a nightmare, especially when word got out. I was 'that creepy kid.' I learned to keep my hands in my pockets and other kids at a distance."

"Then it does work primarily by touch?"

He nodded. "Most of the time. I sometimes get visions. We all have weird dreams from time to time, right? I've learned to differentiate between the I-ate-cheese-before-bed weird dreams and the ones that mean something."

What came to mind was a warm, damp chest pressed against his back, a slow rocking of hips, exquisite friction—and the scent of patchouli and cedar.

Gary mentions cedar and suddenly you know *what that other aroma was? Talk about wishful thinking.*

Sometimes Dan's inner voice could be a real bitch.

"I can understand why you avoided other kids." Gary's eyes were kind. "High school… ugh. Don't even go there. But surely adults are more understanding."

He arched his eyebrows. "Think about Lewis's reaction, then say that again." He drank some water. "To be honest, I'm wary of relationships." *And when was the last time I told anyone this much about myself?*

Maybe it was because Gary was listening that Dan leveled with him. "The thing is, this… gift of mine—although there are times when it feels more like a curse—has made it difficult to get close to people. Imagine being intimate with someone you think could be important to you, and the next minute, your head is spinning because you got a glimpse of something you *really* didn't want to see. I meant what I said to Riley. I can't turn it on and off."

Gary's breathing caught. "That's happened to you, hasn't it?"

He nodded. "I couldn't look at him the same after that." His heart slipped into overdrive. *Why did I do that?* The use of a male pronoun had been deliberate, and he had no clue what had prompted the impulse. *Why should it matter to a straight man that I'm gay?*

Except he was lying to himself. His attraction to Gary lay at the root of it.

Gary wiped his brow. "I think they've just turned the heat up in here." He shrugged out of his sport coat, and Dan drank in the sight of the white shirt that clung to his body, the short sleeves tight around his biceps, the creamy skin of his inner forearm, the—

Oh sweet Jesus.

On Gary's left arm, two words were etched in black. *Never Forget.*

It was him.

Holy fuck, *it was him.*

"Dan?"

His hands shook, and he hid them out of sight below the table, unable to tear his gaze away from Gary's tattoo.

And Gary noticed. He covered up the words with his right hand.

Dan did his damnedest to inject a note of calm into his voice. "I'm sorry. What did you say?"

"I know I said I wouldn't ask questions, and it feels as if that's all I done this evening, but I do have one last question. Do your visions always come true?"

Oh dear Lord.

"When I can make sense of them? Yes. Sometimes trying to work out what a vision is telling me is the hardest part. It doesn't always happen."

Those were the visions that haunted him. Was there something he could have done, some truth he could have grasped but failed to because the message proved too ambiguous?

There was nothing ambiguous about the vision that had visited him time and time again, though. Here at last was his unseen lover.

And he's straight.

Dan had to get out of there, back to the safety of his hotel room. He needed quiet to think things through. Because none of it made sense.

CHAPTER 14

GARY PULLED into the drop-off lane in front of the Fairmont. "If the coffee in your room isn't up to much, I can recommend Jaho Coffee Roaster on Huntington. It's only a couple of streets from here. They close at ten." Traffic roared past: Copley Square was still wide-awake and buzzing.

Dan laughed, but there was a forced quality to it. "If you want to find a good coffee shop, ask a cop."

That made Gary smile. "Sure. But don't ask me to recommend a donut shop. I don't eat them." He glanced at Dan's figure. "Not that you look like a guy who eats donuts." Dan arched his eyebrows, and Gary backpedaled. "I'm sorry. I shouldn't make personal comments." *And I have no idea why I said that.*

Or why he kept looking at Dan every chance he got.

"Hey, don't ruin the compliment with an apology."

Gary noted his relaxed tone with relief. "Are you feeling better?"

Dan blinked. "What do you mean?"

"I got the impression back in the restaurant that something was troubling you. For a moment there, you were… I don't know… I'd say distracted, but it was more than that. You looked like you'd had a shock." Gary had analyzed their conversation, but he couldn't account for the change in atmosphere. The moment had passed, but Dan hadn't slipped back into his earlier, lighter mood.

"I'm sorry about that. I… I remembered something important I had to do. I've calmed down since." His smile wasn't wide enough to create dimples, but he seemed more content than he had been. "Thanks for a great evening. I really didn't want to eat alone tonight."

"Actually, I should be thanking you."

"For what?"

Gary's stomach clenched. "I was certain you were going to ask questions about Cory."

Dan's eyes were kind. "No. You didn't need that, not after today."

Gary's face grew warm, but it was a comfortable warmth. When Dan made no move to get out of the car, he blurted, "You said I'd agreed to your involvement because of Cory, but… I think *you* agreed to it because of the victims."

Dan twisted in his seat to look Gary in the eye. "Because they were all gay men? Like me?" He shrugged. "You could be right." Before Gary could respond, Dan scowled. "No. You've been honest with me—the least I can do is be as honest with you. When I got the call about the case, I'd already been watching the news. I'd had no insights, no visions, but I wanted to help. Seeing homophobia in everyday life is bad enough, but to have some maniac out there picking off gay men?" He swallowed. "He has to be stopped. And I'll do everything I can to help you stop him."

"Thank you." Gary glanced at the hotel's facade, with its flags, its red awnings, and the yellow lights that shone upward from the third floor, bathing the stonework in warmth. "I've never stayed here."

Dan unfastened his seat belt. "The beds are supremely comfortable." He gazed at Gary. "I'll see you tomorrow. I'm going to aim for a good night's sleep. I suggest you do the same—if you can. Try to switch your brain off."

Gary's chest tightened. "Easier said than done." He extended his hand toward Dan, but pulled it back at the last minute. He tensed as Dan held out his.

"It's okay, really."

Gary took it. Dan enveloped his hand and gave it a gentle squeeze. Their gazes met, and Dan stilled, hardly breathing.

Gary shivered. It was as if all the tension had seeped from his body. The constriction around his chest loosened, and warmth tingled through him.

Dan's eyes widened, his breathing ragged, and Gary knew he wasn't alone. *He feels it too.* Then he let go, and the sensations were gone. Gary's heartbeat quickened.

What just happened?

"Till tomorrow." Dan got out of the car and hurried up to the main door without a backward glance.

Gary didn't know what to make of it. His physical reactions to Dan's touch had been pleasurable. But Dan….*He couldn't get out of the car fast enough.*

Gary pulled away from the curb. One thing was certain—he wasn't going to mention it the following day. It would be a distraction, one they could both do without.

What stuck in his mind as he headed home was how good Dan's hand had felt curled around his.

DAN AIMED the remote at the wide-screen TV, flicking through the channels. Nothing registered. His mind was on Gary, his vision—and that tattoo.

Why torture me with a vision that can't come true?

Except it was no longer just the vision. The evening had proved one thing—keeping his thoughts steady around Gary was going to be a real chore.

Keeping his thoughts to himself might prove an even bigger one.

Dan stroked his chin, and a tremor slid down his spine. He could smell Gary's scent on his fingers, only a faint trace but enough to stir his senses. Opening himself up to physical contact was always a gamble; he avoided shaking hands wherever he could. Thankfully he wasn't alone. Lots of people didn't like to "press the flesh," as his grandfather had called it, and generally no one commented on it. Dan made sure his courteous manner assured the greeter that no slight had been intended.

But *oh my God*, when their hands joined….

He could still recall each sensation and reaction: the ache in his chest, warmth spreading out from his groin, the fluttering in his stomach, and the hammering of his heart. His pulse quickened, and he'd longed for more sensation, more of that *connection*. Because he knew with every fiber of his being that Gary had felt something too.

When they broke contact, it was as if someone had turned out the light.

His heartbeat hadn't slowed by the time he'd gotten out of the car. He'd hurried into the hotel, not wanting Gary to see him tremble.

Jesus. All we did was shake hands.

He switched off the TV and climbed into the wide bed, more than ready to leave the day behind. And for once he wished for the vision.

Will it have changed? Will I see him?

Lord, he was a mess.

Did someone up there think it funny to fixate me on a straight guy?

A MOMENT after Gary closed his front door, his phone rang. He answered when he saw it was Nina. "Hey. How are you?" He walked into the living room and sat on the couch.

"Better. I'm only going through one box of Kleenex a day instead of two. That's an improvement, right?" She paused. "Sorry to call you so late, but I thought you'd want to know. A date's been set for the funeral. Next week. Tuesday, June fifth."

"Where will the service be held?" Gary grabbed the notepad and pen from the coffee table.

"Bigelow Chapel."

He gazed at the photo of him and Brad. "Yeah, been there. It's a beautiful place. You probably don't remember because you were only seven, and I don't think you went to the funeral, but... that's where Brad is buried. Mount Auburn Cemetery."

"Oh. No, I didn't remember."

"I'll be there. I'll let the precinct know tomorrow, and I'll take Tuesday off." He scribbled the date and place, then put the pen down. "How are your parents?"

"Still in a state of shock. Dad's coping better than Mom, I think. I've written the obituary and sent it to all the newspapers—the *Globe*, the *Herald*, the *Tribune*, the *Sun*.... It'll be online too. I told Mom and Dad to expect the chapel to be packed. Cory.... Cory went to the memorial service for one of the guys who was killed. Vic something? It was right at the end of last year. He said you couldn't move in the church it was so full. I'm expecting a similar turnout. Cory was a popular guy."

"Yeah, he was."

"I remember him saying he had no idea there were so many gay men in Boston."

That sent a shiver through him. *And right now someone is working his way through them with murderous intent.*

"I'll save you a seat with us, all right?"

His throat seized. "Thanks, sweetheart." The words came out as a croak.

"Okay. That was all."

"Call me if you need anything?"

"I've been recalling things Cory and I said," she blurted. A soft sigh filled his ear. "You're gonna laugh, but... when I was a teenager and you and Cory were roomies in college, I told him you two should date. I said you were perfect for each other. Well, apart from you not being into guys, of course."

"He never told me that."

"Probably didn't want to embarrass you." A pause. "Good night, then."

"G'night, Nina. Next time we talk, I want to hear you've halved your use of Kleenex. He wouldn't want us to cry."

"No, he wouldn't." Her voice grew firm. "He'd want us to celebrate his life."

"Then you'd better start looking for a bigger venue for the reception. There'll be a ton of men who'll want to celebrate him too."

Another pause; then she chuckled. "I'd better get onto TD Garden right away. It can seat thousands. You think it'll be big enough?" She disconnected.

Gary went into the kitchen to make some tea, grateful for the distraction. For all Cory's confidence, he was self-deprecating and never would have assumed he was popular enough to warrant a huge turnout at his funeral. The thought of a crowd of gay men gathered to pay homage to him injected ice into Gary's bloodstream. He could imagine the killer among them, no one suspecting what evil he harbored....

Dan will help us. Dan *had* to help them. And Dan was messing with his head.

What is it about him?

Okay, so he was attractive. Gary worked with a lot of attractive guys—Riley was good-looking enough to be a model, for God's sake—but none of them drew his attention the way Dan did. *So what if he does? It doesn't mean anything, does it?*

Except there was more to this than Dan's appearance. It was the whole package.

He intrigues me. Maybe that's it.

That didn't explain why a simple squeeze of his hand, lasting all of a few seconds, should linger in his memory.

Not linger—more like it was imprinted.

Nor did it explain why Gary's stomach fluttered when Dan focused warm hazel eyes on him.

Jesus. What is wrong with me?

Why did he have the feeling that somewhere Cory was laughing his ass off and saying very loudly, *I told you so. Now get your ass out of that closet.*

His phone's shrill ringtone shattered the quiet, and Gary peered at the screen. Lewis. He clicked Answer. "Something wrong?" Lewis wasn't given to calling him at home.

"Are you sitting down? Because you need to be."

Gary's heart pounded. "What? Tell me."

"I think I've found our man."

CHAPTER 15

OH GOD. "Give me details."

"Riley mentioned something about going through the crossover list again but looking for guys with a link to BDSM. You know, checking for anyone in leather, pics of whips, chains, ropes...."

"That was Dan's idea too."

"Whatever. The point is, I've spent the last three hours on Grindr. I set up a fake account."

"You did what?"

"Hey, if our killer can do it, then so can we. I downloaded photos from BDSM sites—did you know there are *stores* where you can walk in and buy all this sh—stuff? Anyhow, I posted all the photos, and I got a bite. Some guy called Jesse Monroe. I did an online search for him, and there's a *shitload* of pics of him out there in leather chaps, leather jocks, a harness, holding... well, I don't know what the fuck he was holding, but it sent shivers through me, I can tell you."

"So he's into BDSM. So are a lot of gay guys."

"Yeah, but this guy is on our list, and *none* of these pics made it onto his Grindr profile. He arranged meetings with *all* the victims."

"Including Cory?"

"Yup."

"Then we'll have interviewed him already. If he's on the list."

"I checked. We haven't. Don't ask me how we missed him, but at least he's on our radar now." Gary heard the bubble of excitement in Lewis's voice.

"Okay.... Much as I would love this to be our guy, and much as I hate to pour cold water on your enthusiasm, don't you get the sense that our man is an intelligent guy? Would he be that obvious?" The letters, the anagram, the way he'd hidden his tracks....

"Then let's go talk to him and see if he has an alibi for all the murders. Get a sample of DNA. At least *look* at the guy."

Lewis was right. They had to take a look, even if something about the whole business niggled him. "Okay. First thing tomorrow, we'll bring him in for questioning."

"*I'll* bring him in," Lewis fired back. "I'll take Riley with me. Best if you keep out of this. Remember what Travers said."

"Fine. You and Riley can bring him in."

"Great."

"And Lewis?"

"Yeah?"

"That fake account business… I'm impressed." He meant it. He hadn't believed Lewis could be that diligent.

"Hey, we've all gotta step out of our comfort zone now and then, right? I can put up with a few hours of guys asking to see my dick—and worse—if it means we catch the son of a bitch. G'night." He disconnected.

Gary went back to making tea, his mind replaying Lewis's words. The BDSM angle worried him, and he wasn't sure why. But if this Jesse Monroe was on the list and he hadn't been questioned yet, that was enough reason to bring him in.

If they were lucky, he was the missing piece. If his alibis checked out, then it would be back to the drawing board. But if he *was* their man, Lewis would crow about it. Gary could already hear him.

See? There was no need for a psychic.

Gary poured boiling water onto a teabag, absently swirling it in the hot liquid, his thoughts drawn back to Dan.

And if it is our man, Dan can leave.

He'd only been there one day.

Gary wrapped his hands around the cup. *I don't want him to go yet.* The realization forced him to analyze his motives for wanting Dan to stick around, and one thought came to the forefront.

What if Dan had the answers to his questions?

And am I brave enough to ask them?

Tuesday, May 29

"GOOD MORNING."

Gary jerked his head up at the softly spoken greeting. Dan stood in front of his desk, wearing the same suit as the previous day, only with a blue shirt and tie.

Damn. He looks good. Then he shoved the thought from his mind. It had no business being there, not at work. Besides, he wasn't sure if Dan would be able to pick up on his emotions. "Morning."

Dan glanced around the busy room. There were several desks, each one occupied as detectives typed reports, read documents, or made calls. "Where are Lewis and Riley?" He flushed. "If it's okay to refer to them like that."

"They aren't here, so you can refer to them any way you like." He bit back a smile. "You should hear some of the things I call Lewis when he's out of earshot."

"I can imagine." Dan's deadpan delivery didn't detract from the twinkle in his eyes.

"We had a breakthrough," Gary told him. "They've gone to bring in a suspect." He stood. "And in the meantime, I did as you requested. There's a box in the case room, those items you wanted from Evidence."

"Oh good. Then let's go."

Dan followed him to the small room, and once they were inside, Gary closed the door behind them. "I thought you might need a little quiet to concentrate."

"Thank you. It does help."

Gary gestured to the chair, and Dan sat. "How about we do the same thing as yesterday? I hand you an item, and you see if you can sense anything." When Dan regarded him in silence, the skin on Gary's arms prickled. "What have I said?"

"I was thinking…. You really do believe now, don't you?" He smiled. "What a difference a day makes."

"I'm not a stupid man," Gary returned in a quiet voice. "You gave me proof. Why would I not believe in your gift?" He gestured to the evidence box. "Same as yesterday? No information about the victim, just the item?"

Dan nodded. "I'd prefer that." He removed his coat and hung it on the chair, then sat with his hands in his lap, breathing deeply, his eyes closed.

Gary waited by the table, watching as a layer of calm enveloped Dan until his chest rose and fell steadily, each breath slow and even.

"I'm ready," Dan said, his voice low and deep.

Gary reached into the box and withdrew a bag containing a coil of red rope. He removed it from its covering, then placed it on Dan's upturned palms. Dan held it between his hands, his fingertips tracing along its length, his brow furrowing.

Gary understood Riley's remark about finding it fascinating. Watching Dan at work was certainly that. What drew his attention were Dan's long lashes, dark against the cream of his complexion, the clean line of his jaw, the fullness of that lower lip....

Twenty-four hours had elapsed since their first meeting, and if anything, the attraction he'd felt to the slight, handsome man had intensified.

I don't understand why he affects me the way he does.

Cory's voice was in his head. *You sure about that, honey? Or do you just not want to admit the truth?*

Dan opened his eyes and sighed. "I'm sorry. I'm not getting anything." He held out the rope to Gary. "Give me another. I'll try not to take so long this time."

Gary frowned, but when he glanced at his watch, he realized what Dan had meant. Fifteen minutes had elapsed. "Take as long as you need." He replaced the rope in the box and took out another. Once he'd handed it over, he took a step back.

Dan smiled. "You're fine where you are. Besides, that scent you wear? It calms me." Then he closed his eyes again.

Gary forgot about the time, the muffled noises from beyond the door, the murmur of traffic from outside, and focused on Dan, the sound of his breathing, the movement of his hands as he touched the rope, and the tiny changes in his expression.

Dan opened his eyes once more and shivered. Gary checked his watch. Ten minutes had passed. "You felt something."

He nodded. "A lot of rage in this guy."

"Do you mean the killer?"

Another nod. "I think so. There are definitely two different energies connected to this. But there's another emotion—guilt. So much guilt that it almost swamps the anger. And I'm picking up something that can only be from the victim." His eyes widened. "Surprise. He didn't see this coming. It's almost as if...." He closed his eyes once more.

"As if what?"

Dan paled. "He knew him. He knew the killer." He opened his eyes as Riley came into the room, and Gary stilled at the sight of his clearly agitated state.

Riley expelled a breath. "I think you should see this guy."

"Did you bring him in?"

Riley nodded. "Sure, an hour ago, but he's not talking, and he's asked for his lawyer. We've had him in an interview room for the last twenty minutes, and we can't get a peep out of him."

"Did he indicate he was willing to help with inquiries?" Gary asked. Riley grimaced, and Gary stared at him. "Okay, what happened? And why am I only hearing about it now?"

"When we got to his address, there was no answer. Then this old guy from across the hall opened his door and said he'd been about to call the police. He'd heard sounds coming from Monroe's apartment that scared him. Well, then *we* heard something, and Lewis didn't hesitate. He busted the door down, announced we were the police, and charged in there."

"I take it you found something."

Another nod. "He was in the living room, and he wasn't alone. He was dressed up in a harness and boots—that was all—and he was holding some kind of a whip. There was another guy, naked, tied up and gagged, facedown over the coffee table. But there was GHB, a pair of cuffs, rope…. And the tied-up guy was clearly about to be… you know."

"Did Detective Stevens ascertain whether what was going on was consensual?" Dan inquired.

"I took the gag off of him, and the first thing that popped out of his mouth was he was there voluntarily." Riley swallowed. "Lewis asked if he wanted to bring charges, but he said no, absolutely not. *Then* Lewis decided he was too scared to tell the truth. The guy had these marks on his back too, you know, from the whip. Monroe was yelling about his door being busted in, the invasion of his privacy. So Lewis told him to put some clothes on because we were taking him in to answer some questions. He said no at first, but I convinced him what he had to say might help us. He wasn't happy about it, but he agreed."

"And once he got here, he clammed up."

Riley nodded. "Lewis went in there, and as soon as he started asking about whatever it was we'd interrupted, Monroe demanded to be allowed to call his lawyer. I mean, we hadn't even arrested him at that point."

There was a knock at the door, and an officer poked his head around it. Riley went over to him, and they spoke quietly. Riley's groan made Gary's stomach roil. "Now what?"

The officer left, and Riley faced them, his expression gloomy. "Great. Monroe's lawyer arrived. He says he represents the Boston leather community, and there's another guy with him who writes articles on BDSM for the *Huffington Post*, *Out*, and a whole load of magazines I've never heard of. They want to speak to the Chief of Police, and they demand we release Monroe immediately. The lawyer is in with Monroe now."

Dan pulled his phone from his pants pocket and typed quickly. "Wow. News sure travels fast in this town." He held up the screen for them to see. "It's all over Twitter."

"What the hell did you search for to find it so fast?" Riley gaped.

"Hashtag leather, hashtag bondage…."

Riley peered closer. "The other guy, the one who wouldn't press charges…. That's him. He's the one tweeting."

Dan scrolled. "He's not the only one. There's one here from a lawyer's office. Maybe it's Monroe's lawyer. A guy called Adam Winton." He winced. "Oh dear. This does *not* make you guys look good."

Riley scraped his fingers over his scalp. "Fuck."

The door opened again, and Gary froze when he caught sight of Travers's cool expression.

"My office. Now. Both of you." He glanced at Dan. "Not you, Mr. Porter. You have nothing to do with this."

"Actually, would it be okay if I came too? I won't interfere, but I do have some insights that might be valuable."

Travers pursed his lips. "Very well."

They followed Travers through the building to his office, Gary, Dan, and Riley trailing behind him, Gary's face and neck feeling impossibly hot. *I probably look like a school kid being summoned to the principal's office.* Some of his coworkers aimed sympathetic glances in their direction, and others turned away to hide their expressions.

When they entered, Lewis was waiting for them, pacing up and down in front of Travers's desk. Travers pointed a bony finger at the chairs, and Gary dropped into one like a stone. Dan stood behind them, his hands clasped.

Lewis's eyes bulged. "What's *he* doing here?"

Travers's nostrils flared. "If you don't mind, I'll be the one asking the questions. And I agreed to Mr. Porter's presence. Do you have a problem with that?"

"No, sir." Lewis's face was sullen.

Travers addressed Gary. "Did you ask Lewis to bring in Monroe?"

Gary straightened. "Yes, sir. We established a connection between him and all the victims and wanted to investigate it further."

"But you were in charge at the scene." Travers fixed Lewis with an intense gaze.

"Yes, sir."

Travers sighed. "Congratulations. You've only gone and created a PR nightmare."

"All we did was bring in a—"

Travers cut off Lewis's explanation with a hard stare. "Thanks to you, Boston PD appears to be victimizing a well-known member of the leather community."

"Who might have knowledge of these murders," Lewis protested. "And we're not victimizing any—"

There was a knock at the door, and an officer stepped in. "Sir, I have Adam Winton here. He's the law—"

"It's okay, Trent, I know who he is. Let him in."

The officer withdrew, and a moment later, a tall, bald man in a dark suit entered, a briefcase in one hand. He extended the other to Travers, they shook, and Riley stood to let him sit.

"I've spoken with my client." Mr. Winton arched his dark brows. "I assume the police department will replace his front door?"

"We were acting out of concern," Lewis ground out. "A neighbor heard noises that made us fear we were too late to save another victim."

Mr. Winton nodded. "I asked my client about this neighbor. He described him as… let me be sure I quote him accurately…." He removed a notepad from his briefcase and flicked through it. "Ah yes, a 'homophobic asshole.'"

Gary bit his lip.

"Mr. Brading has complained to the concierge on numerous occasions about my client," Mr. Winton continued. "Said complaints have been petty, vindictive, and bordering on hate speech. Your arrival was manna from heaven, and he took full advantage of it." He placed his briefcase on the floor beside his chair. "Now, about the scene your officers interrupted…."

"Scene?" Lewis's jaw dropped. "Excuse me, but—"

Mr. Winton's blue eyes were glacial. "Do you have any firsthand experience of BDSM, Detective?"

"No, but that's not the point."

Mr. Winton blinked. "I rather think it is. Everything taking place in that apartment was consensual."

"Does that include drugs? Because he had GHB."

"Can I say something here?" Dan's clear, deep voice rang out.

Travers nodded. "Mr. Winton, this is Dan Porter, who is helping us with the case." The two men exchanged polite nods.

Dan turned to Lewis. "What you may not know, Detective Stevens, is that GHB is a pretty frequent sex-related drug among gay men. I won't go into details here of what effects it produces, but it *is* commonplace."

"And I suppose *you* have firsthand experience of this?" Lewis retorted, his face flushed.

Gary's chest constricted, but Dan met Lewis's heated gaze, his eyes cool. "Yes, as a matter of fact, I do."

Gary envied Dan his calm.

Dan wasn't done. "You can't assume anyone who has GHB is the killer. That's like saying if someone dies from being stabbed with a kitchen knife, then anyone who possesses a kitchen knife has to be a murderer."

"I've spoken with my client about the dates of the murders," Mr. Winton interjected. "He has alibis for all of them."

"Then we need to check them," Lewis retorted.

Mr. Winton consulted his notepad. "The last murder? Cory Peterson? Mr. Monroe was in Chicago, attending a convention known as International Mr. Leather. Between one and two thousand people attended, and on the day in question, at least several hundred men saw him." He cleared his throat. "Including myself."

Lewis blinked. "How can that many people have seen him? It isn't possible."

"Mr. Monroe is a well-known face at these events. He was on stage for most of the day. Marius Eisler's murder? Monroe was in LA, giving a demonstration of rope bondage at Eagle LA." Mr. Winton regarded Travers. "So unless you're assuming there are *two* killers out there, do you still want to check his alibis? I assure you, they will all stand up to scrutiny."

Travers stood. "Thank you for speaking with us, Mr. Winton. There will be no charges against Mr. Monroe, and he's free to leave." They shook again.

"Now we've cleared all that up, I trust you'll get back to finding the real killer." Mr. Winton's face fell. "I meet a great many gay men, and most of them are frightened by this."

"We're doing all we can," Travers assured him. With a final nod, Mr. Winton left the office. Travers ran his fingers through his hair. "Christ. This is a mess."

Lewis was on his feet, staring at Dan. "So you're into all this? Whips, chains, and drugs? With guys?"

Dan stared at him, but Travers got in first. "I don't give a damn if he is or he isn't. His personal life is none of your affair. Carry on like this, Stevens, and it'll sound as if you're victimizing Mr. Porter on account of his sexuality. I don't have to remind you what a dim view the state of Massachusetts takes of attitudes like that, do I?"

"No, sir."

"For the record, Detective Stevens?" Dan lifted his chin. "Yes, I'm gay. It isn't a secret. No, I'm not part of the BDSM lifestyle, but I know people who are. No, I don't use GHB myself, but again, I've met others who do. It has a not-unearned reputation as a date-rape drug, and in this instance, a maniac is using it to kill gay men. But please don't assume the same of every GHB user." He gave a cool smile. "And now we've got *that* out of the way, let's concentrate on finding the killer."

"I second that." Travers drew in a deep breath. "Damage control time. Gary, you're back as lead investigator, but Riley will be in on all your interviews." He speared Gary with a look reinforced with steel. "I told the chief you were one of the best detectives on the force. Now prove me right." Someone rapped on the door, and Travers barked out, "What is it?"

Officer Dietrich peered around it. "Sir. A call just came in. A body's been discovered." His face was pale. "Looks like another one."

Jesus fucking Christ.

CHAPTER 16

RILEY WAS at the wheel, and Lewis was in the passenger seat. Ahead of them loomed the tall glass-and-steel elegance of the huge apartment complexes on Liberty Drive, and beyond lay Boston Harbor. Blue sky, calm water... and they were on their way to a crime scene.

"Murder doesn't belong in a place like this," Dan murmured beside him.

Gary shivered to hear his thoughts echoed. He glanced at Dan. "Murder doesn't belong anywhere." Dan raked his fingers through his hair, disturbing its perfection. His knee bounced, and his breaths were short.

Gary didn't have to be psychic to read Dan's body language. "What's up?"

He closed his eyes for a second or two before replying. "Are you sure I should be here?"

"Travers okayed it," Riley said as he took a right off Seaport Boulevard. "He agreed with us that it's important for you to see the crime scene."

"He agreed with you and Gary, you mean," Lewis muttered. "No one asked my opinion."

"Yeah, because we knew what it would be." *And this has gone far enough.* They were long overdue for a conversation. Gary leaned forward, pointing. "That's it on the right. Fifty Liberty."

"Pretty swanky neighborhood," Riley murmured as he pulled up behind a police car. "Nothing like the others."

"How is it different?" Dan asked. "That might be important."

"Up till now the victims lived in Dorchester, Roxbury, Jamaica Plain. Average-looking neighborhoods. This is new."

"This place looks like it might have CCTV." Lewis twisted to look at Gary. "I'll check. You guys go on up."

Riley's gaze met Gary's in the rearview mirror, but he said nothing. He switched off the engine, and they got out. At ground level, the words Fifty Liberty stood out from the wall in polished metal.

Gary glanced up the street. "Del's here." The medical examiner's car was parked ahead of theirs.

"He usually beats us to it." Riley led the way across a paved area bracketed by neatly trimmed shrubs. He stopped at the main door, where a police officer stood. "Hey, Lomax. This is getting to be a habit."

"If it is, it's one I'd like to break. Six days since the last one. What's he doing, going for a record?" Lomax gave Gary a nod, then stared at Dan.

"It's okay, he's with us," Gary informed him. He pushed open the door, and they stepped into the cool interior with its marble floors and expanses of glass.

"I'll go talk to the concierge." Lewis strode toward the rear of the lobby. Gary, Riley, and Dan headed for the elevators, where a couple of officers stood talking.

"The medical examiner arrived about five minutes ago," one of them told Gary. "Eleventh floor, Apartment A."

He glanced at his badge. "Thanks, Williams." He pressed the button, and when the doors slid open, they filed inside. More marble covered the floor, and the back wall of the elevator was mirrored. Gary expelled a breath. "Okay, what do we know about the victim?"

Riley consulted his notes. "Dispatch said his name is Robin Fields. They got a call from the concierge. Mr. Fields's cleaner arrived this morning and found him. I did a quick search online." Riley whistled. "This guy could buy the whole building if he wanted."

"What else do we know about him?" Gary asked as the elevator stopped and they got out.

"Apart from the fact that he's a millionaire? Self-made man, made a fortune from the sale of his first company when he was twenty-nine, then kept doing the same thing for the next twenty years."

Gary paused at the yellow tape across the hallway. On the other side of it, an officer walked toward them.

Dan rubbed the back of his neck, and there was tightness around his eyes.

Gary frowned. "Are you all right? It's like Riley said, Travers agreed you should be here." He seemed awful jumpy.

Dan swallowed. "Look, this is my first crime scene, okay? Up till now, I've worked with evidence, the way I did today. Walking into an apartment where someone was murdered? I-I'm not sure what to expect."

Oh God. Gary stilled. "This could be more intense than the… signals you get from items? Is that it?"

"Yeah. And right now I don't know whether I should open myself up to whatever is in there or shield myself from being bombarded by emotions."

Gary squeezed his arm. "If it gets too much, you give the word, and I'll have you out of there in a heartbeat." He was glad Lewis wasn't around. He could imagine the sort of crap he'd come out with.

"What he said," Riley added, his voice warm. "If you can't take it, you get out. Period."

Dan nodded, then cleared his throat. "Thank you."

Gary greeted the officer who held back the tape for them, and they entered the apartment.

The dark brown wood floor contrasted with the deep cream walls. On the left of the entrance hall, a huge painting dominated the space, an abstract in muted shades of beige, bronze, and sand. The narrow hall opened out into a larger area, combining kitchen, living room, and dining table. A corner sofa filled most of the floor space, and along one wall was a unit filled with books, home theater, and ornaments. Above it was the wide-screen TV.

Rob Michaels stood beside the dining table, conversing with an officer. Behind him were floor-to-ceiling windows, affording a view of the harbor. He greeted them, his face grim. "We have to stop meeting like this." He pointed to a door on the right. "He's in there."

"Did he live here alone?" Riley asked.

Rob shook his head. "There's a boyfriend, the concierge says. We're trying to locate him. The victim has lived here for five years." He arched his eyebrows at the sight of Dan.

"Mr. Porter is here to provide us with his insights," Gary told the sergeant. He glanced at Dan. "Okay so far?"

Rob said nothing for a moment, then nodded. "We've already dusted in there for prints, so it's okay to touch whatever you need to."

Gary had a feeling that last part was for Dan's benefit.

"CSI say there are prints all over the place. We'll have the medical examiner print the victim so we can eliminate his. We've got the cleaner's prints too, once she'd given her statement. That just leaves the boyfriend."

"Thanks, Rob." Gary led Riley and Dan into the bedroom, one end of which was taken up with more windows. A couple of Del's assistants stood back from the bed, clearly waiting for instructions.

Robin Fields lay naked on his back, his eyes closed. He'd been a handsome man with graying hair, some of which could be seen on his chest. He was uncovered, his arms by his sides, his legs straight. A pair of cuffs and a tangle of red rope sat on the bed beside the body. Gary noted the marks on the victim's wrists and ankles.

Del glanced up from his position next to the bed. "Your timing is excellent. The officers already took photos, so I'll take the rope and cuffs when you're done." He lowered his gaze. "Victim was forty-nine, according to his ID. Kept himself in good shape." He pointed to the nightstand. "An officer found GHB in there. Not standing on top of it like the others. No apparent cause of death. I'll know better, of course, when I get him on my table." He looked Gary in the eye. "I haven't gotten to the best part."

Someone traced a path down Gary's spine with an icy finger.

Del gestured to one of his assistants, and together they gently rolled Robin Fields onto his side, revealing his back.

What the fuck?

There was no letter.

"What the hell is this? It's like he just played the blank tile in Scrabble. You know, the one that can be any letter you choose." Riley scowled. "This bastard is playing fucking *games* with us."

Dan took a step toward the bed. "Can I…?"

Gary caught up fast. "Del, could you maybe give us a moment?"

Del blinked, glanced at Dan, then back to Gary. "Okay," he enunciated. He gestured to his assistants, who followed him out of the room.

Riley stood by the door. "No one's coming in. Do your stuff."

Dan shuddered, but he approached the body on the bed. He held out his hands, and Gary saw them shake a little. The tremors increased as he lowered them to Robin's chest and forehead, but ceased when he made contact. Dan drew in a deep breath. Gary didn't move for fear of breaking Dan's concentration. Riley's breathing had slowed, his gaze locked on Dan.

Then Dan sighed, and Gary focused on him, his chest aching as a tear fell on the victim's chest. Dan didn't wipe them from his eyes, but stared intently at the body.

What are you seeing? What are you feeling? For the first time, Gary wondered what toll this took on Dan. Did his gift make him especially sensitive to the emotions of others? How did he live with that, day after day? Did he shield himself from people for fear of being overwhelmed?

And what does he sense about me?

There were things Gary never discussed with his coworkers, mainly because it was none of their business, but he had to wonder if all his secrets lay bare before Dan.

His heartbeat raced. *Does he sense my attraction to him?*

Dan straightened, wiping his eyes, and Gary was forced back into the moment. Dan gave Riley a nod. "You can let them back in now." His face was drawn, and Gary knew whatever had passed had sucked the energy right out of him.

Riley opened the door, and a moment later, Robin Fields was carried from his bedroom, followed by Del, who paused as he passed Gary. "I'll get started on this first thing tomorrow. See you back at my place?"

Gary appreciated Del's touch of humor. "It's a date."

Del didn't move. "You don't seem your usual self today."

"What makes you say that?"

"Because apart from the nonexistent letter on the victim's back, something else pretty vital is missing from this crime scene, and you don't appear to have picked up on it." When Gary frowned, Del pointed toward the bed. "There's no condom either. This time the killer didn't gift us with his DNA." His eyes grew cold. "Maybe he thinks we already have enough." With a final glance at Dan, Del left them alone.

Gary kicked himself for his lack of focus. The reason for it was standing beside the bed.

Riley stared at Dan. "Well?"

He pointed to the chair beside the bed. "Can I sit, please?"

"Of course you can." Gary's stomach churned. "You got something, didn't you?"

Dan gave a low nod as he sank onto the seat. "Not that it makes any sense, but...."

"Tell us," Riley demanded in a low voice.

"It's just that... I'm not getting the same emotions as last time. There's no anger, for one thing. And there's something else." He gazed at the surroundings. "This room... I can feel him. The dead man, I mean. The place is practically vibrating with his energy. But what I felt when I touched him? That was from someone else."

"The killer?"

Dan pulled in and slowly released another deep breath. "You're not going to like this."

"Tell us." The hair lifted on the back of Gary's neck.

Dan's eyes met his, and they were full of misery. "I don't think it's the same guy." Another glance toward the bed. "But how can that be? It looks the same as the other crime scenes."

Gary's mind shifted into high gear. "It may *look* the same, but there are two important differences. No GHB left in plain sight and no letter." He peered at Riley. "You thinking what I'm thinking?"

Riley nodded. "This isn't our killer, but a copycat."

Dan's eyes widened. "Seriously?"

"It happens." Gary held up his gloved hands. "Don't get me wrong. I want this to be our guy, but…."

Dan walked over to the nightstand, where a photo sat in a silver frame. "I'm okay to touch this, right? The officer out there said so."

Gary gestured to the frame. "Go for it."

Dan picked it up and gazed at it. "This is the boyfriend." The man in the photo with Robin was maybe in his early thirties. The pair wore ski clothing, and their faces were tanned. The snow in the background was almost blinding in the sunlight. Both were smiling.

"I assume so," Gary replied.

Dan gave a smile that didn't reach his eyes. "It wasn't a question. And you need to talk to this guy."

"We'd talk to him anyway. That's procedure." Riley peered at the photo. "They made a good-looking couple."

"They do, but I don't like his mask." Dan shivered. "Can I leave, please?"

"Of course. Riley, will—"

"I'll stay a while. Lewis and I will catch a ride back to the precinct."

"Thanks." Gary gave the photo one last glance as Dan replaced it on the nightstand.

What did he mean? Neither of them is wearing a mask.

CHAPTER 17

DAN TOOK the coffee with a sigh. "Thanks. I need this." He inhaled its pleasant aroma before meeting Gary's concerned gaze. "Relax. I'm okay now." He was thankful Gary had brought him to the case room. Dan was aware of scrutiny as he walked along the precinct's hallways. He knew from Riley that Travers had informed the Homicide unit of his arrival, and he guessed there had to be guys out there as skeptical as Lewis.

"It shook you up, didn't it?"

Dan forced a smile. "Damn. And there I was thinking I'd hidden it so well." He stared into his black coffee. "Can I ask something? How do you feel when you look at a dead person? I mean, it must be a commonplace event in your job, but...."

Gary leaned against the table. "If I'm honest, my first thought is always the same. 'I hope they didn't suffer.' When it's clearly murder, it... makes me sad, I suppose. Someone was robbed of life. They could've had so much in front of them, so much to live for."

Dan's mouth dried, and he hastily took a drink from his cup. He fought the urge to move closer to Gary, to touch him. Gary gazed at the board, oblivious to the tumult of emotions at war within Dan. "What's on your mind?" Dan's voice was unsteady.

He pointed to the letters. "Seven murders. Six letters. P-R-E-E-X-P. Is the lack of a letter in this case meant to indicate a space? It doesn't make sense. Unless it *is* a copycat, and Robin Fields's death has nothing to do with the others." Gary frowned. "Something at the back of my mind is niggling me. For some reason I keep thinking of Agatha Christie."

"Hey, if you want her for a consultation, you're talking to the wrong person. I don't see dead people, remember?"

Gary chuckled. "Another of my favorite movies. Even if I did piss Cory off the first time we saw it. Not to mention most of the people sitting near us in the movie theater."

"How did you do that?"

"We got to the part where Bruce Willis is having dinner with his girlfriend or wife, and Bruce is doing all the talking. I turned to Cory and said, 'Hey, what if she's not replying because he's dead and she can't see him?' Cory glared at me and said if I'd just guessed the plot, he was never going to the movies with me ever again." Gary smiled. "He lied, of course."

Dan gaped. "Oh my God."

"What?"

He couldn't freaking believe this. "I did the same thing. I mean, I had the same thought, but I wasn't in a movie theater. We were watching it on TV, and the thought slipped out. My dad looked at me and said, 'Well, you'd know, wouldn't you?'" What surprised him was how much the remark still burned.

"You said your parents don't talk about it, but that's not the whole story, is it?"

Dan looked him in the eye. "You know, you may not be psychic, but you're very intuitive." *And attractive. Damn, you're attractive.* But there was more to Gary than his appearance. Not for the first time, it occurred to him that he *knew* Gary. How Gary's body felt against his. The intimate sounds he made when he fucked, punctuating each thrust. The gentle touch of Gary's hands on his body as they rocked together, locked into a sensual harmony.

His name on Gary's lips when they came together.

Back on track. Get your mind back on track, for God's sake.

He drank a little more to steady his nerves. "The best way I can describe it is… there's a wall between us, and they were the ones who built it." Gary flinched, and Dan's throat tightened. "What did I say?"

Gary swallowed. "You got me near the bone, that's all. Not something I want to talk about, okay?"

"It's okay." Dan kept his voice soft and soothing, as though he were inching closer to a skittish horse. And there it was again, the urge to reach out and touch, to *connect*….

The door opened, and the moment shattered. Lewis came into the room. "Officers contacted Robin Fields's boyfriend, Quinn Dalmont. He's here, and he wants to know what we're doing to find Robin's killer."

"He can wait a minute. What turned up on the CCTV recordings?"

"A guy in a hoodie. Couldn't see his face. And he knew where the cameras were, because he didn't look once in their direction. He didn't knock at the door, though. He used a key and strolled right on in there."

"Did you speak to Robin's neighbors on his floor?"

"Yeah. Robin didn't have a lot of visitors. They said Dalmont moved in about a year ago."

"The guy in the hoodie part… that's been in the papers. Interviews with neighbors of the victims."

An officer stuck his head around the door. "The desk sergeant says to let you know this Dalmont guy looks pretty distraught. Says he wants to speak to the detectives in charge, like, now."

"Then let's talk to him." Gary thanked the officer, who withdrew. He glanced at Dan. "You can watch the interview via the camera."

Lewis's face darkened for a second, but he said nothing.

Dan followed them to the interview rooms, where Riley waited for them.

"You and I will conduct the interview," Gary told him. "Lewis, stay with Dan and show him where he can watch."

Lewis's brow furrowed. "I'm not a babysitter."

"No one said you were. For God's sake."

Dan's stomach clenched. He had no idea how Gary and Lewis had gotten along before his arrival, but their interactions left a sour taste in his mouth.

Riley patted Gary's arm. "It's okay. You two go in, but make sure you lead the questions." He fired Lewis a glance. "I'll stay with Dan." Riley gave Dan a warm smile. "You come with me, and I'll get you the best seat in the house."

"Sounds good." He followed Riley into another small room with a wall of monitors. Riley grabbed two chairs and they sat. He pointed to a screen. "This one." He handed Dan a pair of headphones, then plugged them in.

The view wasn't ideal—Dan wanted to zoom in to get a closer look at facial expressions, only the camera angle was fixed—but the sound was crystal clear. Dalmont sat at the table, his eyes reddened and puffy, a crumpled Kleenex clutched in one hand. "He's got good taste. Or someone has," Dan murmured.

"What do you mean?"

He pointed to the monitor. "That suit? Prada. You wouldn't get much change from three grand."

On the screen, Dalmont gave each of them a nod as Gary made the introductions. "Are you the detectives in charge?"

"Yes, Mr. Dalmont. I'm Detective Mitchell, and this is Detective Stevens. When was the last time you saw Mr. Fields?" Dan admired Gary's calm manner.

"Friday. I went away for a few days to see family."

"Did you talk to him on the phone over the weekend?" Gary asked.

Dalmont nodded, wiping his eyes. "He was staying home to get some work done. He... he was planning to buy another company and wanted the time to concentrate. That was why I went away. You know how it gets, two people living in each other's pockets. You need a little space now and then."

"And he seemed okay when you spoke to him?" Dalmont nodded. "How long were you two together?"

"Three years." Dalmont's face contorted, and he covered his eyes with the tissue. "We... we were getting married this year." Then he straightened. "So have you gotten any closer to catching this maniac?"

"I can't comment on the case." Gary's response was quiet and measured.

"You don't need to. The media is already doing plenty of that." He gaped at Gary. "Surely it's obvious the same man is responsible for Robin's death. Robin is the seventh victim."

Dan shuddered. "Mask."

Riley's hand was warm on his. "Hey, you all right?" Dan gave him a hopefully reassuring glance, then refocused on the screen.

"So you and Mr. Fields were monogamous?"

Dalmont froze. "Of course we were. Didn't I say we were getting married? Robin was the only man for me."

"But you obviously weren't the only man for him," Lewis interjected. When Dalmont stared at him, Lewis shrugged. "Hey, just telling it like it is. There was someone else in that apartment, and it wasn't you. CCTV caught a guy going up there. He had a key."

"You mean you've *seen* him? Then why aren't you out looking for him? And I have no idea why Robin would look for sex elsewhere. I didn't think he was a cheater."

"Who mentioned sex?" Gary asked quietly.

Dalmont rolled his eyes. "Are you kidding? With everything that's appearing in the media, you think I can't put two and two together when the police show up to tell me my boyfriend's been murdered in our apartment?"

"Oh, I'm sorry." Gary's tone was smooth. "I didn't realize the apartment was in both your names."

Dalmont coughed. "It was Robin's apartment, but he was going to make half of it over to me once we were married." His expression grew pained. "Except that's not going to happen. It's only now occurred to me—I'm homeless. Unless Robin made some provision for me." He paused. "Do you... do you need me to identify the body?" He grimaced.

"Contrary to what you might see on TV, that's not usually how we do things. Identification will be made using fingerprints, dental records, and DNA. And speaking of fingerprints... we'll need a set of yours before you leave."

"What for?" Dalmont gaped at them. "Are you suggesting I had something to do with this? Because that's... that's horrible. I just lost my fiancé, for God's sake."

"We need them because there were prints all over the place. Once we've eliminated yours, Mr. Fields's, and the cleaner's, any unknown prints could point us to the killer. Okay?"

Dalmont shuddered. "Of course. I'm sorry. I'm not thinking clearly right now."

Gary rose to his feet. "Understandable, given the circumstances. Officer Hollins will take you to be printed. Could you leave us your contact details? In case we need to talk to you again."

"And we will," Riley muttered. When Dan gave him a quizzical glance, Riley's face hardened. "This guy gives me a bad feeling."

Dan patted his hand. "Welcome to my world."

AN OFFICER escorted Dalmont out of the room, and Gary waited for Riley to show. He wanted to hear Dan's reaction too.

"Is it me, or did he not seem all that upset at finding out his boyfriend had someone else in their bed?" Lewis commented. "And I know for a fact the officers who contacted him didn't mention how the body had been found. All they told him was he'd been murdered."

"This feels off," Gary murmured as Riley and Dan entered the room.

"That's what I said." Riley gestured to Dan. "And we both felt it."

"He's hiding something," Dan blurted out. "That's what I meant when I said he was wearing a mask." He shuddered. "When he said Robin was the seventh victim... I felt it most strongly then."

"I thought you had to touch something to know all that," Lewis remarked.

"He said sometimes he gets visions," Riley retorted. "I'm guessing this is one of those times. Like Dan said, it's not exact."

Lewis widened his eyes. "Whoa, there." He glanced at Dan. "Looks like you've got yourself a fan."

Gary let out a sound of exasperation. "*Now* I know why I keep thinking of Agatha Christie. There was this one book where a serial killer was bumping people off alphabetically. I think he got as far as *D* before Poirot got wise."

"What's that got to do with this?" Lewis demanded.

"What I'm getting at is the whole point of the story was that the best way to hide a murder was in the middle of a bunch of murders. Okay, in Agatha's story, the killer bumped off three random people to hide the one murder that mattered. This is the other way around."

Dan's eyes gleamed. "You think Dalmont murdered Robin. That he took advantage of all these killings to make it seem as if Robin was the next victim."

"That's why there's no letter," Riley announced. "Because he didn't know about those." He frowned. "But there's no motive. Why would he kill Robin? They were engaged. Dalmont had no reason to kill him."

"Yes, he did," Dan murmured. When they looked at him, he lifted his chin. "You just haven't found it yet, because it's hidden." He cocked his head to one side. "I know Robin Fields was a wealthy man, but was he a greedy one?"

"Why do you ask?" Gary frowned.

"Because that was part of what I was picking up in that apartment—greed." He met Gary's gaze. "You need to find out what kind of man Robin was. How he died. Who benefits from his death. And whether Dalmont painted an accurate picture of the state of their relationship." Dan crumpled a little. "Sorry, but…." He looked as if all the energy had drained from his body.

What overwhelmed—and shocked—Gary was the need to get closer to him. Something in Dan *tugged* at him, the irresistible pull of invisible yet strong-as-steel threads slowly bringing them together.

Into a collision.

He had to make do with comforting words. "This has wiped you out. Do you need to go back to your hotel?"

"Maybe for an hour? I could come back this afternoon."

Gary smiled. "Sure. Go recharge your batteries. I think we're going to need them."

Dan nodded. "See you all later." He walked toward the door.

"I'll walk you to your car." Riley followed him from the room.

Gary turned to Lewis. "Okay. Start doing some digging. Let's see what we can find out about Robin Fields—and Dalmont too." When Lewis didn't respond, Gary arched his eyebrows. "Something wrong?"

"I agree, Dalmont is kinda suspicious, but don't you think you're relying too much on what Porter says?"

Gary went over to the door and closed it. "Okay, let's have this out. What have you got against him? You've been on his case since he arrived. He's already proved he's on the level. How else could he have known about Cory?"

"That's easy. Someone in the department told him."

Gary stilled. "You really believe that?"

Lewis snorted. "I find it easier to believe *that* than some crap about having visions and knowing things just by touching." He aimed a hard stare at Gary. "And the fact that you aren't even considering my suggestion tells me your judgment is cloudy when it comes to him. Now why would that be?"

Gary ignored the question, although his pulse quickened. "And what if he's right? What if it turns out Dalmont *did* kill Robin?"

"*What if* is a fool's game. I'm going on record to say I think this is a bad idea, putting all our eggs in one basket."

"Duly noted. Except we're not. Let's assume Robin Fields is victim number seven, and the absence of both a letter carved into his back and a soiled condom means the killer was having an off day. So we go down the same route as all the others: Grindr, phone records…." He paused. "Was Robin's cell phone at the scene?"

Lewis nodded. "On the nightstand."

"Okay, so we chalk that up as yet another anomaly. What does that leave us with? A killer who murders six men in exactly the same way, his MO not wavering in the slightest, and then suddenly ditches said MO for his next victim?" He peered at Lewis. "We explore both avenues. We check everything, like we always do. So go check. But before you do…." He drew himself up to his full height and looked Lewis square in the face. "I get that you have pretty fixed opinions about some things. I'm not saying you should keep them to yourself. But if I were to repeat some of those opinions—to Travers, for instance—I've got a good idea what he'd say."

Lewis froze. "Yeah? Never mind Travers. What do *you* say?"

"That you're exhibiting borderline intolerance." *For God's sake, tell him.* "No, that's not right. I think you've already crossed the line."

Lewis said nothing, but his face tightened.

"So maybe it's time for you to decide if you're going to be part of the solution of these murders or a problem to be dealt with." He lowered his voice. "You're a good cop, Lewis. Or at least you were until this. I want to work with the guy who had flashes of inspiration, the one I could rely on. Don't make me take this further up, okay?"

He swallowed. "Gotcha." Lewis walked out of the room.

Gary sank into one of the chairs, his gut feeling as if it were in a twist. They were the same rank, but damn it, someone had to put Lewis straight, and it had to be better coming from him than from Travers. One point Lewis had made had struck home, however.

Is he right? Is my judgment skewed where Dan's concerned?

One thing was certain. Dan Porter messed with his head.

CHAPTER 18

DAN OPENED his eyes. His phone buzzed on the nightstand. He reached for it, his sleep-befuddled fingers missing it the first time before he finally curled them around it, the vibrations traveling up his arm. He stabbed at the screen when his bleary eyes picked out Gary's name. "Hey." His head felt heavy.

There was a pause. "I woke you, didn't I? I'm sorry."

"S'okay. I didn't intend to sleep this long. What time is it anyway?" He focused on the screen. "Oh my God. It's four o'clock." Dan sat up. "Do you need me? I can be there in—"

"Relax. I was only calling to say you could rest easy. Riley and I are going through the crossover list—again—and Lewis is checking out a new lead, but we're almost done for the day." Another pause. "Plus I was worried about you."

An effusion of warmth spread through him. "Thanks for the concern, but you don't need to worry about me." When Gary fell silent, goose bumps broke out on his arms. "Gary? Something wrong?"

"Would it be okay if I stopped by your hotel? Just for a chat."

Dan took in his room in one glance. "Sure. When were you thinking of?" Hopefully after he'd cleaned up the place.

"Maybe in an hour? And to sweeten the deal, I promise not to turn up empty-handed."

You could turn up naked and it wouldn't bother me none.

He chuckled. "Sounds like an offer I can't refuse. Buzz me when you get here. I'll have to come down. It's one of those places where you need a key card to use the elevators. I'll meet you in the lobby."

"See you then." Gary disconnected.

The prospect of Gary's visit sent a welcome burst of energy tingling through him, and he launched himself from the bed, heading for the bathroom. A hot shower would make him feel human again. Except that was bullshit, and he knew it.

He wanted to be at his best for Gary.

DAN EYED the white cardboard box with interest. "What's in there?" He'd picked up a hint of chocolate in the elevator coming up to the room. "And iced coffee... how did you know?"

"It was a hunch. I get them now and then." Gary opened the lid to reveal...

Dan grinned. "Chocolate cream pie. Oh, I like you." He leaned against the seat cushions, holding his plastic cup in one hand, and sucked on the straw. "Damn. You were right. Good coffee."

Gary glanced at the room. "Wow. Very nice. You even get a couch."

Dan studied him. "You didn't come here to bring me coffee and chocolate deliciousness, did you?"

Gary sagged against the cushions. "Why do I get the feeling I'm an open book to you?"

You have no *idea.*

"Maybe you're easy to read. But you did say you wanted to chat, remember? So what are we chatting about?"

Gary took a long drink of his coffee, then put the cup down on the table in front of them. "Something I didn't feel comfortable discussing at the precinct."

Dan arched his eyebrows. "Color me intrigued." Something fluttered in his belly, and his heartbeat quickened.

"When we were in Travers's office this morning... I thought you were brave, by the way, speaking out like that. I meant to say as much at the time, but we got called out to Liberty Drive, and...." Gary's face tightened. "You didn't owe Lewis an explanation. He was being an asshole."

"He's been an asshole since we met in Travers's office. I'm getting used to it." When silence fell once more, Dan gave him a speculative glance. "If there's something you want to ask, please, come right out with it. I promise you, there's little you can say that will shock me."

Except if Gary suddenly pointed to the bed and told Dan he wanted them in it, Dan had a feeling his heart might explode.

Gary said nothing for a moment but took another long drink. He set the cup down, straightened, and looked Dan in the eye. "You said you know guys who use GHB. So… maybe I got this all wrong, but I kind of assumed you learned this in an intimate situation. But at the restaurant, you told me you're wary of relationships, and why. So I guess I was trying to understand how the two match up."

It felt as if someone had turned the room's thermostat way up.

Gary flushed. "Don't get me wrong. I'm glad you have some experience with this. It could be invaluable. God knows who I'd discuss it with if you weren't here." His Adam's apple bobbed sharply. "Actually, I do. I'd have gone straight to Cory." The flush in his cheeks almost matched his hair color. "You know what? This is none of my business. Forget I asked."

Dan grabbed his cup and drank, mostly to get his throat to work. He kept his focus on the clear plastic lid. "I hook up occasionally with guys I meet. I'm not on Grindr, or any similar app for that matter, so I can't help you there. Yes, I've been offered GHB from time to time, and I've always declined. But about what I said at the restaurant—" He raised his chin to gaze at Gary's flushed face. "—I like to keep things casual for a reason. There have been a couple of times where it was more than just sex. And yes, I wanted that. But the closer we got, the more entangled my emotions became."

"And then you saw something." When Dan blinked, Gary continued. "You told me as much at dinner. Remember?"

That whole evening had been reduced to a blur once he'd seen Gary's tattoo.

Dan took a couple of deep breaths. "I don't read minds, okay? But when I touch people, I see things they've done, things they might not want others to see. And that one time, the guy I was falling for?" He shuddered. "He had a cruel streak, something I hadn't even glimpsed until then. You know how it is when you first meet someone. You're on your best behavior, right? You want to make a good impression."

"I guess."

"Well, we'd been together a couple of months, and yes, I had it bad, but not bad enough that I wanted to stick around and see what happened once he got comfortable being with me. Because I'd seen how he'd treated his exes." He drank a little more. "When it happened again with a different guy—different circumstances, though—I got the message. Stick with sex and keep my heart out of it."

Gary's eyes widened. "You can't live like that." His voice quavered. "Shutting yourself off from the possibility of falling in love with someone. Is that what you really want?"

That tremor shook him. "You're a good man. You care for people."

"Of course I do."

"So answer me this. Are *you* in a relationship?"

Gary huffed. "I'm a cop."

"That's not an answer."

"Yes, it is. It takes a special kind of person to put up with a cop's life because there *are* times when that life takes over. There's no such thing as a normal day. There's a lot of stress, emotion, even danger."

"So you don't date? How does that make you any different from me?"

Silence.

Dan sighed. "And I'm *not* shutting myself off. I don't want to stay single all my life. I *want* someone to come home to, someone to share my hopes and dreams. But like you said, it will take a very special person to cope with me. With my gift."

"Now I get why you said sometimes it feels more like a curse," Gary murmured.

"Yes, but I have faith. He's out there, waiting for me."

And I pray to God he's sitting right in front of me.

"Then I hope you find him." Gary glanced at his watch. "I should go."

Don't. Please don't. "Can I ask a case-related question?"

He stilled. "Sure."

"The bottles of GHB at the crime scenes… did they have any prints on them?"

"Not one."

"And what about today?"

Gary smiled. "You're a smart man. There were prints on it, but they belonged to the deceased. Yet another argument for this being the work of a copycat."

"Then might I suggest another line of inquiry? See if you can locate any of Robin Fields's exes. Find out if he ever used drugs during sex."

"You don't think he did, do you?"

Dan shook his head. "It would've been easy enough to press his fingers to the bottle when he was dead, wouldn't it? To make it look as if he was the last person to touch it. And while you're at it, check the papers, the news sites. Maybe word has gotten out about the GHB. I'm not suggesting that's what killed him—I think it was simply there as a prop." He glanced at the box. "You can't leave yet. You haven't eaten your pie."

Gary smiled, and the light in his eyes set Dan's pulse racing again. "Then I'd better stay and eat it."

Dan picked up the remote. "I was going to find a movie to watch. Something familiar that doesn't require deep thought." He hesitated, then continued, "You could stay and watch it with me. Unless you're leaving because there's somewhere else you have to be."

Stay. Please stay.

"I was going home to eat, that's all."

"Then eat with me." Dan grabbed the in-room dining menu.

Gary's eyes twinkled. "I thought the food here didn't grab you."

"They do mac and cheese." He rolled his eyes. "It's pretty difficult to ruin that. *And* there's a blueberry pizza."

Gary's lips parted. "Blueberry… pizza?"

He nodded. "With vanilla cream cheese, hazelnuts…."

"Stop with the sales talk. You had me at blueberries." Then he glanced at the white box. "Except… we've got chocolate cream pie, remember?"

Dan grinned. "Two desserts. Works for me." He handed Gary the remote. "You can choose the movie."

"You sure?"

He smiled. "I trust you." *For reasons I might never share with you.*

That didn't stop him longing to do just that.

CHAPTER 19

Wednesday, May 30

"YOU GONNA tell me where we're going?" Lewis asked as Gary took the turnoff and headed west along the 139. "Apart from seeing this Silver guy."

"To a construction site off 3-A. They're laying a water main. I spoke with the crew's foreman. Silver is there."

"Do we not need the Boy Wonder for this one?" When Gary glanced at him, Lewis held up one hand. "Hey, relax, I got the memo. I was just wondering why you didn't bring him along, that's all."

"Dan's working with Riley. He's taking Dan to Marius Eisler's place and then Cory's." At least those scenes were relatively fresh. He and Lewis were about to interview Anthony Silver, who'd hooked up with Marius and Cory via Scruff. Silver was in construction, presently working out near Duxbury.

"You know what I think?"

Gary chuckled. "No, but I'm sure you're about to tell me."

"I think Riley has a little crush on Porter." Gary stared at him, and Lewis's brow furrowed. "What? It happens, right? And Riley could be bi for all we know."

"And you're okay with that?" Lewis's 180-degree turn made Gary's head spin. "Because up till now, you haven't been the most LGBTQ+ friendly cop I've ever worked with."

Lewis fell silent, and Gary pondered his suggestion. He didn't think Riley was crushing on Dan—he was simply a decent human being. Riley had admitted his grandmother had similar gifts. Maybe he felt comfortable around Dan.

So what's my excuse? Gary couldn't explain why Dan was frequently in his thoughts. What shocked him was the form those thoughts took. He'd been down this road before, a long time ago.

It was a phase back then. It wasn't real.

Except it felt all too real now.

Lewis sighed. "Something you said yesterday made me think."

"Oh?"

"Yeah. When you asked if I was gonna be part of the solution, not the problem. I guess I haven't really been a team player up to now, have I? Well, that's gonna change. I'm having what Travers would call an 'attitude adjustment period.' This case revolves around gay guys, so I need to alter the way I think. And I don't really have anything against them."

"Let me guess. Some of your best friends are gay." Gary couldn't keep the sarcasm from seeping into his voice.

Lewis snorted. "Okay, I wouldn't go *that* far. But Travers was right about one thing. The state takes a dim view of LGBTQ discrimination. I don't want anything on my record."

"So you're playing it safe and losing the attitude? You'll get no complaints from me."

"Besides, I've got a good feeling about this guy."

"Silver?"

"Yup. He's been interviewed a few times, suspected of violence and stalking, but no charges were ever brought against him. Maybe we're about to get lucky." Lewis reached into his pocket and pulled out a packet of gum. He offered it to Gary, who declined, then popped a piece into his mouth. "This case gets weirder and weirder."

Gary knew he was referring to Robin Fields. Examination of his phone and records revealed none of the apps used by the previous victims. The toxicology report would take a day or two, but so far, Del's initial findings were that death appeared to be the result of cardiac arrest. He'd found evidence of heart disease. "What were your thoughts?"

Lewis shrugged. "Maybe the killer tied Robin to the bed, he struggled, and it was all too much for his heart."

"And maybe the GHB helped him on his way," Gary suggested. "We know it has a short half-life, but it'll show up in the urine sample."

"You still think the boyfriend did it?"

"Yeah. At least, that's what my gut is telling me." They'd gotten a search warrant for Quinn Dalmont's phone records. They'd also contacted Robin's lawyer to get access to his will. And Riley was going to check Quinn really was visiting family the whole weekend, especially Monday evening.

Lewis pointed. "That must be it."

Ahead of them were road signs diverting traffic, and beyond, large flatbed trucks were loaded with wide-bore black pipe or similarly sized metal coupling rings. A forklift hoisted a section of pipe like it weighed nothing, carried it through the air on chains, and lowered it into a deep ditch, where guys stood in high vis jackets, waving it into position. All around was the chug of heavy equipment engines, the clang of metal on metal, and the smell of burning plastic, dirt, and cigarette smoke.

A man in a reflective jacket and white hard hat approached them as they got out of the car. "You the cops? I was told to expect you."

They fished out their badges and held them up for inspection. "We need to talk to Anthony Silver," Lewis announced.

The guy pointed to the ditch, where a construction helmet was visible above the mound of dirt. "Ant's down there. I'll get him."

They waited as the guy went over to the edge of the ditch and hollered down into it. A moment later, Silver clambered out.

"He's a big son of a bitch," Lewis muttered as Silver strode toward them.

Everything about Silver was big, from his large hands to his muscular thighs barely constrained by his jeans to his broad chest. He took off his helmet, and his bald head gleamed in the afternoon sun. His goatee was black and his eyebrows bushy.

He came to a halt in front of them. "What can I do for you?" His voice rumbled out of him.

Gary held up his badge. "Anthony Silver?" He gave a curt nod. "I'm Detective Mitchell, and this is Detective Stevens, from Homicide. We'd like to ask you some questions about Marius Eisler and Cory Peterson. Maybe some other men too."

Silver frowned. "Who?"

Lewis arched his eyebrows. "Please, don't even go there. We know you hooked up with both those guys. Scruff ring a bell? We can even give you the dates. But we're not interested in what you got up to with 'em—we're more interested in what you were doing the nights of May fifteenth and May twenty-forth. And while we're at it, March eighteenth, 2016, December second, 2016—"

"Wait a minute." Gary could have sworn Silver paled beneath his tan. "You think I'm the fucker who's killing all those gay guys? Why the fuck would I do that? *I'm* gay, for Christ's sake."

"Then come with us to the precinct. We'll take a DNA swab, and if it doesn't match any of the DNA from the crime scenes, we can eliminate you from our inquiries."

Silver shook his head. "Nope. I'm not your man. And I'm not going to any police precinct."

Gary frowned. "If you're innocent, then why not?"

Silver's eyes bulged. "Because I don't want to end up on some police database where you guys have my DNA forever, that's why not."

Lewis reached into his pocket and pulled out a pair of cuffs. "Look, buddy, we can do this the easy way or the hard way."

Silver snorted. "I'd like to see you try." He glanced around, his fists clenched.

Goddammit, Lewis.

Gary held up his hands. "Listen to me, okay? Just listen." He had a feeling Silver would make a run for it, and the odds of them getting a search warrant, based on what they had so far, were pretty slim. "If you bolt now, you'll only be making it worse for yourself." Gary kept his voice low and even. "All we want to do is ask you some questions. And take a swab."

"Jesus, Ant, do what he says," the guy in the flak jacket whined. "You're no good to your mom if you're in jail for resisting arrest or beating up a cop."

"Yeah, listen to your coworker." Gary didn't break eye contact. "Come with us?"

Silver swallowed. "Okay. Am I under arrest?"

"No, you're coming with us voluntarily. All right?"

"All right. But only so you can take your damn swab. Then you'll know I'm not the guy you're looking for." He turned to his coworker. "This won't take long."

The guy waved his hand. "Just get it over with. And call us if you need us to arrange a lawyer. I've got a few contacts."

"It's not gonna come to that." Confident words, but Silver's gaze flickered toward Gary and Lewis as he uttered them.

You're hiding something.

But was it murder, or some other guilty secret?

GARY WALKED out of the interview room to find Dan standing by the window.

"Well?" Dan broke off when Silver was escorted out by an officer. Lewis followed, pausing in the doorway.

"The officer will show you to the main desk," Gary called after Silver. "If you wait there, I'll be along with your stuff."

"And it had better be all there," Silver hollered back.

Gary waited until he was out of sight. "We're letting him go. We don't have probable cause to apply for a search warrant. The DNA test will take a while, so right now we have nothing to hold him on. However, he can't provide alibis for the dates in question, so we need to find witnesses who can ID him at any of the crime scenes before we can pull him in again." He tilted his head. "*You* might be able to help us, however." He waited for Lewis's customary eye roll or derisive snort, but nothing was forthcoming.

Wow. A leopard can *change its spots after all.*

"Tell me. What do you need?"

Gary held up a brown paper sack. "I've got his personal effects here. How about before I return this to him, we go to the case room and you see what you can learn from them?"

Dan nodded. "Sure."

Another glance at Lewis revealed an impassive expression, and Gary heaved an internal sigh of relief. *Finally.* He wasn't sorry to see the back of Lewis's animosity.

When they got into the small room, Dan sat, his fingers pressed to his temples.

"Is everything all right?" Gary inquired.

"Just a headache. It'll pass." Dan held his hand out for the sack. He reached into it and removed Silver's wallet. He didn't open it, but after placing the sack on the floor, he held the wallet with both hands, his eyes closed.

Lewis watched from the doorway, arms folded, his gaze focused on Dan. "We can't take too long over this," he said quietly. "Silver's waiting. Let's not give him any grounds for a complaint."

Gary narrowed his gaze. "Then let Dan work. Give him some quiet."

After a minute or two, Dan opened his eyes and shuddered. "This guy has a temper."

"Tell us something we don't know," Lewis muttered. When Gary aimed a hard stare at him, Lewis fired one right back at him. "Well, we do, don't we?"

"Showing his photo to any witnesses might bring results." Dan dropped the wallet back into the sack and handed it to Gary. "I don't like the way he makes me feel." He winced, then cupped his head.

"Is your headache getting worse? Do you want some Tylenol?"

Dan shook his head carefully. "Migraine coming, I think. I get them now and then." He gestured to the sack. "This is one nervous dude. Almost bordering on fear." Another wince.

It was something. Maybe Silver wasn't as innocent as he claimed. "We've told him not to leave Boston."

Riley entered the room, holding an envelope. "I've had copies done of the photo we took of Silver. I'm gonna revisit the crime scenes, see if anyone recognizes him. Then I'll interview his coworkers, his neighbors...." He glanced at Dan. "Hey, are you okay? You look awful."

Dan got to his feet. "I think I'll go to my hotel and lie down. Hopefully this won't hang around too long." His eyes were squeezed into slits, his face pale.

"Want me to arrange a ride for you?" Gary asked. Riley was right, he did look as if he was in a bad way.

"No. Believe it or not, concentrating on driving will actually dim the pain a little." He met Gary's gaze and attempted a smile. "Hey, don't look so worried. I'm not about to crash. I've driven in far worse states than this."

"Why don't we call it a day?" Lewis said. "For you, at least. Don't feel you need to hurry back."

Gary stared at Lewis, then looked away, unsure whether to be surprised or shocked by Lewis's solicitous tone. "Lewis is right," he said at last. "Take the rest of the day off, and we'll see you tomorrow. Who knows, we might have some news by then."

"But I haven't told you yet about the visits to the crime scenes with Riley."

"You told *me*, didn't you?" Riley's eyes were kind. "So I'll tell them."

"Okay." The pain had to have been bad, judging by the way Dan was squinting at them. "Till tomorrow." He left the room.

"Poor guy," Riley murmured. "My grandmother used to get terrible migraines after a séance. Maybe it's something to do with being psychic." He held up the envelope. "I'll get right on this." Then he too was out of there.

Lewis unfolded his arms and wandered over to the board to gaze at the photos. "You wait and see. It's not psychic ability that'll nail this guy—just good old-fashioned policing. Like you said." He looked at Gary over his shoulder. "And you know I'm right."

I'm not as sure as you *are that Dan can't help us.*

Gary's stomach churned. He knew it was wrong, but the thought of Dan not being there for the rest of the day sent relief surging through him, alleviating tension he hadn't even been aware of. He recognized the root of that tension, however.

Being around Dan was starting to feel like a constant battle to hide his emotions—and his attraction to him.

An attraction he could no longer deny.

CHAPTER 20

Thursday, May 31

DAN REACHED for his phone and peered at the screen. Seven thirty. His head still felt a little bruised, the way it usually did after a migraine and a bad night's sleep, but at least the pain had gone.

He sat up in bed. Coffee was probably the last thing he should be drinking right then, but he needed a jolt of caffeine. He deliberated calling room service for a pot but changed his mind. Going down to the hotel restaurant would force him to get showered and dressed, and by the time he got his first sip, he'd feel more human.

He hovered by the desk at the entrance to the restaurant until a server showed him to a table. Most of the diners had departed, leaving a few people here and there. A glance at the breakfast menu had him deliberating between a salmon tartine and a classic Benedict, but in the end he chose neither and decided on eggs, potato hash, and chicken sausage. The nausea from the migraine had passed, thank God.

His server approached the table, a pot of coffee in her hand, and he smiled. "If you only knew how much I need this."

She stared at him, her blue eyes wide. "Oh my God. You're him, aren't you? The psychic who's helping the police catch that killer." She placed the pot on the white tablecloth. "And to think, only the other day, I was telling my mom it had been ages since I'd seen someone famous in here."

For a moment he was too startled to respond, his heart pounding. *What the hell?* He took a deep breath, hoping to induce calm.

"Well, I hope you catch him," she said in a decisive tone. "My uncle's gay. Gives me the shivers just thinking about it."

Dan found his voice. "How do you know about me?"

She beamed. "I saw it on my phone this morning when I was coming into work. And when I saw you here, I *knew* it was you right away." She gazed expectantly at him. "What can I get for you?"

Dan had suddenly lost his appetite. "Just the coffee for now." As soon as she walked away from his table, he got out his phone and typed in *psychic Boston police serial killer*. His heart plummeted. There it was, in bold headlines, along with a photo of him.

Then he looked again at the photo's background. *Holy fuck. That's the police precinct.* He went back to his search and found variations of the headline on three more news sites.

His hand shook as he scrolled through his contacts. When the call connected, he fired first. "I thought we had an agreement." His voice cracked.

"I know. I saw it too." Gary sounded pissed. "I was going to call you."

"Want to tell me how I ended up being today's news?" *And who took a photo of me in your precinct?* His stomach roiled.

"It's not only the news. It's on social media. You're all over Twitter, Facebook...."

He swallowed. "Then I need to quit now." He was done. There was no way he was going through this again.

"But...." Gary fell silent.

Dan realized he couldn't leave it like that. He cleared his throat. "Can you get over here? We have to talk."

"Can't we talk here?"

"Are you kidding me?" He clammed up when the remaining guests jerked their heads in his direction. Dan gave them an apologetic glance, then whispered, "I am coming nowhere near that precinct until we've talked. Or did you miss the photo of me? I want whoever took it and leaked this to the media strung up by their—whatever."

"I didn't miss it. Travers is beyond pissed. So am I." He paused. "Okay, I'll come to you."

"And once we've had that conversation, I'm going to get in my car and head home to New Hampshire."

There was a pause. "I'll be there in twenty minutes." He disconnected.

Dan turned off his phone and placed it on the table.

I need to tell him the truth. Before I leave.

CHAPTER 21

GARY GAVE Dan an apologetic glance when he opened the door to his room. "Sorry about this." He held up the paper bag. "I couldn't face breakfast this morning, once I saw what had happened, but now I'm starving." He was momentarily distracted by the sight of Dan in a fluffy hotel robe that hugged his slim body.

Dan gave him a weary smile. "Great minds and all that. I just ordered food for myself. Something ruined my appetite earlier." He stepped aside to let Gary enter. "And my apologies for my state of undress." He headed for the couch, where a tray sat on the table, containing a pot of coffee, two cups, and covered plates.

Gary was about to say Dan's state of dress was fine when he realized he was staring at Dan's ass, the way the robe clung to it, the way it moved as he walked.

For God's sake, focus.

He waited until Dan was seated before launching into the speech he'd rehearsed over and over in his mind during the drive to the hotel. "I know you're angry, and you have every right to be. But… I don't think you should leave. I still feel you could help us solve this case." He clutched the paper bag.

Dan said nothing but lifted the stainless-steel cover to reveal eggs, sausage, and potato hash. He took a mouthful of eggs and a forkful of potato hash.

The silence sent a shiver through Gary. "Won't you even discuss it?" His stomach clenched.

Dan re-covered his food and sat back. He gestured to the couch. "Sit down, please."

Gary sat at the other end and placed his bag on the table.

Dan cleared his throat. "There's something I think you should see." He loosened the soft belt around his waist and opened the robe to reveal his upper body. Gary's heartbeat raced. He couldn't move.

Dear Lord, don't let him be naked under there.

It was such an incongruous thought to be having in the circumstances, especially as his earlier view had already proved the lack of underwear. His face tingled, his cheeks hot.

And then he couldn't breathe when he saw the jagged diagonal scar across Dan's chest. It wasn't a recent scar, Gary could tell that much, but *oh my God*, it was long.

It was a scar that spoke of pain and suffering.

Gary's fingers ached to reach out and trace it, but then Dan pulled the robe shut, and Gary dragged air into his lungs. "What happened?"

Dan leaned forward, picked up the coffee pot, and filled two cups. He handed one to Gary, then sagged against the cushions. "I told you when we first met that I liked to keep my involvement on cases private, staying in the background. Well, that's how it is *now*. In 2013, I was asked to consult on a murder case that was baffling the Chicago police. Actually, I approached them. I'd had a vision, and miracle of miracles, I'd been able to make sense of it. I knew I could help them find the killer."

Gary searched through his memory. "I watched the case at the time. And of course when Travers suggested bringing you in, I looked up your documented cases." He glanced at Dan's covered chest, then raised his gaze. "But what does... this have to do with the Chicago case?"

Dan wrapped his hands around his cup and drank deeply. "I gave them vital leads that brought them closer to the killer. Then a particularly inquisitive journalist discovered this, and suddenly I was front-page news. Everyone was reading about me working with the police and how my help had narrowed the search." He shivered. "Everyone, including the killer."

"But they caught him, didn't they? Jackson Perrault *was* caught."

Dan's eyes met his. "Yes, he was—but not before he caught up with me."

Jesus. "*He* did that to you?" Dan nodded. "But... surely you had police protection. I mean, if you were giving them information, they should've kept you safe."

"Well, that night something went wrong, because I went for a walk, and he was waiting for me." Dan's lip trembled. "Yes, they got him, but only after he'd managed to do this." He covered his chest with his hand. "I'm not going to talk about that night, okay? I'd rather forget it. I didn't come close to losing my life, but...." Another shiver coursed through him. "Let's say it took me a while to face the world again. And even longer to consider helping out another police department."

"Yet you agreed to help us. Because of who the killer was targeting."

Dan nodded again. "I couldn't sit back and watch as gay men were dying. Not if there was a chance I could do something about it."

Gary's pulse quickened. "I… I think you're amazing. It took real guts to step forward and say yes. And yeah, now I get why you made that stipulation."

"Do you also understand why I can't stay?"

Cold inched its way through him. "But… we need you. You *know* we do. I went to see Travers this morning. He's turning the place upside down, trying to find out who leaked the story to the media. No one connected to the newspapers is talking."

"And that surprises you? They're protecting their source."

"But if I tell Travers what happened to you, why you wanted to remain out of sight, he'll protect you. Hell, *I'll* protect you, even if it means you staying at my place or putting an officer outside that door."

Dan arched his eyebrows. "Are you volunteering to be my personal bodyguard, Detective?"

"If it keeps you safe and working on this case? You bet I will." Heat surged through him.

Dan was courageous, and Gary admired him greatly, but it was more than that. Gary was a tangled mess, and he recognized the same heady mix of emotions he'd felt back in high school when he'd crushed on Cory. Not that Gary had ever revealed his attraction to Cory—for one thing, Cory clearly hadn't been interested in him in that way. Then Elsa Makins had come along, letting slip accidentally on purpose via her network of girlfriends that she was interested in Gary.

That had been the clincher. He'd decided his infatuation with Cory was nothing but a phase. After all, there were no other boys to whom he'd felt that same tug of attraction, so he obviously wasn't gay. When he and Cory had reunited as Gary was going through the police academy, he'd been overjoyed to have his friend back—his best friend. The attraction had still been there, yes, but Gary wasn't going to do a thing about it.

And what about now?

He couldn't explain his reaction to Dan—mental *and* physical—but he was definitely drawn to him. No, *tugged* was a better description. When Dan was around, Gary found it increasingly difficult to focus. Despite needing to keep a lid on his emotions in order to do his job, he felt powerless to resist that tug.

"Gary?"

He blinked. "Sorry. I zoned out for a moment."

Dan expelled a long breath. "I said I'll stay."

His heart pounded. "Are you sure?"

"No, but I'm staying anyway." Dan squared his shoulders. "I want to see this killer stopped, and I want to be part of the investigation that stops him."

Thank God.

"I'll go see Travers now. I'll make sure he understands that keeping you safe is a priority." He got to his feet. "Do me a favor? Stay here today? Let me set things up so you'll have protection."

"I don't need protection. Well, not at the moment. And I don't want Travers going to any special lengths to keep me safe. If I'm only ever in two places—here or with you—then I'm safe enough." He smiled. "Though if the offer to be my bodyguard still stands, I won't refuse. What sane man would do that?"

Gary stilled. *Did you just flirt with me?*

Dan stood too. "I'll see you out, and then I'll lock my door. I'll make do with room service for a while."

The thought of Dan holed up in his hotel room while the killer was free to do whatever he desired sent heat flushing through Gary. "It's almost the weekend. I'll make sure I'm not working, and if you want to eat out or go for a walk or something, I'll be here for you."

I want to be here for you.

Dan's smile lit up his face. "Thank you." He glanced at his surroundings. "Don't get me wrong, it's a classy hotel, but all I've seen since yesterday morning are these four walls. A walk sounds awesome." He glanced at his robed body. "And maybe now is a good time to put some clothes on."

There it was again, the tantalizing thought of what lay beneath the layer of fluffy white cotton.

Dear Lord, I need to get out of here.

"I'll see myself out. Lock the door after me." He grabbed his paper bag containing a probably stone-cold McMuffin, and hurried to the door. In the hallway he waited until he heard the lock click into place before heading for the elevator.

As the doors slid shut, he could still hear Dan's words in his head. *Though if the offer to be my bodyguard still stands, I won't refuse. What sane man would do that?*

No, he hadn't imagined it. Dan Porter had definitely been flirting with him—and Gary didn't know what to make of it.

I told him we need him. That wasn't the whole truth.

Gary needed him.

CHAPTER 22

Friday, June 1

GARY KNOCKED on Travers's door, opening it when Travers barked out, "Come in." Travers was sitting at his desk, staring at a computer screen and chewing on the end of a pen.

"How was the training day?" Gary asked.

Travers rolled his eyes. "A waste of time." He flung his pen down with a scowl. "Still no luck trying to find out who leaked Porter's involvement to the press. That photo…. They didn't even bother to blur the background." He leaned back in his chair. "I got your email yesterday. I have to say, I'm impressed Porter still wants to work with us on this. That man has balls." He frowned. "Unlike the spineless little shit who took that photo of him." Travers steepled his fingers. "Okay, bring me up to speed with your progress."

Gary wasn't ready to abandon the topic. "Look, about Dan… I'll be honest. I'm not happy about it. I've promised we'll keep him safe. I know he's not in any danger, but—"

"But we have no way of knowing what will happen. I agree. We don't want a repeat of Chicago. Little wonder there was no mention of this in the records. Chicago PD dropped the ball on that one." He gave Gary an inquiring glance. "What do you have in mind?"

"From now on I'll pick him up from his hotel and take him back there when he's done. I've also told him I'll be with him this weekend. I'm not happy about him being on his own."

Travers picked up his pen. "I'll make sure you aren't called in, then."

"Thank you. He's going stir-crazy. I told him to stay put until I'd sorted things out, but I wanted to talk to you first." His throat tightened. "This is a reminder that I won't be here next Tuesday. It's… Cory's funeral."

Travers's expression grew thoughtful. "Of course."

Gary forced his mind into practical mode. He pulled his notepad from his pocket. "We've been doing a lot of digging into Robin Fields's death."

"Tell me it's yielding results. I need some good news right now."

"Well, it's not looking good for his boyfriend, Quinn Dalmont, that's for sure."

Travers's eyes gleamed. "You think he did it?"

"That's the line we're pursuing. This guy set off some major vibes when we interviewed him. We're certain Robin Fields is *not* victim number seven. Too many anomalies at the crime scene, not to mention Del Maddox reports there's no evidence of penetration. At least not like in the other cases."

"What have you got on Dalmont so far?"

"The only prints in the apartment belong to Fields, Dalmont, and the cleaner. Which means nothing because we have no prints from the other crime scenes. But Lewis found Dalmont on Grindr, using another name. No doubt it's him. A little suspicious for a man who claims he and his fiancé were monogamous, don't you think? Our guess is Fields didn't know about that. We got a warrant to check Dalmont's phone records. Plus we're following a few other leads. When we see what they bring, we'll invite him in for an interview." Gary didn't want to say too much about those leads. Travers liked facts, not hunches.

"Excellent. Then I'll let you get back to work." Travers stilled. "No movement on our serial killer? What about Silver?"

"Still waiting on the DNA results, but Riley's checking up on him too. I'll let you know what he discovers."

Travers nodded. "The social media furor appears to have died down since Tuesday. Thank God. At least there are no more posts on Twitter about Boston PD's discriminatory attitude toward BDSM. And Monroe's lawyer says he won't be making a formal complaint. Yet another thing to be thankful for." His phone rang, and he sighed.

Gary took that as a sign. He left the office and headed for his desk. His phone buzzed, and he smiled when he read the text from Riley.

Office, now. We hit pay dirt.

It was about time they hit something.

He hurried to the case room, to find Riley and Lewis talking animatedly. "I was beginning to think you two had transferred to another precinct," Gary said. "Where have you been all morning?"

"Working," Lewis retorted. "And you're gonna like what we found."

"Where's Dan?" Riley asked.

"At the hotel. And if we need him, I'll go pick him up."

"I don't know him all that well, but I'm betting he hates being in the spotlight."

"You'd be right." Gary couldn't think about Dan right then. He needed to keep a clear head. "Okay, bring me up to speed."

"I just finished checking the street cameras around Liberty Drive." Riley thrust a folder into his hand. "We have to question Dalmont about his weekend with his family. I have no idea where they're located, but I'd be interested to hear how he explains this."

Gary opened the folder and smiled. "Yes, so would I." He placed it on the table. "Have you contacted Uber? They keep records for ninety days."

"Yup. I got them to preserve the account."

Lewis tapped another folder with his index finger. "And I got his phone records. Makes for compelling reading." He opened it, removed two sheets, and handed them to Gary.

Gary scanned the sheet, frowning. "Nothing compelling about this. I can't see how this helps—" He froze as he glanced at the second sheet. "Oh, I stand corrected." He grinned. "Nice work." He handed the sheets back to Lewis. "I have news too. Fields's lawyer sent over a copy of the will. Apparently, Fields made a new one in anticipation of the wedding." His phone rang, and Gary answered it immediately. "Del. What have you got for me?"

"The results of the prelim toxicology tests. Now, you *know* this is merely an indication—"

"Yes, I know it's not accurate proof. So what have you got?"

"I had them test for the substances found in the previous cases. I'm fairly certain the victim's cardiac arrest was brought about by a lethal dose of ketamine."

"Thank you, Del." He disconnected, then looked at his team. "Anything else?"

Lewis nodded. "I spent the morning contacting guys who've hooked up with Dalmont. I managed to interview three of them, and I took statements."

Gary smiled. "Judging by that grin, I'm going to go out on a limb and say you found something."

"Oh yeah. A couple of them told me something very illuminating."

The door opened, and an officer entered. "There's a visitor for you. Says he's Robin Fields's ex. He also says it's important. I put him in Interview Room One."

"I'll be right there." When the officer withdrew, Gary grabbed a notepad from the table. "Two things. Log everything you've got so far. And can one of you call Dalmont and invite him to come talk to us? Make sure he knows he's free to leave when we're done. We don't want to rattle him. Just tell him we want him to make a statement for our records."

"I'm on it." Riley's eyes sparkled. "It'll be a pleasure."

Gary left them and headed for the interview room. It was the most casual of the rooms, usually used with witnesses and relatives. He opened the door, and a tall good-looking man lifted himself out of his chair.

Gary held out his hand. "Detective Mitchell. You wanted to see me?"

The man nodded. "My name is Simon Westfall. Robin Fields and I were in a relationship for ten years. I'm here to ask how your investigations are progressing. Are you any closer to catching his killer?"

Gary gestured to the chairs. "Please, sit." He waited until Mr. Westfall had done so before taking a seat. "You must understand, I can't divulge information about an ongoing case."

"Then is there any help I can give *you* that would bring you closer to catching him?"

Gary studied him. Simon Westfall was maybe in his late forties, early fifties. He wore his almost-white hair cropped close to his head, and there was a distinguished air about him. "Can I ask a personal question? Why did your relationship with Mr. Fields end?"

Mr. Westfall sighed. "Three years ago, he had a late midlife crisis. In other words, his head was turned by a newer model."

"Quinn Dalmont?"

He nodded. "He was twenty-nine to Robin's forty-six years. He was pretty, lithe, and he swept Robin off his feet. Robin said Quinn made him feel young again." He swallowed. "Why do some men want to live forever?"

"Was it an amicable parting?"

"Yes. We stayed friends, for which I'm grateful." A faint smile creased his features. "Ten years is a long time in gay years. Too long to simply break completely with each other. We'd meet for dinner occasionally, and we'd go to the theater and to concerts, something that wasn't to Quinn's taste." He straightened. "But enough about my successor. I'm here because of something I read in the newspapers." He paused. "Robin's death has been linked—in the media, at any rate—to the spate of murders of gay men."

Gary didn't comment.

"Some mention was made of… drugs found at the scene. Now I have no idea how accurate this information is, but I had to see you." He set his jaw. "Robin would never, *never* take drugs."

"Forgive me for another personal question, but I have to ask it. What about during sex?"

Mr. Westfall shook his head. "Never. He abhorred the use of drugs of any description. It was all I could do to get him to take Tylenol for pain relief."

"Maybe he changed during the last three years," Gary suggested.

Another vehement shake of his head. "No. His horror of drugs was rooted deep in his past. I'm not going to divulge his family history, but I can assure you, there is no way on this earth he'd participate in drug use. If you did find such substances in the apartment, the killer brought them with him." His voice was firm, but the pain in Mr. Westfall's eyes was all too apparent.

"Thank you for coming in to clarify that. Was there anything else?"

"No, that was all." Mr. Westfall rose with grace. "And now I'll let you get back to finding Robin's murderer."

Gary shook his hand. "We will, I can assure you of that." He met Mr. Westfall's gaze. "And you *have* helped." He'd provided another piece of the puzzle.

It could also prove to be another nail in Dalmont's coffin.

"THANK YOU again for coming in to make a statement." Gary glanced at the neatly written document Dalmont had signed.

Dalmont waved his hand. "It was no problem. I hope and pray you're getting somewhere with your investigations."

"Actually, we've made a lot of progress during the last two days."

Beside Gary, Riley scanned the statement. "You've mentioned a couple of things here that need a little clarification, if that's okay."

"Oh?"

"You've stated you were away for the weekend, visiting your family."

"That's correct."

"Where do they live? Where did you go?"

Dalmont frowned. "My parents live in Springfield. What does this have to do with Robin's murder?"

"So you were in Springfield the whole weekend?"

"Didn't I say that in here?" Dalmont reached across the table and tapped the statement with a manicured fingernail.

"You did, but we'll come back to that in a moment. Do you know who the beneficiaries are in Robin's will?" Riley removed a sheet from the folder.

Dalmont stuck his chin out. "I haven't seen a copy of his will, so I wouldn't know."

"I see. Well, you'll be delighted to know Robin did make provision for you. According to the will he had drawn up early last month, apart from the sum of ten thousand dollars which he left to Simon Westfall, the remainder of his fortune—comprising his property and all his assets—goes to you, in anticipation of your marriage."

Dalmont's jaw dropped. "I… I had no idea. What a generous man he was."

Gary frowned. "Okay, *now* I'm confused."

"About what?"

"You just stated you didn't know about the new will, and yet…." Gary removed another sheet from the folder, and Dalmont's gaze locked on it like an Exocet missile. "You told Axel Washington all about it on May twelfth."

Dalmont sat very still. "Who?"

"Axel Washington. You remember him, surely. You visited his apartment at 22 Abbotsford Street, Roxbury."

"I don't know anyone called Axel Washington, and I don't recognize that address either."

Riley tapped the sheet. "We have his statement right here, along with the records from Grindr showing the two of you making contact on May tenth and arranging to meet May twelfth. It showed up on your phone records too."

Dalmont reached into his coat pocket and pulled out a phone. "There's been a mistake. I don't have Grindr on my phone. See for yourself if you don't believe me."

"That proves nothing. You could've deleted the app. But for clarification purposes…. Is this phone's number 585-301-4986?" Dalmont nodded, and Gary smiled. "But what about your other phone?"

Beats of silence.

Then Dalmont cleared his throat. "What… other phone?"

Gary peered at the sheet. "484-457-8754." He raised his head. "We have records for both phones, registered in your name. I'm assuming Robin didn't know about the second phone. Was that in case he checked the other one?"

"I can understand why you'd do that," Riley commented. "For a man who claims he and his fiancé were in a monogamous relationship, it might be a little awkward to explain all the hookups." He peered at the sheet in front of them and blinked. "*My*, there were a lot of them."

Dalmont was doing an excellent impression of a statue.

Gary folded his arms. "The GHB we found in the nightstand drawer. Was it yours?"

Dalmont shook his head. "That was Robin's. He…." His face flushed. "I'm sorry, but I feel our sex life should remain private."

"I see. Unfortunately, this is a murder inquiry, so we have to ask these things. Robin liked to use GHB during sex?" Gary leaned back.

"Yes. I wasn't that keen myself, but I went along with it. He said it was better to have both of us take it. Something about the timing of doses. I didn't really understand, but…."

"Something else that was mentioned in the statements we got from Axel Washington, Drew Gorton, and Mike Miller…." Riley pulled them from the folders. "We asked them specifically about the use of GHB during sex. What do you think they told us? Or are you going to deny meeting them for sex?" He glanced at the sheet. "Mike Miller states you and he met up on several occasions, and that you were the one who suggested using GHB. Drew Gorton confirmed the same thing but added that it wasn't the only substance used. He said you used ketamine to… relax certain muscles."

Gary had to admire Riley's tact. Dalmont's flush deepened, and his breathing grew a little erratic.

"So on the one hand we have *you* stating Robin liked to use substances during sex, but you didn't, and then we have his ex telling us Robin had a horror of drugs. Yet the only fingerprints on the bottle of GHB were his.

"Which brings us to the most puzzling part of your statement." Gary opened the folder in front of him and removed a photo. "This was recorded by street cameras on the night of Monday, May twenty-eighth. It shows an Uber pulling up on Seaport Boulevard, one block from the apartment." Gary placed the photo on the table and pointed to the figure getting out of the car. "That *is* you, isn't it?"

Dalmont leaned forward. "He looks a little like me, I suppose. But no, it's not me."

"Well, now you see why we're confused," Riley chimed in. He opened another file and withdrew a sheet. "This is your Uber account. It shows a car picking you up from Six Corners in Springfield at eight o'clock that night and dropping you at Seaport Boulevard."

"That's a trip of around ninety minutes, give or take," Gary added. When Dalmont stared at him, he smiled. "I make that trip once a month, so I know it well. That ties in with the time on the camera footage. The Uber dropped you off at nine forty. Then *another* Uber picked you up at eleven at the same drop-off point and took you back to Springfield."

Riley whistled. "That was some expensive trip, I'll bet." He cocked his head to one side. "Where did you tell your parents you'd gone, for, what… several hours?"

"I'm sure this can be cleared up," Gary said in a pleasant tone. "We can contact them. All we'd need is a statement that you didn't leave until the twenty-ninth." He sat back again and waited for the first cracks to appear.

Dalmont gaped at them, his lips parted.

"You didn't plan this, did you?" Riley said. "You saw the murders and thought we'd simply accept that Robin was the next victim."

"You learned about the new will, and you thought, 'Why wait for him to die naturally?'" Gary said. "The murders were a godsend. It was too good an opportunity to miss." He leaned forward. "If you *had* planned it better, you'd have covered your tracks more carefully. If cameras picked you up on Seaport Boulevard, they could've picked you up in other locations. But *you* only thought about the CCTV in the building, hence the hoodie to hide your face. You forgot to wear the hood up when you got out of the Uber."

"Did you think the ketamine would be missed during the autopsy? Or did you just think the medical examiner would pronounce his death due to cardiac failure?" Riley narrowed his gaze. "We've seen Robin's medical records. We know he had problems with his heart. Which you probably knew all about."

"So how did it go down?" Gary demanded. "Did you come back that night to surprise him with an early return? Did you slip something into his drink? When he was incapacitated, did you undress him and tie him to the bed?"

"Did he wake up and struggle?" Riley's face was hard. "He must have been so scared. Maybe he saw you without your mask on. Maybe he saw the *real* Quinn Dalmont that night. The lethal dose of ketamine would have finished what you started." He locked gazes with Dalmont. "You broke his heart in more ways than one."

"You had plenty of time to clean up after yourself," Gary noted. "Prints didn't matter, though, not when you lived there. But the GHB… that was a different story. You had to clean yours off and then press Robin's dead fingers against it. I'm only guessing he was dead by then, of course. I don't think he'd have even touched it if he'd been alive."

Dalmont's face was like milk. "I want my attorney. I'm not saying another word until he gets here."

Gary nodded to Riley, who intoned, "Quinn Dalmont, you are under arrest for the murder of Robin Fields. You have the right to remain silent. Anything you say can and will be used against you in a court of law. You have the right to an attorney. If you cannot…."

Gary watched Dalmont's face crumple as Riley Mirandized him.

Dan saw through your mask. He saw your greed.

Now all they had to do was find the killer who was hidden from sight.

CHAPTER 23

CHRIST, I WAS a mess.

Some son of a bitch out there went and murdered some rich guy, and suddenly the newspaper headlines were screaming Seventh Victim. Robin Fields? Who in the hell was Robin Fields? Certainly no one *I'd* encountered. Except when I had a moment to calm myself, I saw it in a different light. *I should be flattered. I've got a copycat.*

Don't they say imitation is the sincerest form of flattery?

There was always the possibility that this event could create both a diversion *and* confusion. I was all for anything that hampered the police. I wasn't going to waste any more time on the unknown murderer.

I had bigger problems, in the shape of one Dan Porter.

My first thought when I saw the headlines? I dismissed them as invention. Fake news. Click bait. There was no way of telling what was real and what was fabrication anymore.

Except….

What if there's more to this? What if it is real? What if he's real?

Those questions lingered through Thursday and into Friday, haunting my days, until I could think of little else. My coworkers commented on my distraction, but I didn't enlighten them. There was only one way to alleviate my suspicions and ease my mind.

I didn't dare do anything while I was at work. Too many eyes. By the time my shift had ended Friday evening, I knew I wasn't going back to my apartment. Besides, I hadn't been to my sanctum for a few days, and right then I needed to sit in his presence, to reaffirm my intent. Being in the house would be enough.

Being in that room would be even better.

Crossing the threshold restored a little of my calm. I made myself coffee and got on my laptop to Google Dan Porter.

I didn't like what I found.

He didn't appear to be a fake. He'd successfully helped the police catch a couple of murderers, he'd located a kidnapped girl, and he'd given vital information in a few other investigations.

My heartbeat raced. My thoughts were chaotic.

What if he helps them find me?

I knew they'd get to me eventually, but not yet, not while there was still so much left to do.

Sixteen more degenerates to remove from the world.

What little calm I'd regained fled me. I couldn't think straight. I couldn't breathe. And that meant going to the one place where I could collect my thoughts, focus... plan.

I picked up my phone, got up from my chair, walked out of the room and along the hallway to the door. I unlocked it, then stepped inside.

Sanctum.

I stared at the wall, at his sweet, innocent face. "What do I do now?"

There were only two options—stick with the plan or take a step back and wait.

The second option had its merits. I could let my copycat put them off the scent while I sat back and watched the trail go cold. I'd waited six months between victims, for God's sake. I could wait a little longer.

Only... I didn't *want* to wait.

Two men crossed off in less than ten days. Waiting a few months, although a wise option, felt like a backward step.

But what about Porter? There was always the possibility of exposure before I was able to finish my task.

I gazed at the wall, looking into his innocent eyes. *For you. I'm doing this for you.*

And like a thunderbolt, it hit me.

"I'm safe," I whispered. "He can't see me." Because if he had, the police would have been knocking on my door by now. For some reason I couldn't fathom, Dan Porter's gift hadn't revealed me. If it truly existed in the first place.

There would be no retreat.

No surrender.

No deviation from the plan.

Why should there be, when I was hidden from his sight?

I breathed easier, my gaze falling on the calendar below *his* photo. I went over to it, turned the page, and traced a pristine surface with my fingertip. A death-free month as yet.

Well, not for much longer.

"It's time for another slut to bite the dust." The weekend was coming, and that meant opportunities. All I had to do was decide who was next to shuffle off this mortal coil. Who would be victim number seven.

I didn't need a copycat to muddy the investigative waters. *My* victims had been carefully chosen. My initial rage bubbled up, and I resolved to make sure the police didn't chalk up the death of Robin Fields to me.

I pulled up the image I'd saved of Dan Porter on my phone.

"You can't see me." I grinned. "Some psychic. Why should I concern myself with you?"

Calm restored.

Resolve hardened.

I scrolled through my phone and smiled.

Victim chosen.

CHAPTER 24

Saturday, June 2

GARY'S KISSES grazed Dan's neck, making him shiver. His damp chest pressed against Dan's back as he rocked into him. This was always the part of the vision Dan loved, when their coupling became less frantic and more sensual. He felt cherished, worshipped... loved. But then Gary withdrew and rolled Dan onto his back, and for the first time in thirteen years, Dan gazed into the eyes of the man making love to him.

"Please," he whispered. "I need you." He stroked Gary's face, his fingertips brushing over his beard as he slid them lower to Gary's shoulders.

Gary groaned as he filled Dan to the hilt. "Need you too." He rolled his hips, a sinuous motion that forced a moan of pleasure from Dan's lips. And suddenly they were rocking together, locked into a rhythm echoing that of Dan's heartbeat, both covered in a sheen of perspiration, drops falling onto Dan's face.

Except they weren't drops of sweat—they were tears.

Gary looked into his eyes, his cheeks streaked. "Heal me."

Dan sat bolt upright in bed, his heart pounding. He grabbed his phone from the nightstand, his hand shaking, his breathing erratic.

What are you going to do? Call him in the middle of the night?

He dragged air into his lungs, expelling his panic with each exhalation until at last he was calmer. He threw off the comforter and got out of bed to walk into the bathroom. After drinking a glass of water, he stared at his reflection.

"What is going on here?"

So many things were conspiring to screw up his life and his focus. Learning the identity of the man in the vision. The *change* in the vision. The revelations in the media. His turbulent emotions whenever Gary was near.

"I don't even *know* him." Not even six days had passed since they'd met. Certainly not long enough to tangle Dan's senses into a convoluted mess, but they were. He couldn't deny that.

And now this. *Heal me*. What the hell did it mean?

He gripped the sink, forcing his thoughts back to every occasion of physical contact with Gary. That first burst of recognition when Gary had handed him Cory's ring…. *I knew then, didn't I? I knew he was important.* And if Gary needed healing, Dan would do his utmost to provide it.

But healing from what? His grief over the loss of his best friend?

No. It was more than that; Dan was sure of it.

I need to know what the hell is going on.

Gary had said he'd come to the hotel at some point, but Dan wanted more than a vague arrangement. He returned to the bed, picked up the phone, and composed a short text.

Breakfast here. 8:00.

It wasn't a request. Maybe if he learned more about Gary, more pieces would fall into place.

He hoped. Because right then, he was floundering in the dark.

BREAKFAST HAD been delicious. Having Gary share it with him had been a bonus.

Gary poured another cup of coffee. "This is good."

"If you're anything like me, you need a decent hit of caffeine to kickstart your brain in the morning." Dan wiped his lips with his napkin. "Thanks for agreeing to meet me for breakfast."

Gary cocked his head to one side. "I was glad to get the invitation, if a little surprised at the hour you sent it."

Dan stilled. "Oh God. I didn't wake you, did I?"

Gary chuckled. "One thing I learned long ago—put the phone on silent when going to bed those nights when I'm not on call. I should go one step further and leave it outside the bedroom, but I'm nowhere *near* that disciplined." He leaned back in his chair. "So… want to tell me what you were doing awake at that ungodly hour?"

"I had a dream." That much was true. "And I sent the text while you—while *it* was on my mind." He had to steer the conversation in another direction. "So how long have you lived in Boston?"

"Since I went to college at Northeastern."

"And before that? Where did you grow up?"

"Springfield. It's not that far from here."

"I know where it is. From New Hampshire, remember?"

Gary chuckled. "Ah, but did you also know it's the birthplace of Dr. Seuss?"

"No kidding. And do you like Boston?" Dan smiled. "Stupid question. If you didn't, you'd go someplace else."

"Yeah, I like living here." Gary drank some more. "In fact, that was my plan for today. I was going to show you the sights."

"My own personal tour guide?"

Gary sat immobile, and Dan cursed his loose mouth. It wasn't the first time he'd uttered something that could have been interpreted as flirtatious, but he couldn't help himself. He had to be honest, Gary's proposal didn't appeal. He had a goal—to learn more about Gary—and he didn't think sightseeing around Boston would help him achieve that.

Dan helped himself to another cup. "Actually, I had something different in mind. Well, a different location at least." His heartbeat quickened as the idea took root.

Gary lifted his brows. "Oh?"

He nodded. "Can we visit Springfield?"

That earned him a blink. "Why there?"

His heart hammered. "Show me where you grew up. The places you went to." He held his hands up. "I don't want to be a tourist. I want to see places that meant something to you."

Gary rubbed his chin, his lips pursed.

"I know," Dan said quickly. "It makes no sense, but—" He swallowed. "—I feel safe with you." *So safe, you wouldn't believe.* "And... I want to know more about you."

Gary tilted his head. "Before you leave us to head back to New Hampshire?"

Dan didn't want to contemplate leaving Boston, leaving Gary, just yet. "I guess."

Gary studied him in silence, and for one awful moment, Dan felt certain he was about to refuse. Then he nodded. "Okay. Although I think Boston has more to offer."

"Then we can do Boston tomorrow, if you're free. Today I want to see Springfield."

Gary's smile didn't reach his eyes. "Then you have yourself a tour guide."

Dan got to his feet. "Let me go up and grab my stuff, and then we can head out."

"Sure. I'll wait for you in the lobby." He gestured to his cup. "I'll finish this first. But what do I owe you for breakfast?"

"Nothing. It's on me. And before you get any noble ideas, I've already paid." Dan walked out of the restaurant, heading for the elevators. Gary's smile occupied his thoughts.

He agreed to my suggestion, but he's not happy about it.

Maybe their visit would reveal why.

"YOU'RE NOT enjoying this, are you?" Gary murmured.

Dan jerked his head away from the view of Memorial Bridge. "What makes you say that?"

He shrugged. "Instinct." The Connecticut River Walk was their first stop, and already he was aware of… something he couldn't put a finger on. "I thought you'd like the walk as it was such a beautiful day. But if you don't, there are plenty of other places we can visit." He grinned. "There's always the Dr. Seuss National Memorial Sculpture Garden."

Dan gazed at him with wide eyes. "Seriously?"

"Or there's the Casino, the Basketball Hall of Fame…." He grinned again. "The Springfield Armory."

Dan snorted. "Yeah. I can imagine the fun times you had *there* as a kid." He leaned against the railing and folded his arms, and Gary tried not to let the sight distract him. Dan in jeans and a button-down blue shirt proved to be just as attractive as Dan in a suit.

Let's not be coy about this. Dan in jeans is hot. And the fact that Gary could be honest about that only went to prove how far he'd come. It was useless to deny it.

"Earth calling Gary. Come in, Gary."

He blinked to find Dan regarding him with obvious amusement. "Sorry."

"Do I want to know where your mind took you?"

Hell no.

Dan continued, "Okay, I'll admit, this wasn't what I had in mind when I asked you to bring me here. So let's try an experiment. No hesitation allowed. Say the first place that comes to mind when you recall your childhood."

"Forest Park." No sooner had the words left his lips than he felt as though he couldn't get enough oxygen. "No... wait...."

Dan was already on his phone. "Let me see."

No. No. We can't go there. His stomach roiled.

"Oh, this looks great. Duck ponds, a rose garden, covered bridges, even a zoo...." Dan's face lit up, and right then Gary knew he'd take him there simply to see more of that light.

That didn't mean he'd show Dan *all* of the park.

"Fine. Forest Park it is."

"But let's grab some food to take with us," Dan added. "There are picnic tables where we can eat lunch."

Something coiled around his chest... tighter... tighter....

"There are plenty of places to eat," he countered, striving not to croak out the words. "We don't have to stick to the tables."

Dan bit his lip. "How about we get there first? *Then* we can decide."

"There's a Subway right by here." He pointed to the left along the river walk.

"Great. Let's go." Dan flung out his arm. "Lead the way."

As they strolled along, Gary couldn't keep one thought from invading his mind over and over.

This is a bad idea.

By TWO o'clock, Gary's stomach was growling. "You ready to eat?"

Dan nodded, tossing food to the ducks and other birds who'd flocked to the water's edge. "That's the last of it." He crumpled the plastic bag and tossed it into a nearby trash can. "So many ducks, and different kinds too."

"Yup. They've got mallard, wood ducks, black ducks, common mergansers, and pintails. Not to mention swans, egrets, blue heron, and Canada geese."

The light Gary found so attractive danced in Dan's eyes. "I didn't realize I was in the presence of a waterfowl expert."

He smiled. "My dad used to point out the different varieties every time we came here. I guess it stuck."

Dan pointed to the silhouettes of buildings along the bank. "What are those?"

"They're part of the Bright Nights display." He couldn't hold back his smile. "It's a two-mile-long drive through the park that starts in late November and continues through the holidays. They decorate the trees and shrubs to look like Dr. Seuss characters."

Dan gazed at him for a moment before speaking. "You loved coming here, didn't you?"

His throat seized, and he unscrewed the cap of his water bottle to take a long drink from it. "I did when I was little. I grew out of it." His stomach grumbled. "I really need to eat."

"I saw some benches under a tree near that cute little red bridge. We could eat there. I think there were picnic tables too."

Oh God.

"Gary? Is there something wrong?"

"You know what? I'm hungry enough to squat here and eat." He gestured to the water. "The view is awesome."

Dan chuckled. "Okay. Just be prepared to have lots of beady eyes focused on you while you eat."

Gary didn't care if he got his fingers nipped off by ravenous ducks.

Anything was better than going near that spot.

WHY WON'T you tell me what's wrong?

Because it was clear to Dan that something was bothering Gary. He'd seemed on edge most of the day, although a stroll through the zoo had lightened his mood a little.

Dan didn't understand. Gary had clearly loved the park as a child, but the waves of unease that rolled off him as they walked disturbed Dan's senses.

Maybe it was time to go back to Boston.

"Thank you for bringing me here, but I think I've seen enough."

Gary's quiet exhale and the momentary closure of his eyes spoke volumes. "Okay. I hope you enjoyed your visit."

"I did." *I'd have enjoyed it better if you had, though.* Dan couldn't get over the feeling that he was right on the edge of an important discovery, something that would open Gary up to him, revealing....

That's just it. Revealing what?

There were times Dan hated his fucking gift with a passion.

"Best part?" Gary inquired as they strolled along the path through the water gardens that led to the parking lot.

He forced a smile. "The purring cougars in the zoo. And the timber wolves, Orion and Aurora. The covered bridges were so pretty. I could spend all day here." Dan pointed to where the creek meandered through the trees, a small reddish-brown footbridge spanning its width. "So peaceful." On the other side of the creek were two faded wooden picnic tables set down in the lush green grass beneath the spreading trees. Then he spotted a splash of color. "What's that?" He squinted.

"It's nothing." Gary shivered.

"Something wrong?"

"No, it's nothing."

Dan regarded him. "Maybe someone walked over your grave. Mom used to say that a lot."

"We should go this way," Gary said, pointing to where the path diverted.

That splash of color wasn't calling Dan, it was *tugging* him.

"You wait here. I want a closer look. I'll only be a second." Dan left the path and sprinted over to one of the picnic tables. Under a nearby tree, a small rectangular piece of stone had been erected at its base, the size of a book. Someone had rested a bunch of flowers against it. He walked over to them and squatted. Roses, peonies, lilies, and sunflowers were tied with a ribbon, and among the blooms was a white card. Dan read the words printed on it, and his heart ached for the unknown writer.

Brad, we love you. We'll never forget you. Mom and Dad.

The stone bore a single word and a date: Brad 04.16.95

Tears pricked his eyes, and he resisted the urge to touch the flowers or the stone. He had a feeling that would break him. Dan straightened, turned, and walked slowly back to where Gary stood on the path. As he drew closer, he inclined his head toward the bouquet.

"I think someone must have died here. His parents left flowers."

Gary's chin trembled. "That's awful." There was a tearful quality to his voice.

All Dan wanted to do was draw Gary close and hold him. *He's as affected by it as I am.* But there was no way he could touch Gary.

If he did, there was no telling what he might reveal.

Gary pointed to the parking lot. "Come on. I'll get you back to the hotel in time for dinner."

"Will you stay and eat with me?" He wasn't ready for the day to end, despite the mixed messages Gary was sending.

"To be honest, I'm tired. I think I'll go home."

"Will I see you tomorrow?" Dan asked as they reached the car.

"Sightseeing around Boston? Sure." Gary unlocked the car, and they got in.

Dan stared through the windshield at the dappled shadows cast by the trees. "I have a confession." When Gary turned to look at him, he sighed. "I wanted you to forget about the case for a while and relax." *I don't think I've accomplished that.* Weariness settled on him, and he knew the day had taken its toll.

Gary expelled a long breath. "I'm sorry. I had a lot on my mind, and I couldn't shut it down." The engine burst into life, and he backed the car out of the space.

Dan couldn't shake the idea that whatever occupied Gary's thoughts, it wasn't the case, and coming to the park had only made matters worse.

CHAPTER 25

Monday June 4

GARY GRABBED his coat, his stomach churning. Something had lit a fire under the killer's ass, that was for sure. Three victims in the space of twenty days. Based on the information Riley had provided over the phone, there seemed little doubt the body discovered that morning was the work of their man.

He knew the cause of his upset stomach wasn't only the latest development. *Why should spending a weekend with Dan make me feel guilty?* All they'd done the previous day was visit Beacon Hill, the harbor, Back Bay....

A week had passed since Dan first walked into the precinct, a seemingly innocuous yet at the same time cataclysmic event that had rocked Gary's world to its foundations. Feelings he'd thought long dead had resurfaced, forcing him to acknowledge the truth.

He wanted to be near Dan. To be closer to him.

He's important to me.

"What's wrong?" Dan's voice broke into his thoughts.

He jumped. "Jesus, don't sneak up on a guy like that."

Dan arched his eyebrows. "You make me sound like a ninja. Want me to ring a bell as I approach?"

"Works for me. And what's wrong is Riley called. We've got another one. He's at the scene."

"Then I'm coming too."

Gary wasn't about to argue.

They hurried out to Gary's car. "Do you want details, or would you prefer to go in blind?" he asked as he got behind the wheel.

"What's the name of the victim? And is Riley certain this is the seventh victim?"

"A guy called Jack Noonan. Lives in Dorchester. And yeah, this is our man—unfortunately."

Dan fell silent as the car sped along Dorchester Avenue, and Gary didn't feel the need to fill the air with conversation. They'd talked enough over the weekend, although after Saturday, he'd been careful to steer conversations toward safe topics.

He did *not* want to bring up the visit to Forest Park.

I should never have agreed to take him there. What was I thinking? It was the last place on earth to take someone who was more intuitive than anyone Gary had ever met.

"By the way…." Dan cleared his throat. "Thank you for giving up your weekend. I appreciated it."

He frowned. "I didn't *give up* my weekend. I chose to spend it with you."

"Okay, but…."

"But what?"

"When we were in Forest Park, there was a moment—okay, several moments—when I got the feeling you didn't want to be there."

Shit.

"Look, that wasn't you, all right? That was me. You did enjoy seeing Boston, though?"

There was a moment's hesitation before Dan spoke. "Okay, I'd better come clean. I've been to Boston many, many times."

Gary frowned. "Then… why did you say yes when I suggested showing you around? And then you let me take you to all the tourist spots…."

"I said yes because I got to spend the day with you. Besides, I'd never seen it with you as my guide. That made all the difference." He pointed through the windshield. "I'm guessing this is our stop." Three police cars, Del's vehicle, and an ambulance were parked up ahead. Dan sighed. "I was also hoping you'd enjoy Boston more than you enjoyed Springfield."

Maybe I should just tell him. Gary had to decide which was better—revealing his past voluntarily, or Dan finding out in his own unique way.

He came perilously close to doing that on Saturday.

"Gary." He turned, and his throat tightened. Dan's hazel eyes were warm. "You need to trust me."

That look threatened to unravel him.

"Not now," he croaked. He swallowed. "Come on. Let's see what surprises Kris Lee Arill has in store for us this time."

The officer at the door let them in, and they creaked their way up a wooden staircase to the second floor. As soon as they emerged into the living room, Gary's senses were on alert. Three police officers went quiet and regarded him with impassive expressions. Rob, Riley, and Lewis stood by the fireplace, locked in a quiet discussion, but as he approached, all conversation ceased.

Gary's scalp prickled. *Something's up.*

He turned to Dan. "Can you wait here a sec?"

Dan nodded. "Give me a shout when you need me."

Gary followed Riley and Lewis into the bedroom. "What's going on?" he demanded in a low voice. Del stood by the bed, on which a man lay facedown. Gary glanced at the body, and cold washed over him.

Oh God.

A letter *O* had been carved into the victim's lower back, but that wasn't what sucked the breath from Gary's lungs. A sheet of paper was stapled to the victim's back, and even at a distance, Gary recognized Dan's face.

He walked over to the bed slowly, his gaze locked on the white paper. At the top had been typed Robin Fields, but the letters were almost obliterated by another word in slashes of vibrant red—Fake. Dan's photo was below it, obviously the one from the newspaper, and below that were more letters in red.

Ha Ha Ha.

Christ.

Del coughed. "Our killer doesn't seem to rate Mr. Porter's abilities very highly."

Riley moved to Gary's side. "You have to tell him. He needs to know."

Lewis's splutter broke the quiet. "Are you for real? He needs to walk away from this case, like, yesterday. He's a target." His words rang out, and Gary had no doubt the volume was deliberate.

"So *now* you're worried about him?" He suppressed his rising ire. "Don't exaggerate. Dan's not a target. Far from it. The killer is simply telling us he doesn't see Dan as a threat, and it's not going to slow him down." He knew Riley was right, however. Dan had to know.

He scanned the room. "Same MO, I see." It was all there: the GHB, rope, cuffs, soiled condom…. "No phone?"

"No. No sign of it." Lewis's face contorted. "Jesus. This guy is only twenty-five. He's so young."

"I agree." Del gazed at the body, his eyes dull. "I'll be performing the autopsy tomorrow."

"I won't be there, but I'm sure Riley will." Gary's chest constricted. "I have a funeral to attend."

"I'll be there," Riley assured Del.

"What do we know about the victim?" Gary asked.

"He lived here with two roommates, according to the lady downstairs. She rents out the apartment. Both of them were away this weekend."

"When did death occur, approximately?"

Del stroked his chin. "Last night. I can't be more specific than that right now."

"And did she see anyone?"

"She heard footsteps on the stairs, but she didn't pay any attention to them," Lewis reported. "She said there were always guys coming and going. But she didn't hear anything suspicious." He pulled a face. "The invisibility cloak strikes again."

"The officers have already processed this room. Before I have the body removed, do you want to invite Mr. Porter to…?" Del arched his eyebrows. "I'm not sure what verb I'd use to describe what he does."

"I'll go get him." Gary turned and headed for the door, only to find Dan standing on the other side, his brow furrowed.

"What's going on?" Dan gestured to the officers. "I'm getting some strange glances out here," he added under his breath.

Gary stood aside. "Come see for yourself."

Dan walked into the bedroom and over to the bed. He stood there in silence, staring at the victim, his body language affording no clue to his thoughts. Gary forced himself to watch without comment. At last, Dan turned to face him.

"You were going to try to hide this from me, weren't you?" Dan rolled his eyes. "If the whole of Boston knows about my involvement, it's a safe bet the killer does too. And *he* thinks I can't help you." Before Gary could respond, Dan forged ahead. "So let's prove him wrong." He glanced at Riley. "Is it safe to touch stuff in here?"

"Yup. Already dusted for prints. Do you want us to leave you alone to concentrate?"

Dan shook his head. "By now you know what to expect."

Del asked his assistants to withdraw but made no move to follow them. Gary gave him an inquiring glance, and he shrugged. "I'm curious. How did Shakespeare put it? Something about more things in heaven and earth.... But if Mr. Porter wants me to leave, I'll do so."

Dan waved his hand. "You can stay. Just give me a moment. This could all be for nothing."

"Let's hope what we've had so far doesn't turn out to be a flash in the pan," Lewis murmured. Gary aimed a glare in his direction, but Lewis wasn't looking.

Dan touched the victim, and Gary couldn't miss his flinch. "There it is again."

"There's what?"

"Surprise." Dan met his gaze. "He knew the killer." He picked up the cuffs and closed his eyes, and it felt as if the air became electrically charged. The hairs on Gary's arms stood to attention.

Then Dan opened his eyes, and Gary knew. "You felt something."

"It was more a case of hearing something. A phrase. Except it feels more important than that. Almost as if...." He stared at the body again.

"As if what?" There was an undercurrent of excitement in Riley's voice.

Dan took a step back. "It's a mantra."

"*What* is?" Gary demanded.

Dan expelled a breath. "It's as if the killer was repeating it, over and over, while he was...." He shuddered, then inhaled deeply. "*I'm doing this for you.*" He returned to the bed and laid his hand on the victim's back. Dan jerked his head up to stare at Gary. "I'm not getting any feeling of pleasure from the act. Raping them—"

"Then it *was* rape?" Riley's face fell. Gary caught Del's sharp intake of breath.

Dan nodded. "It was against their will. But isn't rape more about power than sex?" He stepped back, scraping his fingers through his hair. "This feels as if it's a means to an end. It's one of many steps he goes through before he kills them." His eyes locked on Gary's. "But that mantra—his motive lies in there. I'm sure of it." Then his shoulders slumped. "God. That wiped me out."

"Take Dan back to the precinct," Riley suggested. "Lewis and I can finish up here." He peered at Dan. "Unless you want to go back to the hotel?"

Dan's expression was grim. "Not today. I want to spend some time with all the evidence from the crime scenes." Another glance at the body.

"So he thinks I'm a joke, does he? He won't be laughing when I help you catch him." His facial muscles were tight, his jaw set.

Gary regarded him with warm approval.

Looks like the killer isn't the only one with a fire lit under him.

"DAN. DAN."

He blinked. "What's up?"

Gary stood beside him, a twinkle in his eyes. "Do you know what time it is?"

He glanced at his phone and blinked again. "Seriously?"

"Time to call a halt. For one thing, you need a decent meal inside you, not a couple of protein bars." He gestured to the evidence bags piled high on the table. "Did you get anything?"

"Not really." His neck was bent, his shoulders drooped. "I didn't want to leave until I—"

"Enough." Gary's voice was low and firm. "Leave it for tonight. You can spend all day in here tomorrow. I won't be around, so that'll be one less person to distract you."

Dan regarded him steadily but said nothing. He couldn't deny Gary was a distraction, albeit a welcome one at times. Then he remembered where Gary would be, and his heart quaked. *You shouldn't be alone. Not tomorrow. Not when it's time to finally say goodbye.* Then cold surged through him. *And what about when it's time for me to leave? What if I don't want to say goodbye?*

Gary grabbed Dan's jacket from the back of the chair. "And now I'll take you to the hotel."

He was too tired to argue.

As they walked to the car, he was aware of Gary's scrutiny. When they reached the parking lot and Gary still hadn't spoken, Dan came to an abrupt halt at the gate. "Why don't you come right out and say whatever's on your mind?"

Gary lowered his gaze. "Maybe Lewis is right. Maybe you need to walk away from this."

He was shocked into silence.

Gary aimed his key fob at the car and clicked. "Come on. Let's get out of here."

The car sped through the Boston streets, and with every mile Dan's mind lurched further into panic mode.

I can't go. Not yet.

He didn't dare speak for fear he'd blurt out something that was better off hidden, but the nearer they got to the hotel, the tighter his chest became.

Fuck it.

"I can't," he blurted.

"Can't what?"

"Walk away from this."

"Why not?"

Dan swallowed. "Because… I haven't done enough yet. I haven't given you something concrete to work with, something that brings you closer to catching him."

"I disagree."

"Go on, then. Tell me precisely what information I've provided that has given you—"

"Dan."

He wasn't listening. "I can't leave yet because I have to help you find Cory's killer. That's… that's very important to me."

Gary frowned. "Why Cory's killer in particular?"

"Because…." Heat bloomed in his face. "Because he was important to *you.*"

They stopped at the lights, and Gary glanced at him. "There's something you're not telling me."

He resisted the urge to laugh out loud. *You have* no *idea.* "Not here. When we're at the hotel." *When you're not behind the wheel of a vehicle.* What Dan had to tell him was going to be a shock, and he didn't want to be responsible for Gary losing control.

His mind was made up.

He was going to tell Gary about his vision.

What terrified him was how Gary would react.

CHAPTER 26

GARY WALKED over to the couch and sat. All the way up to the room, he'd mulled over Dan's words.

I have to help you find Cory's killer. That's… that's very important to me. Because he was important to you.

"So what couldn't you tell—"

Dan picked up the menu and thrust it into his hand. "Choose what you'd like for dinner, and I'll order it. You were right, I do need to eat something."

Gary put the menu on the table. "Food can wait. We need to talk first."

"I can recommend the lobster roll. It's delicious. The ribeye and fries are pretty good too, and they do a mean Cajun shrimp and grits, if you're into grits."

What the fuck?

"Dan." Gary got up from his seat, went over to Dan, and guided him to the couch. "Stop babbling about the menu and tell me whatever it is you're trying so hard not to say." When Dan still hadn't sat, Gary sighed, placed his hands on Dan's shoulders, and exerted pressure, forcing him onto the couch. Gary retook his seat and waited.

Dan swallowed. "I swear, I have *never* needed a drink as badly as I need one now." He licked his lips, the pulse in his neck visible, his elbows pressed into his sides.

Gary's breathing hitched. "What are you so afraid of?" He placed his hand on Dan's knee. "You said earlier that I needed to trust you. Well… trust *me*. Whatever it is, you can tell me." He withdrew his hand.

Another sharp swallow. "And what if… what if what I have to tell you changes everything?"

The thought crossed Gary's mind that Dan knew about Brad, but he dismissed it. That wouldn't account for the fear rolling off him. "Tell me and we'll see," he said, his voice as soothing as he could make it.

Dan laced his fingers, his gaze focused on them. "I know I only met you last week, but…." A breath shuddered out of him. "I've known you for much longer than that. Except I didn't know it was you." He raised his head. "Does that make sense?"

"No, but don't stop, not now you've started."

Dan sucked in a deep breath. "For many years now, I've had a recurring vision. It never deviated, not once—until the other night."

"Was that the dream you were telling me about? The one that woke you?"

Dan nodded. "I need to tell you about the original vision. In it, I was...." He shivered. "I was on all fours on a bed, and someone was fucking me. I never saw their face because they were behind me, but I knew it was the same man every time."

"How could you know that?"

Dan lowered his gaze. "There was a... scent that never changed. And the man had a tattoo on his inner left arm."

Tumblers clicked into place. "Describe the tattoo." Gary's voice cracked.

It seemed as if time froze, awaiting Dan's response. "It was only two words. Never Forget."

Oh dear God in heaven.

Before he could manage to speak, Dan plowed ahead. "Fucking makes it sound so... coarse, but it wasn't like that. You—he—was gentle too, holding me as if I were something precious and fragile. That scent of patchouli and cedar permeated the vision. And then that first day, in the case room, when I smelled it on you...." He swallowed. "I told myself it was a coincidence. I would've gone right on believing that but for two things."

"You saw my tattoo in the restaurant," Gary murmured. "When I removed my coat. I remember. And I thought you were going to ask what it meant, so I covered it with my hand."

Dan locked gazes with him. "Do you also recall what you asked me right after that moment? You asked if my visions always came true." Gary opened his mouth to speak, but Dan wasn't done. "Look... I know you're not into guys, so please, don't say a word. I don't want you to feel under—"

"You said you'd have gone on believing it was a coincidence but for two things. You saw my tattoo. So what was the second thing?"

Dan didn't break eye contact. "It was... the way you made me feel."

"Explain." Christ, his heart was pounding.

"I *wanted* it to be you, okay? Because you were perfect for me." His words rang out in the quiet room.

Gary's world stopped turning.

"But what I want doesn't matter," Dan protested. "Go back to your question about my visions. *This* one… this vision I've had for more years than you'd probably believe… this is a first, because it can't come true."

Years? Holy fuck.

Then it hit him. He accepted Dan's vision. Had he *even for a moment* considered it preposterous that Dan should have such a vision?

No, not for a second. Because every sense he possessed was *screaming* at him that he wanted to be that man.

His future teetered on a precipice. Dan was right—this changed everything.

Gary took a deep breath. "And what if it *could* come true?"

CHAPTER 27

DAN COULDN'T breathe. Couldn't move. Because this was one dream he did *not* want to wake up from. Gary hadn't moved either, his gaze locked on Dan's face.

One of them had to break first.

"What are you saying?" Dan's voice was rough to his own ears.

Gary raised his chin higher. "I'm saying… you walked into my life and turned it upside down, inside out, back to front…."

"But… you're not gay."

Gary maintained eye contact. "No, I'm not. So imagine how it feels—for the second time in my life—to find myself attracted to another man."

Dan closed his eyes, overwhelmed for a second or two by the memory of strong emotion. "Cory." When he opened them, Gary's eyes were huge.

"How did you—what did you feel when I gave you Cory's ring? Was it more than you said at the time?"

"I've been waiting for that question. What surprises me is that you didn't ask it at the time. I did wonder why. And to answer your question, no, I didn't feel anything other than the strong connection the two of you shared." He stilled. "You loved him."

Gary's mouth opened and closed, but no words fell from his lips. He got up from the couch and walked over to the window, pressed his palm to the glass. "He was my first crush. Except… I think I always knew it was more than that. He didn't feel the same way about me."

Dan rose and went to him. He stood behind Gary, aching to touch him, hold him. "He loved you, though. Like a brother." *Christ, the smell of him….*

Gary didn't turn his head, but nodded. "I know. And that's how I came to feel about him. I told myself it was only a phase. I dated girls. I was perfectly happy dating girls. I never looked at a guy the way I looked at him. Until you."

They were close enough that Dan felt heat radiating from Gary's body. His heart thumped, his pulse raced, his breathing was shallow. "Look, you don't have to say these things. Just because I had a vision doesn't mean we have to—"

"Oh for God's sake." Gary spun around, grabbed Dan by the shoulders, and flipped them, shoving him against the cool glass. "Stop talking and kiss me."

Then his lips met Dan's in a searing kiss that exploded Dan's senses. His hands were on Gary's neck, then his broad shoulders, stroking, caressing, exploring. Gary moaned into the kiss, and the sound reverberated through Dan, beating a path to his dick.

Christ, is this real?

Dan gasped, pushing him away. "Wait—"

Gary halted, shaking. "Do you really want me to stop?"

"I want you to slow down." Dan cupped his cheek. "Breathe, sweetheart." A tumult of emotions was at war within him. "I want you too, but you have to be sure about this."

"So sure you wouldn't believe." Gary swallowed. "You have no idea what I've gone through this past week. Every time we were together, I couldn't think straight. All I wanted to do was hold you. Be close to you. Touch you." Another swallow. "I tried to ignore my feelings, but the more I did, the worse it got, until I thought I was about to explode."

"Then you're not saying all this because of my vision?"

Gary smiled, and the light in his eyes sent Dan's heart soaring. "Touch me again." When Dan frowned, he gently brought Dan's hands to his face. "Touch me. *Connect* with me, if you can. I want you to tell me what you feel."

Dan breathed deeply, Gary's face warm against his palms, his beard soft, and opened himself up. "Oh my God." Warmth surrounded him. He trembled as wave after wave of emotion surged over him until he was swimming in an ocean of desire, arousal, need—all focused on *him*. And through it all, he was aware of Gary, the light in him, the gentleness.

"Am I speaking the truth?" Gary demanded.

"Yes," Dan whispered.

"Do you want this as much as I do?"

"God yes." The words were almost a sob. Then soft lips met his, Gary's beard grazed his skin, and they were in each other's arms.

Where they belonged.

He couldn't stop touching Gary. He wanted to learn every line of him, from the curve of his pecs to the curve of his ass. Gary seemed intent on a similar mission, and when his fingers strayed to Dan's crotch, Dan didn't hesitate. He covered Gary's hand with his own, molding it around his erection, loving the groan that fell from Gary's lips.

"Can I?"

Dan swallowed. "You don't have to ask." Then his breath caught as Gary unfastened his pants, lowered the zipper, and stroked Dan's length through the soft cotton layer of his briefs. "As long as I can do the same."

Gary froze for a second; then they fumbled with buttons and zippers until clothing was discarded and they stood facing each other, both of them trembling. Dan stroked Gary's firm chest, trailing his fingers lower until at last he curled them around Gary's thickening flesh, the skin warm and smooth beneath his fingertips. He glanced down at it and licked his lips.

"Oh sweet Jesus," Gary groaned.

That was all the invitation Dan needed. He sank to his knees and took Gary into his mouth. Gary's soft cry sent the blood rushing south, and he began to worship with lips and tongue, one hand holding Gary steady, the other stroking Gary's warm, furry body. Gary laid his hands on Dan's head, cradling it as he rocked his hips, a gentle motion at first that gathered speed until he pulled free.

"I don't think my legs will hold me up a second longer."

Dan got to his feet, took him by the hand, and led him to the bed. He gave a gentle push, and Gary fell backward onto it, his erection rising into the air. Dan climbed onto the bed, straddled Gary's head, and twisted to gaze at him over his shoulder.

"You know what comes next, right?" Without waiting for a response, he leaned forward, his face inches from Gary's crotch, and went back to the task of blowing Gary's mind. He shuddered at the feel of Gary's tentative tongue. "Oh, yeah, don't stop."

It was apparently all the encouragement Gary needed.

The air filled with a soundtrack that heightened his arousal, and Dan gave himself up to his senses. The heady musk emanating from Gary was as erotic as the vibrations caused by his moans, and he knew it couldn't last long. Everything was conspiring to send him hurtling toward his climax: Gary's mouth on him, his hands stroking Dan's ass, hips, thighs....

With a cry he came, shuddering with each jolt of pleasure that coursed through him. Seconds later Gary's groans mingled with his, and Dan's lips, cheeks, and chin were coated with warmth. When the tremors ceased, Dan shifted position to lie beside him.

Gary rolled him onto his back, his welcome weight pinning Dan to the bed. He stretched out his hand toward the nightstand, pulled a Kleenex from the box there, and proceeded to remove all traces of his load from Dan's face. Once he'd discarded the crumpled tissue, he focused his attention on Dan. Gary's lips brushed against his neck, and Dan shivered, craving more of Gary's touch, more of his kisses.

I could never have enough of him.

Gary propped himself up on his elbows and gazed into Dan's eyes. "Wow."

"Good wow?"

He chuckled. "You have to ask? That was amazing."

"You were pretty awesome too. For a first timer." He bit his lip. "Is it something you'd like to do again?"

Gary grinned. "I repeat… you have to ask?" His gaze grew serious as he stroked Dan's cheek. "Is it always like this? So intense? So overwhelming?"

He took a deep breath. "No. This was a first for me too."

And I think that was because it was you. The emotions he'd felt when they'd touched earlier only amplified their connection.

"You feel good under me," Gary murmured. He rolled his hips, and Dan knew there was more to come.

He looped his arms around Gary's neck. "You feel good on top of me." He spread his legs, drawing them up to wrap them around Gary's waist. Desire trickled through him, and he whispered, "You'll feel good inside me too."

Gary's eyes widened. "Now?"

He chuckled. "Not right this minute." He kissed Gary on the lips. "What do you think of that idea?" Not that he'd force the issue if Gary wasn't keen. Dan had been with enough guys to know not everyone was into anal.

It didn't stop him hoping, however.

"Well, actually, I—" Whatever Gary had been about to say was lost in the growl that erupted from his stomach.

Dan blinked, and a moment later, the bed shook with their laughter. He kissed the tip of Gary's nose. "Message received. I'll order food." When Gary didn't move, Dan cleared his throat. "Er…. To do that, I need to get out of bed."

"Mm-hmm." Still no movement.

He chuckled. "Gary…." When Gary rolled off him with a sigh, Dan leaned over and kissed him again, this time a lingering meeting of lips. "I promise, once we've dealt with your demanding stomach, we'll pick up where we left off."

Gary's breathing quickened. "About your… suggestion…."

His hesitation was adorable.

Dan sat up. "There's no rush, okay? You choose the pace. You're in charge."

Gary shifted onto his side. "I was going to ask… would it be okay if I stayed here tonight? And I'd be happy if all I did was hold you all night long."

A layer of peace settled on him. "That sounds perfect." He reached for Gary's hand. "I know I said I couldn't leave yet because I had to help you find Cory's killer. That was the truth. But there was also *this*." He laced their fingers. "I can't walk away because of this… connection."

Gary shuddered. "Thank God for that." He stared at their joined hands. "And about me choosing the pace. Are you okay with the slow lane? Because I've never moved this fast in my life, and I want to reduce speed and enjoy the journey."

Warmth spread through Dan until he felt it in his fingers and toes. "The slow lane works for me. Especially as I didn't exactly come prepared for such a… trip."

Gary's brow furrowed and then cleared, a flush rising up from his chest, reaching his cheeks. "Oh. Yes."

"Do I *need* to be prepared?"

Gary's grin was all the answer he required.

Tuesday, June 5

GARY SURFACED from sleep. A warm body lay in his arms, and his nostrils were filled with the scent of clean hair and bed-warmed skin. He didn't want to know what time it was.

Then he remembered, and his throat seized, an ache spreading through his chest.

It was time to say goodbye.

Dan stirred and rolled over to face him. "Hey." His voice was soft.

"Good morning." If it hadn't been for Cory's funeral, it would have been the perfect morning.

"Did you sleep okay?"

Gary pushed the hair back from Dan's face. "Better than I have for a long while." He kissed Dan's forehead. Dan tilted his head, clearly seeking his lips, but Gary chuckled. "Nope. That's all you get. I didn't bring a toothbrush."

"There's a wonderful goodie bag in the bathroom," Dan told him. "I think there's a toothbrush in it." He searched Gary's face. "No regrets about last night?"

He smiled. "Only that it had to end."

"And do you want it to end?"

Another soft kiss to Dan's forehead. "No." There was a rightness to waking with Dan in his arms that he couldn't deny.

"I'm glad." Dan sighed. "And about today…."

He'd been thinking about that too. "You know it's the funeral." Dan nodded. "Well, I'd feel happier if you didn't go to the precinct today. Stay here."

"I wasn't intending to go there."

Relief flooded through him. "Oh, good."

"I was thinking of going with you." Dan's eyes focused on him. "If that's okay."

Gary didn't say a word, but pulled Dan into his arms and held him tightly.

Dan's lips grazed his ear. "I'll take that as a yes."

He breathed Dan in. "Thank you." Gary released him. "So when we've had breakfast, come back with me to my place. I'll need to change."

"I don't have a black suit, only the dark blue one."

Gary smiled. "Cory wouldn't have minded. I wasn't going to wear a black one either. I can hear him now. 'Bitch, please. Where are the rainbows, the sequins?'"

Dan laughed. "He was a character, wasn't he?"

"You would've liked him." He shook his head. "And none of this would have surprised him." His chest tightened.

Dan sat up. "You. Bathroom. Now."

"Are you always this demanding first thing in the morning?"

His eyes sparkled. "When I'm getting impatient for my first kiss of the day? You bet your ass."

Gary swallowed.

You bet your fur.

His phone buzzed on the nightstand, and Dan peered at it. "They won't call you in to work today, will they?"

"No." He peered at the text from Riley, and his face tingled.

My thoughts and prayers are with you.

He showed it to Dan, who smiled. "He's a good guy. Wish I could say the same about Lewis."

"He has his moments." When Dan gave him an incredulous glance, Gary shrugged. "Just not enough of them." Then he pushed such thoughts aside. Dan coughed, and Gary lurched from the bed. "Okay, okay, I'm going."

He stood in front of the mirror, peering into the bag provided by the hotel. When he straightened and saw his reflection, the reality of his situation finally hit home.

I spent the night with a guy.

What shocked him was how much he wanted to repeat the experience.

GARY SCANNED his rack of shirts, searching for his pale blue one. "You think that suit'll be okay?" he called out to Dan in the bedroom. He'd laid the dark blue double-breasted on the bed.

"Perfect. Except we'll match."

Gary smiled. As if he cared about that.

"Did Cory have any brothers or sisters?"

"A sister, Nina. She's great. Well, she is now. She was a real pain in the ass when she was a kid."

Silence.

"Dan?" When there was no reply, Gary walked out of the closet and came to a dead stop. Dan stood by his bedside chair, holding Brad's sweater.

His heart fluttered. "Where did you find that?"

"It was here." Dan sank onto the chair, still clutching it.

"Are you all right?"

He stroked the soft garment. "Never Forget," he murmured.

Pain lanced through Gary's chest.

Dan raised his head and met Gary's gaze. "Can you talk about him?"

He swallowed hard. "What do you already know?"

"That whoever this belongs to, you love him very much."

Gary walked over to the bed and sat on the edge. He held out his hands, and Dan placed the sweater in them with a reverence that was touching. "It belonged to my brother, Brad. And you're right. I adored him."

"Past tense." Dan paled. "Wait—Brad? That stone in Forest Park…."

He nodded. "My parents put it there."

"But what happened?" Dan got up from the chair and joined him, his hand resting lightly on Gary's back.

"Ever since we met, since that first physical contact, I've been waiting for you to announce you knew about him."

Dan sighed. "What did I say that day? I can't turn it on and off. I knew you were hiding something—I just didn't know what." He moved his hand in slow, soothing circles on Gary's back. "You don't have to tell me. Not if it brings you so much pain."

"Yes, it hurts, but I want to tell you." He sucked in a couple of breaths. "When I was fifteen, Brad was found dead in Forest Park. Murdered. He was twenty-two years old."

"Aw, no." Dan uttered the words in a strangled gasp.

Now that he'd started, he had to finish. "It made headline news in Boston for all of a week. The investigation dragged on for months, until finally they closed the case, unsolved."

"The police never discovered who killed him?"

He shook his head. "His body was discovered by two tourists in the park. He was lying on top of one of the picnic tables."

"How was he killed? Were they sure it was murder?"

"No doubt about it. Unless his heart managed to carve open his chest, wrench itself from his insides, and place itself in his hand." Dear God, it still hurt to say the words, even after all those years.

"Jesus."

"My parents never recovered from their loss."

"Neither did you." Dan touched the sweater. "So much pain woven into this." He traced over the hidden tattoo with his fingertips. "You didn't need this. Brad's death left its mark on your life, your soul."

"From the day Brad died, I've felt like an orphan. There was nothing I could do to penetrate the wall of grief they built around themselves. I had to cope with my own grief as best I could. Hell of a way to grow up fast."

Dan leaned into him. "How did you survive?"

"I would've gone under if it hadn't been for Cory. He was the one who got me through high school. He made sure I studied, covered for me when I ditched class, because Lord knew there were days when I couldn't face school." He smiled. "He wrote absence notes from my mom and forged her signature."

Dan laid his hand on Gary's thigh. "It's because of Brad that you became a cop, isn't it?"

"Yes. I knew when I was sixteen what I was going to do with my life. But I wasn't going to be just any cop, no sir. I was going to be a homicide detective." Gary hugged the sweater to him. "I had my future all mapped out. I would find the person who murdered my brother, and then my parents would *see* me, recognize me again, and realize they still had one son."

Dan kissed his temple, and the sweetness and intimacy of the gesture eased the ache inside him. "You let all your pain, grief, and loss fuel your ambition."

Tears pricked the corners of his eyes, and he wiped them away. *I've wept enough.* Except he knew the day would bring more tears before it was over.

"Is that everything? There's nothing else you want to share with me?"

"Only my gratitude." Gary cupped Dan's cheek. "And I have a lot to be grateful for."

"Me too." Gary gave him a speculative glance, and Dan smiled. "For a moment there, I thought I was the butt of some big cosmic joke."

"I don't understand."

"Well, how would *you* feel if the man you've been seeing in your dreams for thirteen years finally shows up, and he's straight?"

Gary chuckled, until Dan's words sank in. "That long?"

"I'd almost given up hope."

"Well, now you've met me, I hope I'm not a disappointment."

Dan studied him in silence until Gary was aware of the throb of his heartbeat. Then he cradled Gary's head in his hands, and their lips met in a leisurely kiss.

Gary breathed again.

Cory, you were right about one thing. I was single because I was waiting for the right person to come along.

The right man.

CHAPTER 28

GARY PAUSED at the large wooden doors of Bigelow Chapel. "Are you sure about this?" The gray stone facade stood out against the lush green of the gardens surrounding it. Quiet organ music filtered through from the interior, mixed with the low hum of voices.

Dan frowned. "I'm here, aren't I? Why would I change my mind?"

All the way to the chapel, one thought had occupied Gary's mind. *I'm being selfish.* He wanted Dan there, but it wasn't until they'd left his apartment that he realized what he was asking Dan to do. An intuitive, sensitive man, who was also a psychic, was about to walk into a chapel filled with mourners. A lot of emotion. Grief, maybe even anger and fear.

"If it gets too much, say the word and we'll leave."

Dan gazed at him with wide eyes. "You think I'd let you walk out of Cory's funeral service? Don't worry about me. I'm made of stronger stuff than that." Then Dan slipped his hand around Gary's. "I'm here for you, okay? If you need to lean on me, then you lean." He smiled. "I think Cory would approve."

Despite his aching heart, Gary chuckled. "Cory would be dancing in the aisle." He took a deep breath, and they entered the chapel.

Little had changed since Brad's funeral. The vaulted ceilings were as elegant and imposing as ever, and the sunlight spilling through the Great Rose Window above their heads illuminated the stonework with splashes of color.

Hey, Cory. God sent you rainbows.

"So many people here," Dan murmured. "Looks like it's standing room only."

"Nina said she'd save me a seat. I'm sure there'll be one for you too."

"And if she asks who I am?"

Gary smiled. "Let's go with friend for now."

The chapel was packed. On either side of the center aisle, the wooden chairs had already filled, and more mourners stood in the alcoves framed by graceful arches.

He leaned into Dan and murmured, "Cory would have loved this. All these men, here for him." The mourners were predominantly male, and amid the sea of black, he caught sight of yet more splashes of subdued color. He smiled to himself. *Sorry, Cory. Not a sequin in sight.*

He walked slowly toward the front, his chest tightening at the sight of the empty trestle before the altar where the coffin would be laid.

Then Nina stepped into view, looking elegant in a dark blue dress suit and matching hat. Gary forgot his own grief and hurried to greet her. They hugged, and when she released him, she smiled. "Great minds and all that. You didn't wear black either." She glanced at the mourners. "We're not the only ones." She gave Dan a quizzical glance.

"This is my friend, Dan Porter."

Nina's brow furrowed and then smoothed out. "Mr. Porter. Thank you for coming."

"I didn't meet your brother, but I know he was important to Gary."

She swallowed. "Yeah. Gary was the brother he never had." She pointed to a couple of empty chairs on the second row, each with a white Reserved card on them. "I've put you behind us."

Gary glanced at her parents, who stood talking with an elderly couple. "How are they doing?"

"As you'd expect. We just need to get through today. It'll be better after that, right? When we've all moved on?" She gazed at him with hope.

"Unfortunately, grief doesn't work like that." Gary kissed her cheek. "You never forget, you just have to accept it and carry on living."

"I tried to help. Once they'd made the arrangements, Mom let me pick the music."

He stilled. "Oh dear Lord."

Her eyes glistened. "Cory would love it. That's all I care about right now." She gazed at the crowds of people. "Maybe I should have booked TD Garden after all."

The celebrant approached them. "I think we're ready to begin," he said in a low voice.

Nina straightened. "On with the show." She removed a Kleenex from her purse and wiped her eyes. "God bless the guy who invented waterproof mascara." She squeezed Gary's hand. "We'll talk more later."

Then she took her place on the front row between her parents and a tall young man who Gary assumed was her fiancé, David.

"That was an odd phrase to use to describe a funeral," Dan murmured as they shuffled into their row.

The congregation rose as music filled the air, and Gary suppressed the urge to laugh as Liza Minelli's voice poured from the sound system.

"Cabaret."

Yeah, Cory would definitely have approved.

Everyone stood as the pallbearers carried the casket solemnly to the trestle, then laid it there with reverent care. Gary's chest grew tight.

He shouldn't be in there.

Dan took his hand. "We'll catch him, okay? So Cory—and everyone who knew him—can be at peace."

Gary squeezed his hand. "Yes."

He half listened as the celebrant spoke of Cory, and although he shared amusing anecdotes, none of them captured the real Cory, the boy in Gary's head, the young man he'd loved. He focused on the polished casket, remembering their times together, the laughter, the tears…. And when the celebrant asked for a moment's silence so everyone could reflect on Cory's part in their own lives, Gary bade a silent goodbye to his first love.

When the service was finally over, all the mourners made their way out into the bright sunshine to the strains of Eva Cassidy's emotional rendition of "Somewhere over The Rainbow." Gary had to admit, the music choices had been inspired. Outside, people gathered in groups, filling the paths that led to the chapel and talking in low voices. Nina, David, and her parents stood by a long black car. She beckoned to him.

"Come with us. There's room."

Before Gary could respond, Dan cleared his throat. "Listen, you go with them. I'll go back to the hotel."

Nina frowned. "That invitation was for you too, Mr. Porter. Any friend of Gary's…." She bit her lip, and her eyes met Gary's.

Oh God. She saw us holding hands. He couldn't be certain of that, but it was a possibility. And judging by Nina's expression, she wasn't in the least bit surprised.

Fuck it.

He took Dan's hand in his, then smiled. "We'd love to."

In high school, I chose a different path, but Dan has brought me back to the life I could have had if Cory had loved me the way I loved him. Gary wasn't going to waste a single day of his new life.

CHAPTER 29

I STOOD AT the back of the chapel with two coworkers, three people in a sea of mourners. I wasn't surprised by the number of gay men who'd turned up to bid Cory Peterson farewell.

He probably fucked at least half of them.

When the suggestion was made at work to attend the funeral, I'd agreed immediately. After all, I'd missed the first five. It was time I saw the results of my handiwork. As I walked into the chapel, I'd received nods from so many familiar faces. No one was surprised to see me there.

Why would they be? They knew me.

Some of them were already on my Potentials list.

But then another familiar face appeared, and suddenly I was cold.

What's Dan Porter doing here?

I watched as he and another man walked toward the altar, my blood like ice. Less than forty-eight hours after my last victim met his maker, and he just *happened* to turn up at Peterson's funeral? I took a closer look at the guy with him. There was something familiar about him too. Then it came to me where I'd seen his face before. In the newspapers, alongside Mr. Psychic.

He's one of the detectives looking for me.

I couldn't breathe.

Couldn't think straight.

Do they know I'm here?

Can Porter sense me somehow?

I might have laughed off Boston PD's decision to involve him, but having him there, mere feet away from me, was unnerving.

Don't lose your cool now. Remember, smart people don't get caught—only stupid people do.

And I was smarter than most of the men in that chapel.

I debated getting closer to him, if only to prove to myself that I was invisible, but brushed aside that idea. *Keep him at a distance. This is a marathon, not a sprint, and there are still fifteen more to go.* I tried to ignore him, to stop waiting for him to turn around and point a trembling finger at me, declaring in a loud voice that I was the killer.

He doesn't know I'm here. I'm safe.

I relaxed a little when one of Peterson's family greeted the detective warmly. *Maybe he knows them. Maybe he's built up a rapport with them.*

I still wasn't going anywhere near either of them.

Instead I contented myself with staying where I was, studying the men surrounding me. Who would be next?

Eenie….

Meenie….

Minie….

Moe.

CHAPTER 30

DAN GAZED at the passing scenery. "So… was that deliberate? Holding my hand in front of Nina?" Not that he'd minded, but it had taken him by surprise.

"Yeah." Gary glanced at him. "You okay with that?"

"Me? Sure. I just wondered why you chose to do it then. It must have been a shock for her. I mean, she's known you how long?"

Gary stared at the road ahead. "She said recently she'd once told Cory that he and I should date."

"Wishful thinking? Or did she have a sense about you? Either way, she didn't appear shocked." Dan spotted a familiar landmark. "You're not taking me back to the hotel, are you?"

"Uh-uh. You're staying with me tonight. And until we catch this guy, you'll be with me at the precinct, or I'll be with you wherever you are."

Dan stiffened. "You can't keep me wrapped up, you know. I refuse to be afraid all the time."

"And what if I need to do this?" Gary paused. "I have to keep you safe, okay?"

Warmth rushed through him. "I know. I do understand. But he's not after me. However…." Warmth gave way to heat. "I have no objection to a police presence in my bed every night from now until I leave. Wherever that bed may be."

Gary fell silent for a moment. "Was that an invitation?"

He shrugged. "I could make it a demand, if you'd prefer that."

"Noted."

The CVS sign on the next corner propelled Dan into action. "Could we make a quick stop?" he asked, pointing.

"Sure. What do you nee—oh. Right." Gary swung the car into the parking lot. "You don't need me to come inside with you, do you?"

Christ, he was adorable.

Dan patted his knee. "I think I can manage this one." When the car came to a halt, he got out, his heart hammering.

One step closer to his vision.

But will it be as good as it is there?

God, he hoped so.

"I COULD KISS you all night long," Gary murmured against his lips. They were lying on his bed, shoes and jackets discarded, and Dan's shirt was open about halfway.

"Me too, but if we do that, we miss out on some really good stuff." Dan pulled back and looked him in the eye. "You do still want this? I mean, we don't have to."

Gary responded the only way he knew. He kissed Dan's neck, moved his fingers lower, seeking Dan's nipple beneath the layer of crisp cotton. Dan's low whimper went straight to his groin.

"Dear Lord, the way you smell…." Dan inhaled deeply.

"You seemed to like it, so I thought—"

"Like it? No. I love it. That scent has been in every vision I've ever had of the two of us, which makes it right." He locked gazes with Gary. "I want to breathe it in when you're inside me."

Gary groaned. "Can you *not* say things like that, please?" Any more and he was in real danger of shooting before he got to where he longed to be.

Dan cupped Gary's burgeoning erection. "Can I suck it?"

Another groan rolled out of him. "Don't ask, just do it."

Dan's nimble fingers dealt with the fastening on his pants, and Gary shuddered to feel a warm, wet mouth on him. He did his best to keep still, but the urge to thrust was huge. "Can I do the same to you?" His first experience of 69 had only made him yearn to do it again.

Dan jerked his head up, and it was as if someone had switched the thermostat to Inferno. Clothes flew to the floor. They lay on their sides, and Gary's lips were inches from Dan's pretty cock. He kissed the head, and Dan shivered. "Please."

Invitation accepted.

Gary slid his arm under Dan's hips, one hand curled around warm, solid flesh, and licked a path from root to head. Exhilaration burst through him, and the dual sensations of sucking and being sucked sent Gary perilously close to the edge, just like their first time. Their heads bobbed, settling into a rhythm, Dan's moans reverberating through his shaft, sending delicious trickles of electricity that tingled and teased. And when Dan broke off to beg Gary to fuck him, Gary shifted with an eagerness that surprised even him. The sight of Dan's ass, tilted, waiting, Dan twisting to look at him, to watch him…

Gary wanted time to stand still.

He wanted to burn into his memory that initial glorious tightness around his shaft when he slowly inched his way into Dan's body. To remember the feel of Dan's hips as he held him steady, driving deep into him, their bodies smacking together, accompanied by their mingled grunts and cries. The look in Dan's eyes when Gary turned him onto his back and raised Dan's legs to his shoulders before entering him again.

I don't want to forget this. Not one second of it.

DAN'S HEARTBEAT raced, his body covered with a sheen of sweat. "Oh Lord, you feel…."

"Tell me." Gary thrust, and Dan groaned.

"Don't stop," he pleaded. He was racing toward his orgasm, and he couldn't delay it a minute more. It was nothing like any previous sexual encounter. Each sensation felt more acute, and he'd had to fight to stop himself from coming the moment Gary penetrated him for the first time.

Gary leaned in and kissed him, rocking his hips in a deliciously slow motion. "We're not stopping till you come," he whispered.

Dan held on to him, wrapping his legs around Gary's waist, his heels digging into Gary's firm asscheeks. "Which will be any second now," he gasped. Gary drove into him, and Dan nodded, his eyes locked on Gary's. "Harder," he begged. Gary did it once more, only this time he set off fireworks inside Dan, making him moan. "Again." His body shook as he came without a single touch, and he clung to Gary, loving how Gary buried his face in Dan's neck, kissing him there, his beard gently rasping the skin, Gary still inside him. Gary's back was slick beneath his fingers.

"My turn." Gary moved slowly in and out of him, hips rolling sinuously, Dan's leg on his shoulder, Gary's hand working him with leisurely tugs. Then he picked up the pace, his gaze focused on Dan's face, and suddenly they were locked together, body and soul. Dan was caught up in a circle of not only his own desire and need, but Gary's too.

He stared at Gary, his chest heaving. "I feel you. Oh dear Lord, I *feel* you." And just like that, something rocked into place and the connection intensified, sending his heart soaring. He felt the throb inside him and came a second time, a thing he'd never experienced before. Gary stilled, and Dan tightened around his shaft, determined to milk it of every last drop.

Jolts shook Gary's body, and he slid his arms under Dan's pits, their damp chests meeting. Dan held on to him, not wanting to shatter the moment. Gary's lips brushed against his neck. "That was...."

"Yeah, I know." Dan was lost for words, and that was so right. Words couldn't do justice to what he'd experienced. If anything, they'd rob it of its intensity and power.

All he knew was, one time would not be enough. He had a feeling a *lifetime* wouldn't be enough.

And there it was, the innate knowledge that Gary was the one he'd been waiting for his whole life.

But has he been waiting for me?

Gary had a life in Boston. A life without Dan.

And once the killer is caught, will our connection be severed?

Only one person could answer that, and his arms were presently wrapped around Dan.

We need to talk.

CHAPTER 31

Wednesday, June 6
9:00 a.m.

DAN KNEW he was being paranoid, but he couldn't shake the feeling that everyone in the precinct, right down to the janitor, knew exactly what he and Gary had been doing the previous day. Officers and detectives filed past him after roll call had finished, and Dan was conscious of their scrutiny. Maintaining a minimum safe distance from Gary would be torture, but it was for the best. Besides, he was there to do a job, and that meant keeping his focus.

Yeah, right. All he had to do was glance in Gary's direction and heat swept through him in a rush as he was transported back to his bed, lost in his memories, Gary's scent, his taste, the feel of his hands on Dan....

But where do we go from here? What happens when we catch the killer and I have to go home?

Questions he couldn't answer.

Gary coughed, and Dan flushed. "Now that I have your attention... Lewis wants us in the case room."

"There hasn't been another one, has there?" Dan felt sick to his stomach at the idea that the killer had murdered again, only three days since the last victim had been discovered.

"No. I would've heard before now if there had been. But he needs to bring us up to speed on yesterday's events."

"I doubt he wants to bring *us* up to speed," Dan murmured when they reached the door to the case room. Then he clammed up as they entered. Riley wasn't there, but Lewis was fixing a photo to the board.

He turned to face them, his expression neutral as he glanced at Dan. "So do you want the good news or the bad news?"

"Good morning would be nice. So would coffee." Gary closed the door.

"Coffee can wait. Travers was here before I left last night."

Gary sighed. "I'm guessing we're starting with the bad news. What did he say?" Dan walked over to the board to gaze at the photos.

"The chief tore him a new one yesterday. Will Freeman said the windows rattled, he was that loud. Seems the LGBTQ community is putting pressure on us now that the body count has reached seven. Did you see the headlines this morning?"

"Now why would I do that? Perfect way to ruin my day."

Heat bloomed in Dan's face, and he turned his head away. There had been no time to look at phones—they'd been engaged in far more engrossing activities.

"Same story there," Lewis grumbled. "Attacking Boston PD for its lack of results. And now for the *really* bad news. If we don't find this guy sooner rather than later, they're calling in the FBI. The only reason the feds aren't already knocking on our door is because they can only do that if requested."

Gary sighed. "It's not as if we didn't know they'd be involved at some point. So what's the good news?"

"Riley arrested Silver for assault."

Dan jerked his head in Lewis's direction. "What happened?"

Lewis folded his arms. "Mystery solved of why he didn't want us around. The day before we turned up to interview him, he'd beaten up his boyfriend. Said BF finally got up the nerve to come in and tell us what happened. Says he'll be a witness. Seems it was one beating too many." He smiled. "And because I'm in such a good mood, I'll go fetch us coffee." He strutted out of the room.

Gary met Dan's gaze. "Alone at last," he quipped.

"Stop that." Dan touched his face. "I swear, I burn up when I so much as think about—"

"What?" Gary moved closer.

"Stay back." Dan strove to make his voice menacing, but it was an epic fail. "You keep away from me."

"Why? What do you think I'm going to do?" Gary teased. "Kiss you?"

"Riley could walk in at any second," he remonstrated. To his relief, Gary laughed, and Dan sagged. "Christ, you really had me going there." He sank into one of the chairs. "Actually, I'm glad I have you alone for a second. There's something I need to ask you."

"That sounds serious." Gary cocked his head. "What's on your mind?"

He took a deep breath. "Look, I know this is fast, but then again, not really when you factor in I've been dreaming about you for thirteen years, but—"

"You weren't making that up?"

He blinked. "Why would I lie about it? That's the only reason I'm still here. You already know why I avoid relationships, but when it comes to you...." Another inhalation. "I guess what I'm asking is if you want us to be together, once this case is closed."

Gary walked over to him, taking slow measured steps. He stood over him. "What do your senses tell you?"

He swallowed. "That even if I hadn't had that vision, we're meant to be together."

Gary expelled a breath. "Then it's not just me." He bit his lip. "If you only knew how badly I want to hold you right now." His eyes sparkled. "Take my hand. You'll know in a heartbeat."

A lightness suffused him. "You can hold me tonight, okay? For as long as you want."

"After we've been shopping," Gary added. When Dan gave him an inquiring glance, a flush rose up to stain his cheeks. "Well, you only bought a packet of three condoms, and we used the last one this morning."

Dan put his shoulders back. "About that. There *is* an alternative."

"What do you mean?"

He raised his chin and looked Gary in the eye. "We get tested so we both know we're in tiptop shape. Then we ditch the condoms." His heart quaked. "Unless...."

"Unless what?"

There was no way around it. "Look, I'm a one-man guy, but you're new to all this. For all I know, you might want to... explore your options." *But please don't.*

Gary said nothing for a moment; then he took Dan's hands in his and helped him to his feet. "The only man I'll be doing any exploring with is you." He didn't let go. "Now, am I telling the truth?"

A wave of emotion crashed over Dan, leaving him weak yet exhilarated. "Oh God."

"I'll take that as a yes." Gary shivered. "What have you done to me, Dan Porter? I've had relationships—not long-lasting ones, granted, but I put that down to not meeting the right girl." Hazel eyes met his. "Not one of those women made me feel the way you do." He shuddered out a breath. "I look at the length of time we've known each other, and I think, this can't be happening. It can't be real."

Dan's heart thumped. "I know, but—"

"So yes," Gary interjected. "Let's get tested." Dan stilled, and Gary leaned in to kiss him chastely on the lips. "The only man I want is you," he whispered.

If Gary hadn't been holding his hands, Dan swore he'd float up to the ceiling, he felt so light. Then he pulled free. "I wouldn't want Lewis to come back with the coffee and find us."

"How do we go about getting tested?"

"Leave that part to me." He swallowed. "And I'm glad it's going to be just us. I was getting ready to tell you all about Truvada." He peered at Gary. "Unless you already know what that is."

"Cory mentioned it once or twice."

Dan nodded. "It goes by other names too, but only because the full-length version is a mouthful. That's why we keep it simple and call it PrEP." He locked gazes with Gary. "I'm not on it, by the way, but so many guys are these days. One pill a day. God bless medical science." He let out a sigh of relief. "If we're going to be monogamous, there's no need for it."

Thank you, God. As soon as Gary had said Dan was all he wanted, Dan felt as if his heart was singing.

Gary froze, his eyes wide. He walked slowly over to the board.

"What is it?" Dan's scalp prickled.

Gary stared at the photos of the victims. "PrEP… what's the full-length version?"

"Pre-exposure Prophylaxis." Then he followed Gary's gaze to the paper where Riley had written the letters carved into the victims, and his blood ran cold. "Oh my God. That's it."

CHAPTER 32

COLD SPREAD out from Gary's core. "We've been blind."

Dan was at his side. "I did the math. There are twenty-two letters. He's just getting started, isn't he?"

"Then we're going to do all we can to make sure he doesn't achieve his goal." He glanced toward the door as Lewis entered, carrying cups of coffee in a cardboard tray. Riley was behind him. "Great timing. We've got work to do."

Riley took one look at his face and came to a dead stop. "You've got something."

Gary picked up a pen and handed it to Dan, who wrote Pre-exposure Prophylaxis below the photos of the victims, then underlined the first seven letters. He stepped back, and Gary pointed to the board. "Recognize anything?" He caught Riley's sharp intake of breath.

"What's that?" Lewis peered at it.

"It's a medicine for people who don't have HIV but are at very high risk of getting it," Riley said in a low voice.

"And who are those people?"

"Anyone who shares needles to inject drugs or has a partner who is HIV-positive or has multiple partners.... A lot of gay men are on it because they don't want to use condoms. Some still use them, however, because it doesn't prevent STDs."

Lewis stared at him. "How come you know all this?"

Riley's gaze was cool. "My brother is gay, all right? And even if he wasn't and we didn't talk about everything under the sun, I'd still know what it was, because *I* don't live under a rock." He turned to Gary. "What do you need me to do?"

"See if you can get the medical records for all the victims. I want to know how many of them were on PrEP." He couldn't shake the ice that had settled in his veins. "I have a feeling it's going to be all of them."

"If they were on PrEP, they'd have to get tested every three months, usually at a sexual health clinic," Dan added.

Gary nodded. "Lewis, make some calls. See if any clinics have our victims on their files." *Finally*. This could be the break they needed.

"How many clinics are we talking about?" Lewis demanded.

"That's what you're going to tell me."

"I'll work on the medical records," Riley said. He shook his head. "How did you figure this out?"

"I wouldn't have managed it on my own. Dan pointed me in the right direction."

Riley smiled. "Thanks, Dan. We owe you." He hurried out of the room.

"I'll go look up clinics." Lewis grabbed a cup of coffee and followed Riley.

Gary handed Dan a cup. "I think you've earned this." Dan took it and gazed at the board, his head tilted to one side. "What is it?"

Dan wrinkled his nose, his brow furrowed. "I'm thinking, that's all."

"Then think out loud." Gary leaned against the table, his own cup in his hand. "What's on your mind?"

"I'm not a detective. I don't see how my musings could be useful."

"Let me be the judge of that." He took the cup from Dan. "You get your coffee when you've told me what's bothering you."

Dan let out a mock gasp. "Oh. *Now* I see. You're mean." Before Gary could protest, he returned his attention to the board. "I keep going back to that feeling… that the victims knew their killer."

"Okay. What about it?"

Dan glanced at him. "You remember I registered surprise? Well, what if…?"

"Don't stop there."

Dan studied the board. "What if they were surprised because they knew him but didn't think he was gay?"

"That doesn't make sense. He contacted them all on Grindr. Why would he be on Grindr if he wasn't gay?"

Dan arched his eyebrows. "You said Lewis was on Grindr. Is *he* gay?" Gary blinked, and Dan nodded. "Exactly. Think about it. Kris Lee Arill approaches them, but we know he uses fake photos. He arranges to meet, probably using WhatsApp. And when he turns up…. *Bam*. It's not the guy they expect, but they know him, or at least recognize him. But maybe they didn't have a clue he was into guys. *That's* why they're surprised."

"And none of them show him the door, because…?"

Dan's brows lifted again. "He's obviously a good-looking guy." He sighed. "I don't think that theory holds water."

"Keep going. Any more theories?"

"Just one. I think you've been looking in the wrong direction."

"What do you mean?"

Dan held out his hand. "Coffee, now. I need caffeine to make my brain work."

Gary chuckled and handed it to him. "Continue. Which direction should we have been looking in?"

Dan smiled. "What if Grindr—and all the other apps—were red herrings?"

Gary became still. "Continue."

"You've assumed he uses the apps to choose his victims. Okay, let's also assume Riley is going to come through that door and tell you *all* the victims were taking PrEP. What if *that's* how he chooses them? Think about what I said when I first saw the letters. He's giving them a tramp stamp. That fits. Maybe he sees anyone taking PrEP as promiscuous. God knows he wouldn't be the first to leap to *that* conclusion." He took a long drink.

Gary couldn't drink. His pulse quickened, and adrenaline shot through his system. "Let's take the assumptions a stage further. You said if they were on PrEP, they'd need to get tested. What if that's where they knew him from? They'd seen him at a sexual health clinic."

"So he *is* gay after all?" Dan gaped. "What is he doing, making a tour of all the clinics, picking out guys to be next on his list?" A violent shiver rippled through him. "It gives me the creeps."

"You still feel he's doing this out of some desire for vengeance?"

Dan shuddered. "I can't get those words out of my head. '*I'm doing this for you.*'" He whooshed out a breath. "Wow. What a mind trip. One minute I'm bringing up us getting tested, and suddenly I've steered the investigation onto a new path." He drained his cup. "What else can I do for you? I'm on a roll."

"I think you've done enough for today. Besides…." He studied Dan's face, noting the faint shadows under his eyes.

"What?"

Gary bit back a smile. "You look as tired as I feel."

"And that surprises you? Seeing as neither of us got a lot of sleep last night?"

He did *not* want to think about that right then, not with the prospect of Lewis walking in there at any minute. "Look, we've got calls to make, records to chase up. Why don't I take you back to your hotel and you can have a nap?"

Dan frowned. "Firstly, I don't need you to take me anywhere. There's this wonderful thing out there called Uber."

"Indulge me." Gary closed the gap between them. "I want to make sure you're safe, okay?"

"We've talked about this already. And I'd agree with you, one hundred percent—*if* the killer had left a very different note on Jack Noonan's body." Dan gripped Gary's shoulders. "He didn't write some dire warning that I would be next if I interfered, did he? If he'd done that, I promise you, I'd have you at my side twenty-four seven. But think about it. He *laughed* at me, Gary. He doesn't think I can find him. I don't think I'm even on his radar. So please, don't be worrying about my safety. Not when you have far more important things to think about."

"And if I wanted to take you back to the hotel so I'd have the chance to be alone with you for a short while?"

Dan's breathing quickened. "Can't argue with that, especially when you're standing close enough that I can still smell the shampoo you used this morning, and you *know* where that thought took me."

Lord, his dick reacted. "You said firstly. What else?"

"Secondly, I'm not a kid that you can send to bed."

"Not even if I have an ulterior motive?" Closer. "Not even if I want you to recharge your batteries before I see you this evening?"

Jesus, the size of Dan's pupils….

"Do I need to recharge them?"

Gary hoped his grin was answer enough. "So… do I take you to the hotel?"

"Sure." Dan's eyes twinkled. "Can't argue with that either."

He felt a pang of guilt. He hadn't lied—Dan did appear fatigued—but underlying his suggestion was the need to put a little space between them. Dan had provided them with new avenues to explore, but Gary couldn't think clearly when he was near.

For the first time since Cory's death, he felt as if the killer was finally within their reach—and he intended keeping Dan out of the killer's.

CHAPTER 33

10:30 a.m.

DAN CLOSED the door to his room. Gary had been correct—he was bone tired. He kicked off his shoes, removed his jacket, and loosened his tie. The bed had been made, and the sight of plump pillows and the smooth white comforter proved too tempting to ignore. He grabbed the Do Not Disturb door hanger and hung it outside. He took his phone from his pocket and put it on silent. After placing it on the nightstand, he undressed, pulled back the soft cotton bedding, and climbed in.

God, that feels good. The mattress topper was supremely comfortable, and the pillows were the perfect shade of firm. He closed his eyes. His intention had been to search for a clinic where they could get tested, but he was too tired to think straight.

It can wait. I'll find one after my nap.

11:30 a.m.

GARY STARED at the list he'd written on the board. *Am I on the right track?* If Dan was correct, the killer was out for revenge. He cast his mind back to his psychology classes in college and when he was training to be a homicide detective.

Maybe I need a refresher course.

A much simpler—and faster—solution was to call in an expert.

Riley came into the case room as Gary scrolled through his contacts and placed a call. "Kathy, are you available for a quick consult?"

"I will be in a few minutes. I'll come to you. Are you at your desk?"

"No. If you come down the hallway toward Homicide, we're in the small room on the right. You can't miss it. Some joker pinned a notice to it."

"See you there." She disconnected.

"Kathy Wainwright's coming?" Riley asked.

"Yeah. I want to pick her brains."

"You might've warned me." Riley straightened his tie and checked his shirt.

Gary cackled. "Will you relax? You've already said she doesn't want a boy toy." He bit his lip. "You might want to smooth your hair down at the back, though."

"What?" Riley jerked his head. "Why isn't there a mirror in here?" He reached around to brush his hair flat, and then narrowed his gaze. "My hair is fine, isn't it?"

Gary grinned. "Gotcha." That earned him a glare.

"Why didn't you take that sign down, by the way?" Riley inquired.

Gary snorted. "I do that and there'd be another to replace it. Besides, Serial Killers 101 had a ring to it. And most of the guys out there are only jealous." He chuckled. "Will Freeman is working on a case of a woman who shot her husband. She claims she didn't mean to do it and that the gun 'just went off.' He told me he'd love to be investigating a serial killer."

"He wouldn't love the pressure," Riley mumbled. He pointed to the board. "What's that?"

"I got to thinking about the similarities between the cases, so I made a list."

"We did that three victims ago."

Gary nodded. "This time, I'm coming at it from a different angle." He glanced at Riley. "Any news on the medical reports?"

Riley nodded. "You were right. They were all on PrEP. How's Lewis doing with the clinics?"

"I'll ask him when he shows up." There'd been no sign of him.

"Why do you want to talk to Kathy?"

Gary stared at the board where he'd written *I'm doing this for you.* Under it, he'd written Anger and Guilt. "Something Dan said has got me thinking." There was a knock at the door, and Kathy entered.

She gave Riley a bright smile. "Hey there."

Gary pointed to an empty chair. "Take a seat." He waited until she'd sat, then pulled up another chair and tugged it to face hers.

"You were right about the sign. Subtle, very subtle. Who was the artist?"

Gary frowned. "What artist?"

"The joker who drew a box of Cheerios lying on the ground, bleeding. Cereal killer?" Her eyes twinkled.

He hadn't even noticed.

She stared past him to the board, and her face grew solemn. "Tell me you're getting closer to catching him," she murmured.

"We're working on it."

Kathy snapped her attention to him. "Okay. What can I do for you?"

"Let's pretend that sign out there is for real. Serial killers. Why do they do it? What motivates them?"

She pursed her lips. "That assumes there *is* motivation. The media would have us believe they kill because they simply enjoy the act of killing. There could be multiple motives. Anger, financial gain, psychosis, sexual need, exhilaration...."

"What about revenge?"

"That too." She tilted her head. "Is that your theory?"

"That's all it's been until now, but I think it's time we explored it some more." He looked across to where Riley stood, his back against the wall. "Who's our whiz kid when it comes to searching the net and finding a needle in a haystack?"

"Barry Davies," he replied without hesitation. "The guy's a genius." He paused. "What do you want him to look for?"

Gary got up from his chair and went over to the board. "What are the constants for each of the crime scenes?" He pointed to the list and worked his way down it. "A bottle of GHB. Rope. Cuffs. Possible link to BDSM. Victims with a very active sex life. Multiple partners. And they all died from a fatal drug dose."

"You missed out the condom. And the letters."

Gary shook his head. "No, I deliberately left them out. Let's assume everything I've listed here is important. I want Barry to look for guys who died as the result of an overdose. Then cross-reference *them* with gay men who were sexually active, gay men with established links to BDSM. Not guys who were murdered, okay?"

Kathy let out a soft sound. "Oh. I get it. You think your killer is murdering these guys in the same way someone close to him was killed, is that it? He's replicating the way they died."

Gary nodded. "Like I said, it's just a theory. There's a pattern to all this—let's assume it's deliberate."

"How far back do you want Barry to look?" Riley asked. "And where?"

Gary stroked his beard. "The first victim died in March 2016. Start there and go backward. And let's stick to Boston for now. Tell him to keep going until he's got enough data to analyze. If nothing turns up, we'll widen the field."

Please, let something turn up.

"I'm on it." Riley met Gary's gaze head-on. "Expect results. He's fast." With a nod to Kathy, he left the room.

Kathy got up from her chair and went to the board. "Can I ask you something?" She pointed to where he'd written Anger. "This one I get. If your theory is correct, someone the killer loved died a wrongful death, and he's out to avenge him." Then she pointed to Guilt. "This intrigues me, however. What made you come up with this?"

Gary hesitated for a moment. "You know who's helping us on this, don't you?"

Her gaze grew thoughtful. "That psychic who's worked with the police before? The one in the newspapers?"

"Yes." Gary tapped the board where "I'm doing this for you" was written. "He feels this is the killer's mantra. And these"—he indicated Anger and Guilt again—"were the two strongest emotions he encountered when he was at one of the recent crime scenes."

She studied the words in silence. At last she took a step back. "We won't find out if he's right until we catch the killer." She breathed deeply. "I'll watch this case with great interest." Kathy gave him a speculative glance. "Why did you ask me to consult on this? As far as I see, you've got a good grasp of what might motivate him."

"I wanted to check that my theory made sense."

"It does." She heaved a sigh. "Seeking revenge for a wrongful death does *not* justify what he's done. He's destroyed lives, and I don't just mean the victims."

Gary swallowed. "And we're making sure *we* avenge *their* deaths."

Kathy gave him an approving glance. "Good luck." She exited the room.

Gary walked over to Cory's photo. *We're getting closer, Cory.*

God, he prayed he was right.

CHAPTER 34

4:00 p.m.

DAN OPENED his eyes and stretched. *I needed that.* He reached for his phone and blinked when he saw the time. *Five and a half hours? That was some nap. Guess I* really *needed that.*

He propped his head up with pillows and clicked on Google. He wasn't sure what time Gary would finish work—not for a few hours yet—but he had to eat sometime, right? The least Dan could do would be to surprise him with a dinner reservation.

And he knew exactly where to look.

He threw back the comforter and ambled over to the window. Outside it was a lovely late afternoon, and it called to him. Since their weekend together, Dan had left the hotel for two reasons—to go to the precinct and for Cory's funeral.

Then he remembered he had another search to do.

He went back to the bed and picked up his phone. The first clinic that popped up looked promising, and he had to smile at its name. *How apt.* When he scrolled through the information, he realized the clinic would close in an hour. But as he went to click on Call, he hesitated. Instead he clicked on Uber. With so little time available, it made more sense than getting his car from hotel parking, then trying to find a place to park near the clinic.

It was too pleasant an afternoon to stay indoors, and the clinic was less than half an hour away by car. He could check it out, see what appointments were available for the coming week, then grab a coffee and find a bench in the sunshine. By the time Gary was finished, he'd be back at the hotel.

A brief pang lanced through him. *Gary won't be happy about me leaving the hotel without him.* But it wasn't as if he was in any danger. The killer wouldn't be lurking someplace, waiting for him to venture out into the open, ready to pounce.

Like I said, I'm not even on his radar.

When he saw an Uber could be at the hotel in five minutes, he made a mad scramble to pull on his jeans and a shirt.

This won't take long.

4:20 p.m.

GARY FINISHED reading the final autopsy report on Marius Eisler, which had come through at last. There were no surprises. If anything it was a carbon copy of the previous four. The tox screen had revealed Rohypnol and ketamine. Although the victim's body had stopped processing the substances biologically, the markers for them remained. Del had declared death to be due to a fatal dose of ketamine.

He picked up the statements from Jack Noonan's landlady and roommates. Nothing new in them either. There were the same comments about the number of guys who visited the apartment. Lewis had observed that they could expect nothing else, not when all three occupants were gay.

Concentration proved difficult, but Gary knew the cause of it. There was a fluttery, empty feeling in his stomach, and every time his phone buzzed, he seized it, only to put it down, disappointed, when it wasn't what he'd expected.

He was waiting for something to happen.

Riley burst into the room. "We've got something."

"I thought you said Barry was fast? It's been five hours."

"Hey, he hasn't stopped since I saw him. And it's paid off."

Gary's heart pounded. "Tell me."

"He cross-referenced all deaths in Boston and came up with nothing. Then he widened the net to Massachusetts, and one name emerged that met all our criteria." Riley consulted his notes. "Paul Philip Ludlow. Died in 2014, in Lowell, aged twenty-six."

"How did he die?"

"He took bath salts—"

"Isn't that some kind of designer drug? Like meth?"

Riley nodded. "The medical examiner postulated that he'd probably suffered from paranoia and psychosis due to the drug. Anyway, he cut off his own penis."

"Jesus." Gary winced.

"He'd been alone for the weekend. By the time his roommate returned to the apartment, Paul had died, not from blood loss but from the drug."

"Now tell me how he fits into this."

Riley glanced at his notes. "Paul was gay, and there was evidence of numerous sexual partners. He was also a sex worker. His roommate—who was also his boyfriend at the time—said Paul had gotten into chemsex. Quote from his statement: '*I tried to stop Paul's downward spiral, but to no avail.*'"

"Okay, that's two off the list. What else?"

"There was evidence someone had been with him before he died, but inquiries revealed nothing. GHB was found at the scene, along with the bath salts." Riley paused.

Gary's skin tingled. "And now it makes sense."

"What do you mean?"

"We've always wondered why GHB was left at each crime scene but never turned up once in a tox screen." He shook his head. "Our killer was making a statement. What about rope and cuffs?"

"They found those too. Then I had an idea. I called that lawyer, Adam Winton, and asked him to do a little digging for me. He just called me back." Riley's eyes gleamed. "Seems Paul Ludlow was a frequent flier at a BDSM club here in Boston."

Gary beamed. "Well done, Riley. Now, did Paul have any family?" It had to be what they were looking for. Paul's death ticked all the boxes.

"His parents died in 2008, caught up in a freeway shootout. That left one older brother, Christopher." Riley cocked his head. "Want me to see if there are any uncles, cousins?"

"What about this boyfriend?"

He peered at his notepad. "His name is Christian Davis. I've emailed you Barry's findings and the last known contact details for the boyfriend and the brother."

"Either one of them could be out for revenge," Gary mused. "But it's a start. Find out what you can about both guys."

Riley grinned. "Already did. The boyfriend is in Florida now. The brother was living in Boston when his brother died."

"Then let's make some calls." Gary brought up the email and clicked on the number for Christopher Ludlow. He grimaced when it went to voicemail. *Damn.* "Mr. Ludlow, this is Detective Gary Mitchell from Boston PD. Could you call me back on this number when you receive this message? Thank you." He disconnected.

"I don't know about you, but I need coffee." Riley smiled. "I'll bring one for you too." He left Gary to his calls.

Next stop was Christian Davis, who answered within three rings. "Hello?"

"Mr. Davis, my name is Detective Gary Mitchell. I'm with the Boston police department. Paul Ludlow's name has cropped up during the course of our investigations, and I was wondering what you can tell me about him." He kept his voice smooth.

"He died four years ago. How can he have anything to do with your investigations?"

"I can't divulge that, I'm afraid. Right now I need whatever information you can give me about him."

There was silence for a moment. When Christian finally spoke, his voice cracked a little. "He was such a lost soul, you know? Losing his parents like that...."

"You said in your statement that you tried to stop him taking drugs."

More beats of silence.

"Mr. Davis, please. This could be important." He needed to keep Christian talking for as long as he could. Anything to formulate a clearer picture of the guy.

Is he the kind of man who could kill to avenge a lover's death?

Finally, Christian sighed. "We had an open relationship, because that was what Paul wanted, and I... I didn't want to lose him. So I ignored the hookups. After all, they left, but I was still there, right?"

Gary caught a tremor in his voice. "You loved him very much." When Christian didn't respond, he continued. "You were okay with him being a sex worker?"

"Yes, because that was work. To him, it was another way to earn a dollar. Not that he got a lot of business. Why pay for sex when your phone tells you there's a guy feet away from you who's looking for a good time?"

And maybe you weren't as comfortable with his work as you make out.

"What about the drugs?"

Christian sighed. "That was... difficult. He started using during sex. Not with me, however. I wasn't into that. So he hooked up with guys who were happy to use with him. I did try to get him to stop. I just didn't get very far." He paused. "I kept hoping. I thought I could turn him around. But he relied on it. I swear, sometimes he took drugs simply to get a boner. And then he wanted... harder stuff." His voice quavered. "I guess he found it in the end." Gary caught a stifled sob. "I know why he used. Why he went with so many guys. He was trying to numb the pain, that was all."

"The pain of losing his parents in the shooting?"

"Oh God, that was only the start of it. He could've come through that, I know he could, but he felt so abandoned."

"What do you mean?"

"The one person he needed wasn't there for him—his brother, Christopher. I did my best to support Paul, to be there for him, but I guess I wasn't the one he needed. I laid into Christopher at the funeral, I can tell you. He was so busy with school, he had no time for Paul. And Paul fucking *needed* him. Christ, the number of texts Paul sent, and Christopher hardly ever replied." He made a strangled noise. "I hope his guilt fucking *chokes* him."

Guilt....

Gary stared at the board where Guilt stood out, its black letters stark against the white. *Dan, you nailed it.* Gary trusted his gut instincts, and right then they were telling him Christian Davis wasn't their man. His heartbeat raced, and he quivered with the effort of controlling his emotions. "Do you know what his brother was studying?"

"Sure. He worked in some hospital where he had a job collecting blood after surgery. He'd clean it up, and it would go back into the patient. I never even knew that was a thing. But then he started training to be a physician's assistant. I think he'd just finished when Paul died." Another pause. "Is any of this gonna help you in whatever you're doing? Because you've gone and opened up a wound I'd thought was healed." His voice cracked.

Gary could have told him that some wounds never really healed.

"You've been a great help, really. Thank you. And I'm sorry to have caused you so much pain." He said goodbye and disconnected. No sooner had he put his phone down than it vibrated. He glanced at the screen. It was a text from Dan.

Don't be mad, but I had to get out of here. I've got us a table tonight at the Noodle Barn. And I hope it's okay, but I'm on my way to make us an appointment for a test. The clinic isn't open on weekends, so I'll try for the latest appointment I can get before then. You can tell Travers you're going to the dentist. I thought we could go together. Tell you all about it later.

Gary smiled to himself. *He doesn't let the grass grow under his feet, does he?*

Lewis came into the room. "My calls paid off. All the victims attended the same sexual health clinic."

Gary couldn't contain his grin. "I call that a result."

"The doc got a little snotty with me at first—client confidentiality, right?—but when I said all these guys were dead and she'd be helping with a murder inquiry, she changed her tune."

"Which clinic? And where is it?"

"It's in Dorchester." Lewis snorted. "Wait till you hear the name of this place. It's on Dix Street, a stone's throw from Dorchester Avenue, and they called it… the Dix Center. Kinda appropriate, don't you think? And about as subtle as a train wreck." His eyes sparkled. "Wanna bet our guy met up with all his victims while they were waiting to pee in a cup? Great place to meet guys, right?"

Riley walked in with the coffee as Gary grabbed his coat. "Are we going somewhere?"

"Yup. We're going to a sexual health clinic to take a look at their clients. Because maybe one of them is our man. And on the way, I'll tell you what I learned from Christian Davis."

"Who?" Lewis asked with a frown.

Gary thought fast. "I'll tell you when we get back. It doesn't need three of us." Without waiting for a reply, he headed out the door, Riley behind him.

When they reached the car, he called Dan, but it went straight to voicemail. He pulled up Dan's text and reread it. *Where is he going to make that appointment?*

His stomach churned. He called Lewis. "Did you find many sexual health clinics in Boston?"

Lewis huffed. "There were quite a few if all you wanted was a therapist or treatment for erectile dysfunction. This one was the only clinic that fit the bill."

The churning in Gary's stomach increased.

I'm getting a bad feeling about this.

CHAPTER 35

4.30 p.m.

THE SPARKLE in the clinic receptionist's eyes was becoming familiar, and Dan exited quickly before she could ask if he was *that psychic*. Five days since his photo had appeared in the newspapers and people didn't seem to have forgotten it.

He walked down the porch steps, removing his phone from his pocket while trying not to stumble at the same time. He frowned when the screen didn't light up.

Not again.

It wasn't the first time his phone battery had lost all its power in a very short space of time. Maybe he needed a new phone. He pictured his power bank, sitting on the coffee table in his hotel room. *Fat lot of good it's doing there*. He pocketed the phone with a sigh. *So much for sending Gary another text*. Then it hit him. *Or ordering an Uber. Damn.*

He peered up Dix Street. At the end of it, traffic roared past. He'd find it easier to hail a passing cab there. Dan walked slowly, enjoying the sun's warmth on his back. On one side of Dix Street were several three-story buildings, similar to the one that housed the clinic. He imagined they had an exorbitant price tag, even if Dorchester wasn't the swankiest of neighborhoods.

"Excuse me?" A man was walking toward him. He was casually dressed, maybe close to Dan's age, with blue-gray eyes set in a long, thin face. His beard was flecked with gray at the chin, and he seemed a little breathless.

"Can I help you?" Dan kept his tone neutral.

The man took a step forward. "Don't I know your face from somewhere?"

Dan groaned inwardly. *Another one.*

Then the stranger smiled, and his face was transformed. "Got it. You were in the paper. You're Dan Porter. You're helping the police catch this maniac who's been killing gay guys."

There seemed to be no escape. "Guilty," he admitted.

The man's gaze narrowed. "Then you catch him. So many of my friends are scared right now. It feels as if there's a new victim every other day."

Seeing as there had been two since Dan's arrival in Boston, he had to agree. The guy showed no sign of moving on, and Dan strove to be polite. "Well, I have to be going."

"Actually… I was going to call the police."

Dan frowned. "Why?"

The man pointed to the Dix Center. "I work there. It's a sexual health clinic."

"I know. I was just there to book an appointment."

He widened his eyes. "Oh. Then you're probably already onto this guy."

"What guy?" His pulse quickened.

"Working there, I get to know a lot of the guys. There's one in particular I think you should check out. Can I tell you about him? Then maybe you can relay my information to the police."

His heartbeat quickened. "Yes, I can do that." Maybe this was the break Gary needed.

"Wanna grab a coffee? There's a place right around the corner."

The last place Dan wanted to be was a coffee shop. "Sorry, but… I've heard 'Aren't you that psychic?' more times than I wanted to."

The man nodded. "Hey, I get that. I was just as bad, right? But I was going to suggest I grab two coffees to go. There's a Dunkin' Donuts up on Dorchester Ave and a playground nearby. We can sit on a bench or something." He glanced up and down the street. "I don't want to be overheard. You never know who's listening, right?"

Dan smiled. A public place sounded perfect. "Sure. And seeing as you're buying me a coffee and you already know my name, can I at least know yours?"

The guy smiled. "It's Christopher Ludlow."

CHAPTER 36

4:45 p.m.

CHRIST, MY hands were shaking as I dropped the Rohypnol into one of the cups.

How did this happen so fast?

I was still reeling from the shock of hearing that voicemail from the detective in charge of the case. *How did the police get onto me?* I analyzed my movements. I'd done *nothing* that could've led them to me, I was sure of it. But when Dan Porter strolled into the clinic and I saw him through a crack in the door, I thought I was about to have a heart attack.

How? *How?*

I had to think on my feet. No, more importantly, I had to get out of there. Because maybe I wasn't as invisible as I'd thought.

I'd left by the rear door, making sure I couldn't be seen from reception. Then I walked briskly out onto the street, got into my car, and drove. Except I hadn't reached Dorchester Avenue before my panic receded and lucidity returned.

Smart people don't get caught, remember? Only stupid people do that.

I had to formulate a plan, but there was no time.

What does he know? What brought him here?

Cold logic reasserted itself. Why the hell was I fleeing?

I drove the car into the first available parking lot, which was at Fields Corner East, my mind in overdrive. I got out, locked it, and glanced at my surroundings. The familiar sign gave me an idea. I headed quickly back down toward Dix Street. As soon as I turned the corner, I spied Porter ahead of me, coming out of the clinic, so I forced myself to walk calmly until I caught up with him. I felt naked without the hoodie. Someone could have seen us together.

It was far too late to be worrying about that.

Maybe when I was finished with Dan Porter, it would be time to pack my bags and move on. Leave the car at the bus station, buy a ticket to anywhere, and keep going. I wasn't done yet, but that didn't mean I couldn't continue my task someplace different. I could even start again.

God knew I'd have enough candidates.

I glanced through Dunkin's window to where Porter stood under the trees, waiting for me. I still couldn't decide if he was oblivious to me or a supremely good actor. Even if he knew nothing, there was always the risk that would change when I handed him the cup.

Will he see me?

My heart hammered. It was a chance I'd have to take. Besides, once he drank the coffee, it was only a matter of ten minutes or so before the drug would take effect.

I could keep my distance for ten minutes.

I walked out of the shop and over to where he stood. "One black coffee." I held my breath as he took it.

"So where did you want to sit?"

Nothing. No reaction.

I was almost giddy with relief. Before the day was out, he'd know exactly who I was and how blind he'd been, but until that point, I needed him to trust me.

I pointed. "Over there." I led him through the parking lot and across the street to the playground. He followed me through the gap in the fence, and we went into the children's park with its monkey bars, jungle gym, and slides. On the other side of the fence, a T-ball game was in progress, little kids in their uniforms, watched over by a couple of coaches. I pointed to a bench that overlooked the children's park, and we sat, the traffic loud behind us as it roared along Dorchester Avenue.

I held my breath once more as Porter drank from his cup, suppressing a sigh of relief when he leaned back against the seat.

"So… tell me about this guy."

I feigned concern. "He's… he's a troubled soul."

"How so?"

I wrapped my hands around my cup. "These guys talk to me, you know? They confide in me. And ordinarily I wouldn't reveal anything they share, but…."

"But this particular man worries you?"

I nodded. "It wasn't until the newspapers started printing details about these deaths that he spoke to me about his past and I realized he might be… involved somehow." I took a drink and waited while he did the same.

That's it. Drink some more.

"What's his name?" Porter asked.

"Lee." It was the first name that came into my head, but hey, it fit. "He had a brother, Paul, a sweet, gentle young man by all accounts. Anyway, they lost their parents in a tragic accident, and then it was just the two of them. Paul was in college when they died. Eventually he graduated but showed no signs of wanting to return home. Lee was engrossed in his own studies, and maybe that was why he didn't see what was happening."

I cursed myself every day for not seeing Paul's struggles until it was too late.

"And what *was* happening?"

My stomach roiled. "Paul got in with the wrong crowd. And one day the police turned up on Lee's doorstep with the news that Paul was dead, aged twenty-six. He'd taken drugs, and the dosage proved fatal. But when Lee learned more about the way Paul had been living, the… activities he'd participated in, the more convinced he became that Paul's death had come about because of his associations with certain men." I had to fight nausea as I told him about the drugs Paul had taken, the club he'd frequented, the things they'd found in his apartment when he died. "The day Lee told me all this, he also said those men were to blame for his brother's death. They'd corrupted him."

Porter's breathing hitched. "I can see why you might think he was involved if he was set on getting revenge for his brother's death. But… there's something wrong about all this." He swallowed, then took several slow blinks. "This killer has covered his tracks… every time… so why would he suddenly tell you all this? Especially when it… throws suspicion on himself."

I knew exactly what was happening to his body right then. The initial effects of the drug would be nausea, dizziness, confusion, and disorientation. He'd feel too hot yet too cold. It wouldn't be long before his blood pressure would drop, he'd become drowsy, then black out.

Porter tugged at his shirt collar, his breathing labored.

"Are you all right?"

He gave a slow shake of his head. "No, I feel awful."

"Can I help?"

Porter tried to stand but fell back onto the bench. "If I can just find a taxi, I can—"

"Look, let me take you to a clinic. If you won't let me treat you, at least let me find you a doctor."

Porter clutched his stomach.

I helped him to his feet. "My car is right across the street. It isn't far." I guided him through the park, heading for the gap in the fence, my hand around his back.

I knew the second realization hit. Porter stiffened, his eyes wide. "Hey… wait a minute…." His speech was slurred, and I knew I didn't have long to get him to the sanctuary of my car.

When the lights changed, I walked him across the street, ignoring his slurred entreaties, my heartbeat racing.

This is a mistake.

Get him out of sight.

There was no one in the parking lot when I reached the car, but the damage had already been done; we'd been in plain sight. I opened the back door and almost shoved him onto the seat. The drug had him in its grip, and by the time I got behind the wheel, he'd passed out.

I twisted to gaze at him. "Sweet dreams, Dan Porter."

CHAPTER 37

5.15 p.m.

"REMIND ME again what we're doing here?" Riley asked as they stopped the car in front of the Dix Center. It was located on the first floor of a triple decker. A rainbow flag hung from the front porch railing, and there was another in the window.

Gary couldn't tell him the real reason—he was following a hunch, and he hoped to God he was wrong. *Why am I filled with this sense of foreboding?* "I'm hoping we'll learn something."

Riley was the first up the steps to the door. He scowled. "The clinic closed fifteen minutes ago."

Gary gazed at the cars parked out front and another in the alley between the property and the house next door. "Ring the bell anyway. There might still be someone here."

He hoped.

After Riley had pushed the bell insistently, the door opened, and a young woman glared at them. "Can't you read the sign? We're closed." They held their badges up for inspection, and she stared at them. "You'd better come in." She stood aside to let them enter, and Gary glanced at her name tag.

"Thank you, Emma. Can you tell me who's in charge of the center?" He took in their surroundings. The front room of the house was the reception area, with chairs along three walls. To the right was a door labeled Treatment Room #1, and farther along was another. A restroom sat between them. The walls were covered with posters of all kinds providing information on different types of STDs and treatment, safe sex practices, and safer drug usage. There were clear plastic bins standing around, and on closer inspection Gary saw they were filled with condoms, lube, female condoms, and dental dams. Behind the reception desk were more posters featuring different vaccines for hepatitis and diagrams of genital regions.

Emma retook her seat behind the desk. "There's only Dr. Priest and a PA still here. I'll get her."

"Can I help you?" A tall, dark-haired woman in a white coat emerged from the treatment room. "I'm Dr. Priest."

Gary flashed his badge again. "Detective Gary Mitchell, Homicide. We need to see a list of men who use this center for testing. Specifically linked to use of PrEP."

She arched her eyebrows. "You should know I can't share that information without a warrant." She stilled. "Is this about the call I had from a detective earlier? Regarding the seven men who've been murdered?"

Emma gasped, and all heads turned in her direction. "Oh God. I should've *known* something was wrong when that guy came in here. He said he was here to book a test, but I recognized him right away." She shivered. "He was probably checking the place out for vibes or something."

And there was that sense of foreboding again, only heavier. "What guy?"

Emma frowned. "That psychic who's helping you. The one in the papers."

"Dan Porter was here?" *So where is he now? And why isn't he answering his phone?*

"Yes. About forty-five minutes ago." Emma peered at her monitor. "He made two appointments for Friday afternoon, one for himself and another guy." She blinked. "Wow. Talk about a coincidence." She raised her head to give Gary an inquiring glance. "Didn't you say your name was Mitchell?"

Oh God.

"Yeah, he told me he was here to make an appointment," he said quickly, before she could say anything else.

Beside him, Riley coughed, and Gary caught his blink before he turned his face away.

Guess the cat is out of the bag. Riley was no slouch in the brains department. Then Riley stiffened. "Is this everyone who works here?"

Gary peered past Riley's shoulder to a whiteboard on the wall next to the treatment room. It had photos stuck on it—head shots—and what looked like names written under each one.

"Yes," Dr. Priest told him. "The receptionists, doctors, PAs, nurses...."

Riley turned slowly. "Boss? You'd better see this."

Gary moved in closer to look at the photo Riley indicated. It showed a thin-faced man with dark brown hair, a mustache and beard, and intense blue-gray eyes. What made Gary's heart beat faster was the name beneath it.

Christopher Ludlow.

Gary turned to Dr. Priest, his mouth dry. "Has Mr. Ludlow already left the premises?" Beside him, Riley snuck his hand under his jacket, heading for his holster.

"He left a little early today, about four twenty-five. Said he wasn't feeling well."

Emma frowned. "I didn't see him leave."

"I think he went out the back way."

Damn.

Riley got out his notepad. "How long has he worked here?"

"I'd have to check." Dr. Priest disappeared behind the reception desk.

Riley glanced at Gary. "Try Dan's number again," he said in a low, urgent voice.

Gary's stomach clenched when he got voicemail again.

"Chris is a great guy. Everyone likes him," Emma said with a smile.

Riley ignored her. "If the doc is right, Ludlow left right before Dan did. What if he left because he *saw* Dan? That's why he went out the back, to avoid running into him."

Gary had another theory, one that came with icy fingers that ghosted his nape. "What if he went out the back way because he didn't want anyone to see him and Dan in the same place?"

Riley paled. "Jesus."

"2014."

Gary was lost for a moment. "Excuse me?"

"2014," the doctor repeated. "That's when Chris joined us."

"Do you have an address for him?" He crossed mental fingers. *Don't tell me we need a warrant before you'll give out that information.*

Dr. Priest cleared her throat, but Emma got in first. "He lives just down the street. Number seventeen. He has a place on the third floor." Her eyes sparkled. "We all joke about it when he gets in late."

Gary grabbed Ludlow's photo. "I'm taking this, okay?"

Dr. Priest opened her mouth to speak and then swallowed. "Oh my God. O-okay."

Gary and Riley hurried out of the clinic and up the street to number seventeen. He bounded up the front porch steps and found the buzzer for Ludlow.

Be here. Be here. And be alone.

The door opened, and he tensed, only to find an elderly lady peering at him. "Who did you want?"

"Mr. Ludlow, third floor."

"He's not home yet. I always hear when he comes home. You could wait for him, though. He won't be long. He already went by here."

"You saw him?" Riley asked.

She nodded. "He walked up the street, talking with some man. I was sitting in my window at the time." She smiled. "I love that. People-watching is *far* more interesting than whatever I can find on TV. And when my daughter goes to work, I have to do something to pass the time."

Gary held up the photo. "This is him, isn't it?"

She smiled. "Sure."

Riley got his phone out and held it up. "Do you recognize this guy?" One glance told Gary it was the photo of Dan.

She squinted at it. "Yeah, that was the man with him. He looked kinda familiar. Chris won't be long, I'm telling you. He was probably going to the store. He does that sometimes after work. There's a convenience store around the corner. He brings me a donut sometimes too." She leaned forward, and her voice dropped to a whisper. "But I don't let my daughter find out about that."

Riley looked into the street. "Does he have a car?"

"Yes."

"Which one is his?"

She frowned. "That's the weird thing. I saw him drive off in it, and then not long after, he walked back. Then they both headed for the Ave."

Gary didn't think it weird. He thought it was chilling.

"Do you know the make of the car?" Riley seemed to be thinking more clearly than Gary was, thankfully.

Her wrinkled brow furrowed even more. "I'm not very good with cars, I'm afraid." Then her face brightened. "It's black. Does that help?"

Gary thanked her, and they walked briskly to their car. Riley drove up the street, both of them scanning ahead for any sign of either of Ludlow or Dan. When they reached Dorchester Ave, Riley pointed to the right. "The old lady mentioned donuts. There's a Dunkin' sign. Let's check in there."

It was worth a shot.

They turned into the parking lot in front of the small mall. Dunkin' Donuts was off to the right, with tables and chairs out front. Inside, most of the tables were occupied, but there was no sign of them.

Riley flashed his badge, then held up the photos. "Have either of these men been in here? Within the last hour."

The girl behind the counter peered at the photos. "I haven't seen him," she said, pointing to Dan's photo. "The bearded guy... maybe he bought coffee? I couldn't swear to it."

Gary asked to speak to the manager, and the girl scurried toward a door at the rear. When the manager appeared, Gary didn't waste time with explanations. He showed his badge. "Do you have security cameras?"

"Yes. There's one in here, and another that shows the parking lot."

"We need to see your footage for the past hour."

The manager frowned. "I'm sorry, but I can't share security footage just like that, even if you are the police. There are procedures for that kind of thing."

"And I would be following those procedures," Gary remonstrated, "but this happens to be urgent. A man's life might be at stake."

He hoped to God he was wrong about that.

The manager widened his eyes. "Oh, I see. Well, maybe this once." He took them to a small back room where two monitors sat on a shelf above a PC. "We had them installed a while back. The place got broken into twice. I mean, what are they going to steal from here?" He tapped the keyboard, and the footage ran backward, a counter at the bottom of the screen showing the time.

"Stop." Riley pointed to one of the screens. "There he is." Ludlow picked up two cups, walked away from the counter, and halted at the table by the window, his back to the camera.

"Is that the man you're after?"

Riley ignored the manager, his gaze locked onto the screen. "What's he doing?" he murmured.

The manager rolled his eyes. "Adding sugar, sweetener, or creamer to the coffee, I imagine."

Riley's gaze met Gary's. "Or something completely different." He addressed the manager. "Let's look at the parking lot camera." The manager scrolled back, and Gary's breathing hitched.

"Wait. There." The screen froze on an image of Dan and Ludlow walking across the lot. They reached the street, then crossed it when the lights changed.

They thanked the manager and hurried out of the shop. On the other side of the street was a children's playground, but no sign of Dan or Ludlow.

Gary was starting to get a very, *very* bad feeling.

Little kids played on the jungle gym and slides, watched by adults, and beyond the park, a T-ball game was in play. Gary pointed to a guy who was obviously a coach. "Let's see if he saw anything." He walked quickly to him. "Excuse me?" Another flash of his badge. "Sorry to interrupt your game, but did you or any of the players see these two men here a little while ago?" Riley held up both photos.

The coach peered at them. "Yeah. They were sitting over there in the children's playground, talking."

"Did you see where they went?" Riley asked.

The coach pointed toward the parking lot across the street. "They headed in that direction. But I think there was something wrong with this guy." He indicated Dan's photo. "I was about to go over to them and ask if I could do anything, but the tall dude helped him to a car. He looked awful."

Gary's heartbeat stuttered. "Did you happen to notice the make of the car?"

"I think it was a black Honda Civic, but I can't be sure."

Riley thanked him, and they dashed around the fence to the street. "So he's taken Dan somewhere in a car, and definitely not back to his apartment."

"But where?"

Riley unlocked the car. "Let's go back to the clinic."

The tires squealed as Riley turned out of the parking lot and drove down Dorchester Avenue toward Dix Street. By the time they reached the clinic, Dr. Priest and Emma were standing on the front porch as the doctor locked up.

Gary got out of the car and ran over to them. "Does Mr. Ludlow have another address?"

"I don't think so," Dr. Priest replied.

"He didn't always live on Dix Street," Emma piped up. She glanced at the doctor. "This was before you came here. When he first joined us, he was living someplace else, but he wanted to be closer to the clinic." She frowned. "I don't know where he lived, though."

Gary thanked them, and they got into the car.

Riley's face was grim. "Ludlow's our killer, isn't he?"

"It's too much of a coincidence for him not to be. Everything fits."

"I don't like this. He's been so careful. Why would he take chances like this?"

Gary had been pondering the same thing. "Maybe he panicked. Think about it. Remember that note he left at the last crime scene? He thinks he's invisible. Then he gets a voicemail from me, and then Dan walks into his clinic."

Riley nodded. "So right now, he's not thinking straight at all." He shivered. "Doesn't that make him more dangerous?"

The question mirrored Gary's conclusion, and cold surged through him. He got his phone out and scrolled. "Lewis? Start checking public records, the County Clerk's office, local assessors.... See if you can find a property registered to Christopher Ludlow. Then search records to find the license plate of a black Honda Civic belonging to him."

"Okay."

"And Lewis? I need it, like, yesterday."

"On it." Lewis disconnected.

Gary pointed to the street ahead. "First stop is the hotel, just to make sure we're not panicking over nothing. Dan could be sitting in his room as we speak."

Except if that was the case, Dan would have his phone charging, and he would've answered Gary's calls.

Please be safe. Please be safe.

He'd lost Brad, Cory.... He couldn't lose Dan.

CHAPTER 38

7:00 p.m.

DAN FELT as if his eyes had been glued shut, it took such an effort to open them. He was seated on a chair, and although he couldn't make out details yet, he knew the room was shielded from daylight. There was a lamp somewhere. He wondered for a moment why he couldn't move his arms. Then he realized they were tied behind the back of the chair. His ankles were bound to the chair legs. His head was like lead, and he closed his eyes again.

"Welcome back to the land of the living, if only for a brief spell."

And there it was, confirmation of what he'd learned before whatever drug Christopher had used had dulled his senses.

He's going to kill me.

Dan squeezed his eyes even tighter, his stomach roiling. *I'm not ready to die.* Because if that were to happen, then he really was the butt of some enormous cosmic joke. *Why draw Gary and me together, connect us, only to rip us apart?*

Keeping his eyes shut was *not* going to make this nightmare go away. He'd have to face it sooner or later.

He opened them to find Christopher in a chair facing him. Dan's gaze was drawn instantly to the wall behind him, and his heartbeat quickened. A large photo had been placed in the center, and on the left were images of the seven victims, each one crossed in red.

Christopher's eyes were watchful. "I didn't give you a full dose. The side effects usually peak within two hours, but they can persist for longer. I wanted you awake. You're probably feeling disoriented. That will pass."

"Let me guess." The words came out as a croak. "Rohypnol."

Christopher grinned. "Clever man. You gave me quite a shock when I looked out of my treatment room and saw you there. How did you get onto me so fast?"

"I wasn't looking for you. I only went there to make an appointment for a test."

His face hardened for a second, and then he schooled his features. "A clever *gay* man, I see." His brow furrowed. "You really didn't suspect me?"

"All I know about you is your name and that you work at the clinic. And only because you told me." That wasn't the whole truth. He'd learned a little more than that when Christopher had put his arm around Dan to guide him to the car. "What do you do there?"

"I'm a physician's assistant."

Dan managed to raise his eyebrows. "And why would I suspect *you*? Aren't you trained to save lives, not take them?" He gazed at the wall once more, and cold settled on him in a heavy layer that seeped into his bones. "Oh my God. That guy you were telling me about? The one you suspected? You were talking about yourself." He stared at the center photo. "That's Paul, isn't it? Your brother."

"Right again. You'll have to say hello for me. Because you'll be seeing him long before I do."

Dan knew Christopher's words were meant to strike fear into his heart.

It was working.

"They'll come looking for me."

Christopher smiled. "Not if they don't know where to look. No, they won't ever find you." He stroked his beard. "I *could* make you victim number eight, but I don't know enough about you for that. So you'll be nothing more than a spare."

"They can track my phone," Dan blurted.

"Not if I've removed the battery. And I did that as soon as you were out." He got up from his chair and walked over to a desk. Dan took that time to assess his surroundings. The room contained nothing but the desk and two chairs. Long curtains hid the windows, and he had no clue where he was.

Christopher opened a drawer. "Your phone can join my collection."

"I have an appointment at your clinic on Friday."

He gave Dan a smile that chilled his blood. "Then I'm afraid you're going to miss it."

Gary, where are you?

Why couldn't I have been born telepathic instead of psychic?

LEWIS WAS waiting for them as Gary pulled into the precinct parking lot. "Any luck at the hotel?"

"No sign of him since he left there in an Uber this afternoon," Gary informed him. "I've tried tracking his phone and Ludlow's. Neither are showing up." He gave Lewis a hopeful stare. "Tell me you had better luck."

"I found a property registered to Christopher Ludlow in Quincy. Pawsey Street. And the license number of his car."

"Then why are we still here? Get in the car and let's go."

Lewis leaned in and grabbed his arm. "Hey, wait a sec. We don't have a warrant. What's more, we have no hope of getting one. We've got DNA that *might* be Ludlow's, but we can't prove that. Even if we had Ludlow's to compare it to, the test takes too long. Dan could be dead by then."

"We've got probable cause, all right?" Riley leaned across Gary, his voice rising. "A witness saw Ludlow take Dan to a car, and Dan was apparently in a bad way. Ludlow works as a PA at the clinic all the victims attended. Not to mention how his brother died. So I say we burn rubber and pray we're not too late. As for what we'll do when we get there? I guess we're playing it by ear." And with that, he gestured to the back seat. "Well, get in, then."

Gary was offering up the same prayer.

7:20 p.m.

THERE HAS *to be a way to slow him down.*

Christopher had started talking about Paul, and so far, there seemed no stopping him. Not that Dan was complaining. The longer he talked, the more minutes ticked by, giving Gary and the others a chance of finding him.

What chance? They don't even know who they're looking for.

Dan tried hard not to believe that. Chance had brought him to that clinic, to the very man they sought. He had to believe it was also at work to guide them to him. And in the meantime, Dan needed to touch Christopher and pray he learned *something*, no matter how small.

Remember the guilt? So overpowering you could've drowned in it? Work on that.

Christopher was keeping his distance.

Come here. Let me touch you. Just once. Dan prayed once would be enough.

He stared at Paul's photo. *He's the key, the lever.* Dan forced himself to speak calmly. "Killing all these men won't get you closer to the truth."

Christopher frowned. "What truth?"

"The knowledge that's eluded you. The man who was responsible for your brother's death."

He sneered. "I already know. It was someone exactly like the sluts I've already dispatched."

Dan kept up a silent litany to whoever watched over psychics and police officers. "And what if I could give you a name? Don't you want to know?"

Stupid question. The longing on Christopher's face....

He straightened his expression. "What are you talking about?"

Dan attempted a shrug. "You know all about me. You know how I work. It was in the papers, remember?"

That earned him another sneer. "Didn't work so well for you this time, did it? You didn't have a clue who I was when I approached you on Dix Street. And I don't believe in your *gift*."

"You should. Because it's real."

"Oh really?" Christopher retook his seat, leaning forward, his elbows on his knees. "We've got time to waste. No one is coming. So how do you intend proving any of this?" His tone held amusement.

Come on. Give me something to wipe that smug smile right off of his face.

Something to shake him, and maybe buy Dan a little more time.

"I work primarily by touch." Dan cocked his head. "Do you have something that belonged to Paul? Something personal?"

"What if I do?"

"If you give it to me, there's a good chance I'll know who was with him when he died." He hoped. He *really* hoped. *Please, God, just this once? Let it work because I need this.* Dan breathed deeply. "You said the police told you there'd been someone else in Paul's apartment that night. Don't you want to know who?"

Christopher swallowed, and Dan knew he had him on a hook. "Yes, I want to know."

Dan glanced around the bare room. "Well... what do you have of Paul's?"

Christopher didn't move for a moment, and Dan's heart hammered. *Come on, come on, you know you want this.* Then he got up and walked over to the desk again. He opened another drawer and withdrew a small carved box. He placed it on the table, opened it, and removed a gold chain. "I bought him this for his eighteenth birthday. He was wearing it the day he died."

Dan gave him a hard stare. "I can't touch it if my hands are tied, can I?" He was clearly no physical risk to Christopher, too slight to even contemplate overpowering him.

Christopher regarded him in silence, and as the seconds ticked by, Dan's pulse quickened. *He's not going to do it.*

"Will one hand be enough?"

Thank you, Lord. Dan nodded. Christopher put the chain on the table, went behind Dan's chair, and freed one hand. Dan kept still as he fiddled with his bonds, not wanting to give him a thing to worry about.

Christopher placed the chain almost reverentially into Dan's palm, and for one brief moment, Dan grasped his hand until Christopher pulled free.

It was enough. The emotions he'd felt as he'd held items from the crime scenes surged over him in a tide, only stronger and more vibrant.

I have you.

Dan held the chain tightly and closed his eyes. The image that came to mind sent a violent shock wave through him, and he had to take several deep breaths to recover his control. He knew what he'd seen was the truth. The visions never lied.

Oh my God. Now *what do I do?*

"What did you see?" Christopher demanded.

Dan had to take a moment to force calm into his voice. "The police got it wrong."

"What do you mean?"

"There *was* a guy with him. They hooked up, and then he left. But Paul needed a hit, a fix. There were no drugs in the apartment, so he called a number someone had given him. A dealer. *They* brought the stuff that killed him. It was nothing to do with the guys he'd been hooking up with."

Christopher gaped at him, shaking. Then his face hardened once again. "You almost had me doubting myself for a moment. No. So what if it was some low-life drug dealer who ended his life? His 'lifestyle' and subsequent death had been the result of the men he'd associated with. *They* corrupted him. *They* were the ones who got him into drugs. *They* convinced Paul he was gay. *They* sucked him into a world where he did not belong." He locked gazes with Dan, his face red. "They killed him."

And just like that, Dan knew he'd run out of chances.

Except....

Go with his feelings of guilt. Don't let him off that hook.

It was all Dan had left to play with.

CHAPTER 39

7:30 p.m.

GARY SAT behind the wheel. They'd parked on Rhoda Street, across the corner from Pawsey, which wasn't as populated. He pulled up Google Maps. "There's only the one house at the end," he commented. "Behind it is nothing but salt marsh."

It was a lonely house, no doubt about that, and it gave him the shivers.

What is Ludlow doing in there?

"I want a closer look." Lewis got out of the car.

"Wait." Gary unfastened his seat belt and followed him. Riley too. "Lewis," he called out urgently. "What are you going to do? Walk right up to it and peer through the windows? You know we can't do that, right? Curtilage—ring a bell? Property boundaries?" Not that he hadn't had the same idea, but there were laws about this kind of thing, and *one* of them had to stay within the lines.

Lewis scowled. "There's a car parked up at the house. At least let's get close enough to see if the license number checks out."

They could do that. "Okay, but don't get *too* close."

They walked about halfway up the street, keeping to the left where they were in the shadow of trees from a nearby property. Lewis squinted at the car. "Yup. That's the one. So it's a safe bet Ludlow is in there."

"Then let's go knock on the door," Riley suggested. "We can do that."

The side of the house they could see was in darkness. No sign of life. Beyond the house was the ocean, its waters reflecting the changing golden light in the sky.

Christ, this is excruciating.

Gary wanted to break down the door and charge through that house until he found Dan. Because everything in him was yelling that Dan was in there.

"Did you hear that?" Lewis said suddenly.

Riley frowned. "Hear what? The only things around here making any noise are the bugs."

"Thought I heard a scream."

"You're hearing things."

Gary caught up fast. "No, he's right. I heard a scream too."

Riley jerked his head from Gary to Lewis, and back to Gary again. "Oh. Fuck, I'm slow." His eyebrows scrunched together. "Are we sure about this?"

"Yes, we are." Because one way or another, they were going into that house.

"I'm gonna go back to the car and call this in," Lewis announced. "We need backup." And before Gary could argue, he ran toward Rhoda Street.

"Wait till he comes back," Riley urged. "At least until we know help is on the way." He cocked his head. "You got a plan?"

No, but Gary was working on it.

Hold on, Dan. We're coming.

7.35 p.m.

"AND WHAT about the part *you* played in Paul's death?" Dan demanded. Pissing Christopher off was risky, but he had to do something.

Christopher's face darkened. "Shut up."

"You've lived with the guilt ever since he died, haven't you?"

"Shut up!"

Before Dan could twist the knife a little more, his pulse quickened, his breathing grew shallow, and his stomach clenched.

Gary is near.

He had no clue how he knew that, but with each passing second, his assurance grew.

He's coming for me.

Dan raised his chin and forced steel into his voice. "You can't deny it, can you? Yes, you're angry at all those guys, but you're also angry at yourself. Don't bother lying to me. I felt it when we touched."

"You don't know anything."

Dan stilled. "You think? That guilt you've been carrying around ever since Paul died? I knew about it before I even laid eyes on you. Everything you touched when you killed those men? It *reeked* of guilt. Anger. Remorse."

Christopher's eyes grew flinty. "You're lying."

Dan locked gazes with him. "Except you *know* I'm telling the truth."

Come on, Gary. Please, be fast. I need you.

7:40 p.m.

"DAN'S IN there." Gary shivered. "We have to move now."

Lewis's brow furrowed. "Why not wait?"

"Because he's running out of time." Gary strode past the house and around it, searching for any sliver of light from inside that would point the way. To the rear of the house were french doors, and despite the curtains across them, a thin bright line showed at their base.

"I'll go to the front and knock." Lewis sprinted away from them.

Riley peered at the doors. "Thank Christ," he whispered. "The frame is made of wood. We can break that down. If we need to."

Gary had a feeling they'd need to. And then he froze.

Gary. I need you.

He didn't know if he'd imagined Dan's voice in his head, but it sounded so real, and the edge of fear running through it was enough to force him into action.

"We're going in."

7:45 p.m.

"I DIDN'T KNOW, all right?" Christopher's cheeks were flushed. "I thought he was okay. I asked him enough times to come home, and when he didn't, I figured he was getting along fine. He was twenty-six years old, for Christ's sake. He wasn't a kid. He'd been through college. He could take care of himself."

"But he couldn't, could he?" Dan's heart pounded. "I'm going to make sure no more gay men pay the price for your overwhelming sense of guilt."

"And how are you going to do that from the fucking *grave*?" Christopher yelled. He lurched out of his chair and towered over Dan, his hands clenching and unclenching. "Tell me, Mr. Psychic. Did your gift reveal exactly how I killed those men? Did you feel the fear that seeped from their pores, only they couldn't move, thanks to the ketamine? Did you feel the prick as I slowly pushed the needle into their bodies? No? Then maybe it's time you did. Because we are fucking *done*." He yanked open the drawer, and Dan's throat seized when he saw the small bottle and the hypodermic. Christopher inserted the needle into the neck of the bottle with precision, pulling on the stopper to draw out the clear liquid. Dan's heart fluttered; he was unable to tear his gaze away from the sliver of metal in Christopher's hand that was coming at him, closer, closer, closer....

Strong fingers gripped his arm, holding him steady, and the metal tip scratched the skin on Dan's neck.

Dan filled his lungs and screamed at the top of his voice, "Gary!"

And before the cold needle entered his body, from beyond the curtains, a voice yelled, "Police, Mr. Ludlow!"

Christopher froze. "What the fuck? No. *No!*" He jerked his hand, and the movement scraped the needle over Dan's skin.

It wasn't intentional, but it unfroze Dan. *Now. Move.* He threw himself forward, toppling the chair and knocking Christopher to the ground. As Christopher scrambled to his feet, the sound of wood splintering and breaking glass filled Dan with blessed relief, and both Riley and Gary tumbled into the room.

"Careful! He has a syringe!" Dan hollered.

Gary lunged, flattening Christopher against the floor, and Riley grabbed his wrist, forcing him to drop the needle. Then he was on him too, cuffs in his hands, grabbing Christopher's arms and tugging them behind him. Once they had him pinned, Gary jerked his head up to stare at Dan with wide eyes.

"Did he inject you? Do we need paramedics?"

Dan shuddered, his legs shaking. "It didn't go in."

"Thank God." Gary waited until Christopher stopped struggling. "Christopher Ludlow, you are under arrest for the murders of Trey Hopkins, Denver Wedel, Geoff Berg, Vic Zerbe, Marius Eisler, Cory Peterson, and Jack Noonan, and for the abduction and attempted murder of Dan Porter. You have the right to remain silent. Anything you say can and will be used against you in a court of law. You have the right to an attorney. If you cannot—"

Christopher craned his neck to glare at Dan, his face red, his cheeks blotchy. "You know what? I made a difference. I wasn't the first, and I will *not* be the last."

Dan's throat was still raw from his scream, and he simply stared at Christopher.

Gary continued Mirandizing him, and by the time he'd finished, Lewis came in through the busted doors, along with three uniformed officers. Gary and Riley got off of Christopher, and two officers hauled him to his feet.

"Get him out of here," Lewis told them. "But take him out the front way. We wouldn't want him to cut himself on all that glass, right?" The officers held Christopher firmly between them, and the third officer went ahead to open the front door.

Dan waited until they were out of sight before allowing himself to breathe more evenly. *It's over.*

Gary unfastened Dan's ankles and wrist and rubbed them. "Are you okay?" He and Riley helped Dan to his feet, and Riley righted the chair so he could sit.

"I'm gonna get one of the boys to call Dispatch," Lewis said. He stared at the wall. "Jesus, would you look at that? The CSIs are gonna love this."

"I've seen enough, thank you," Dan croaked. Lewis strode out of the room.

Riley cleared his throat. "I'm gonna give you two a moment alone, okay? I'll be right outside that door."

Dan blinked, but Gary didn't miss a beat. "Thanks, Riley. Appreciated."

Riley paused. "And by the way? Whatever you have going on? It's no one's business but yours, so in my book, that means nobody needs to know about it." Then he stepped carefully over the busted door frame and glass, and out into the evening air.

Gary knelt in front of Dan. "I thought I'd be too late." Then he leaned in, and Dan lost himself in a fervent kiss.

"I knew you'd come," he murmured between kisses.

Gary looked him in the eye. "I heard you."

Dan managed an eye roll. "I think all of Boston heard me scream your name."

"I'm not talking about that. I mean *before*."

He frowned. "What?"

"I *mean*, I heard your voice inside my head. I could feel the terror like it was my own. You kept crying out that you needed me."

"But… you couldn't have. My gift doesn't work like that."

Gary held up his hands. "Hey, I'm just telling you what I heard, okay? It *was* your voice. I didn't imagine it."

Dan kissed him. "I believe you. Now, are you going to tell me how Riley seems to know about us?"

"Later. When I've got you far away from this place and the doc has checked you out. He drugged you, didn't he? He put something in your coffee."

Dan gaped. "How did you know that?"

Gary smiled. "A lot has happened since I left you at the hotel this morning. And once you've been declared fit, I'm going to take you back there, and I'm not going to leave your side all night."

"What makes you think I'd let you?"

Dan needed to be held, reassured… treasured. But his joy at being rescued was tempered with the shock of what he'd seen when he'd held Paul's gold chain. He couldn't keep quiet about that, even if it meant one man's life was going to change dramatically. *I was given this knowledge for a reason.*

Yeah. Sometimes he hated his gift.

CHAPTER 40

Thursday, June 7

LIEUTENANT TRAVERS poured whiskey into five paper cups. "You had an eventful day, didn't you, Mr. Porter?"

"This is obviously some new meaning of the word 'eventful' that I haven't previously encountered." Waking in Gary's arms that morning, it had seemed like a really bad dream—until he saw the red scratch on his neck in the bathroom mirror.

Yeah. That had been a little too close for comfort.

Gary leaned forward, picked up two cups, and handed one to Riley. "The doc says Dan was lucky. Ludlow could just as easily have pushed the needle in."

"But he didn't," Dan remonstrated. He took a cup and gave the other to Lewis, who took it almost absentmindedly. And then Dan's fingertips brushed against Lewis's hand, and it was as if Dan had delivered an electric shock. Lewis straightened in his chair, his eyes alert.

None of the others appeared to notice.

Travers raised his cup. "Well, you did it. One serial killer off the streets, no more calls from Adam Winton, and the chief is off my back. I call that a successful conclusion."

"Amen to that," Gary murmured.

"Ludlow isn't talking, by the way," Travers remarked.

"Did he really believe he could kill twenty-two men and not get caught?" Riley shook his head. "Because that *was* his plan."

"Ludlow can clam up all he likes. We've got enough of his DNA to sink him," Gary declared emphatically. "Not to mention a drawer full of the victims' phones. It still amazes me that he kept them. What were they, trophies?"

"Maybe he saw it as confiscating the tools those men had used to ensnare Paul. The apps, the messaging…. And maybe he truly believed he was invisible to the police." Dan was still in awe of how Gary, Riley, and Lewis had pieced it all together, especially Lewis. Travers had listened as they'd recounted the events of the previous day, Dan chipping in here and there to share what he'd learned about Christopher.

"I think you were very brave, Mr. Porter, keeping him talking like that. You had no way of knowing help was on the way."

"I wanted him off balance," Dan told Travers. "Once I knew what lay at the heart of all this—his guilt—I kept pushing the knife in." He shivered. "Perhaps I pushed a little too far. He was more than ready to dispatch me by the time the cavalry arrived." He had to resist the urge to take Gary's hand, even though he needed that physical connection.

"There *is* one more thing I'd like to know." Travers gave Dan a keen glance. "Did you really know who was responsible for his brother's death, or was that a ruse to play for time?"

Dan's heartbeat quickened. He could lie—or he could do what his conscience demanded. He took a sip from his cup, and the liquid warmed him. "That wasn't a ruse. As soon as I held that chain, I knew." He closed his eyes momentarily, not missing someone's sharp intake of breath.

Can I do this?

Then he gave himself a mental kick. He'd known all along that he didn't have a choice.

Dan opened his eyes and placed his cup on Travers's desk. "He blamed Paul's death on the gay men who he thought had sucked him into a sordid life that eventually killed him. He truly believed they'd *made* Paul gay. That they'd introduced him to a life of sex and drugs. From what Gary told me, Paul's boyfriend refuted that. Maybe that was why Paul didn't come home after college. He'd been living as an out gay man and thought his brother would disapprove." Dan stared at the cup. "That's mere supposition on my part. I couldn't see that in my vision." He inhaled deeply. "But one thing was crystal clear. It had been Paul's choice to buy drugs that night. It had nothing to do with sex, and everything to do with getting high and numbing the pain. So the person who sold him the bath salts? *They* dealt the fatal blow that caused his paranoia and psychosis, and ultimately led to his death."

Travers frowned. "So... who was it?"

There was no turning back.

His heart hammering, Dan turned to look at Lewis. "Do you want to tell him, or shall I?"

Lewis gaped at him. "What are you talking about?"

"Is it someone Lewis knows from his time in Vice?" Travers demanded. "Someone he put away?"

Dan sighed, his stomach hard. "I wish I could say yes, but I can't. The thing is… Lewis sold Paul Ludlow the drugs that killed him."

The silence he'd expected fell with a thud.

Lewis's face was white. "Whatever you think that twisted gift of yours is telling you? You're wrong."

Travers sucked air through his teeth. "That's a very serious accusation, Mr. Porter." Beside Dan, Gary and Riley had become so still.

"You think I don't know that? You think I haven't wrestled with this ever since I saw his face? Lewis might have been an asshole toward me from day one, but this…." Dan shuddered. "This was just fucked up."

Lewis staggered to his feet, spilling his whiskey onto the carpet. He put the cup on Travers's desk, his hand shaking. "Okay, I'm not going to sit here and listen to another word of this crap."

Gary grabbed his arm. "Steady there. And sit down."

Lewis's eyes bulged. "You're gonna believe this guy over *me*? Christ, you've worked with me. I ain't no stinkin' drug dealer."

"No, you're not," Dan confirmed. He fixed his gaze on Lewis's face. "But you were then, and we both know that's the truth. It wasn't a long career, I grant you. Maybe Paul's death shocked you back onto the right path again."

"Mr. Porter, I'm grateful for all your assistance on the case, but—"

"I think we should hear him out," Gary interjected. "Lord knows he hasn't been wrong so far."

Travers gaped at Gary. "You're serious."

Dan put down his cup. His own hands were trembling too. "Lewis…. When I held Paul's chain, I saw your face. I can even describe what you were wearing at the time. I didn't want to believe it. But then… a lot of things fell into place. Why you wouldn't shake hands with me the day we met. Why you've been so careful to avoid all physical contact with me. Why you kept pushing for me not to work on this case. And when that didn't work, you leaked my involvement to the press. I'm going to bet if we check your phone, we'll find that photo you took of me here in the precinct."

Travers gazed at Lewis with wide eyes. "Stevens?"

Dan pushed ahead. "The day we met, you didn't make a secret of how hard you've had to work to get where you are, about your impoverished beginnings. I'm only guessing here, but I assume you got your hands on the drugs during a bust, and somehow they didn't make it to the evidence locker." Judging by the way Lewis jumped at that, Dan figured he'd nailed it. "You decided you'd make some money on the side." He cocked his head. "Gary said you joined Homicide four years ago. Paul Ludlow died four years ago...." He glanced at Gary. "Where did Paul die?"

"Lowell, Middlesex."

Dan nodded, his calm returning. "And where did Lewis transfer from?"

Silence fell, broken only by Lewis's labored breathing. Finally, Gary spoke. "Chelmsford PD."

Dan studied his clasped hands. "I don't have to ask if Lowell is in Chelmsford's backyard, do I?" He raised his chin and sighed. "Your faces say it all." He faced Lewis, and his stomach clenched to see the expression of horror in his eyes. "Paul Ludlow died, and you got scared. You stopped. That's why you transferred out."

Lewis glared at him. "How the fuck can you know that?"

Dan pointed to Lewis's cup of whiskey. "Because you forgot. You finally let your guard down, and I touched you." For a moment he wasn't certain if Lewis would try to bluff it out, but then Lewis slumped in his chair, and Dan knew he'd had the fight knocked right out of him.

"I knew it was a mistake bringing you in on this." Lewis grabbed his cup and took a long drink from it, his Adam's apple bobbing. "As soon as you held that ring and you knew who Cory Peterson was, I realized you were no hokey fake. You were the genuine article. And every day since then, I've been afraid of you, of what you'd see. Jesus, I've been so fucking scared." He nursed the cup in his hands. "There was always a chance someone in the press would say who leaked the info, but when that didn't happen, I figured I was safe as long as I stayed the fuck away from you." He met Dan's gaze. "You were right, okay? About everything. And when you touched me just now...." Lewis shivered. "I knew the game was up."

"Watson." Travers addressed Riley in a quiet voice. "Take Stevens out of here. Get a statement. I'll deal with this mess later."

"Sure." Riley got up and walked over to where Lewis sat. "Come on." He touched his shoulder.

As Lewis followed him to the door, Dan blurted out, "I had to say something. You know that, right?"

Lewis paused. "Yeah, I know. I was a fool to think I could hide it forever. It's a miracle I made it this far." And then he walked out of the room.

Dan sagged into his chair. "That was… intense."

Travers cleared his throat. "Mr. Porter, you've been… amazing. I can't thank you enough for all you've done." He expelled a breath. "Even though you may not have wanted to do some of it."

"I was glad to help with the case. I'm only sorry about the collateral damage." He'd ruined a man's life.

No, I haven't. Lewis did that four years ago. It was his choice, remember?

"I know you must be anxious to get back to New Hampshire," Travers continued.

Not as anxious as you might think. He wasn't ready to leave Boston yet.

Gary. He wasn't ready to leave Gary.

"However, I had an idea. I need to see if the chief will run with it—so technically I shouldn't even be mentioning it until he gives me the go-ahead—but I wanted to see if it was something you'd consider."

Gary chuckled. "You're being way too mysterious. Just come right out with it."

Dan nodded. "You've got me intrigued too."

Travers sat back in his chair, his fingers laced. "You have an incredible gift, Mr. Porter. Would you consider using that gift to help us on a more permanent basis?"

What the…? "In what way, exactly?"

"We have a backlog of cold cases, some dating back many years, long before DNA testing had even been thought of. But with present-day technology and *your* gift… I feel we could solve some of those cases." He shrugged. "No one likes to admit defeat. I'm sure Detective Mitchell will understand how much it would mean to some people to be able to close the book on the death or disappearance of a loved one, even after so many years." Travers smiled. "It's just an idea, but… at least think about it."

Talk about coming out of left field…. "I'll consider it. I make no promises, mind you."

"That's all I ask. And besides, the chief might listen to my proposal and the first thing out of his mouth is going to be 'We don't have the budget.'"

Gary stood. "If that's all, I'm going to take Dan back to his hotel. After everything he's been through the past few days, I think it's time he got some sleep."

Dan had to fight the urge to smirk.

Travers glanced at the wall clock and nodded. "It's time we all got some sleep." He got up and walked around the desk, his hand extended. His eyes twinkled. "Shaking hands with you is a risky business. Who knows what deep dark secrets you'll uncover."

Dan chuckled. "The fact that you're willing to take my hand says a lot." They shook. "Thanks for the whiskey."

"Dutch courage, I suppose. It can't have been easy, telling us about Lewis." Travers frowned. "You think you know a man...." Then he straightened. "Good night, Mr. Porter. And Mitchell... well done."

They walked out of the office. Gary was silent, and no psychic ability was required to know what was running through his mind.

"I know," Dan murmured. "The shock I felt when I touched Paul's necklace.... I didn't want to believe it, but I had to accept it. The visions don't lie, and it explained too many things."

"You couldn't lie either," Gary observed. "But you were right. It had to come out. And it's no one's fault but Lewis's. He chose that path."

"And then he walked away from it," Dan added. "Don't forget that part." He was still ruminating that unexpected proposal. "Travers wants me to work with you on those cases, doesn't he?"

"That was my impression."

"That bit about closing the book on the death of a loved one...." He speared Gary with a look. "He was talking about your brother, wasn't he?"

Gary paused at the door to the case room. "It's not something I've ever talked about, but it wouldn't surprise me if he knew." They went inside, and Gary walked slowly to the board. "I'd better take all of this down and file it."

Dan sat. "Something occurred to me in the middle of the night."

Gary chuckled. "I know. I was there, remember? I don't know what woke you, but I was more than happy to help you get back to sleep."

Dan tried not to think about Gary's methods. That would have to wait until they were alone. "You and Christopher Ludlow...."

"What about us?"

Dan did his best to formulate his thoughts. "You both lost a brother. Their deaths devastated both of you. And yet you went in completely opposite directions. He wanted to avenge Paul's death. You wanted to become a detective to solve deaths like Brad's."

"At first, all I thought of was finding Brad's killer. As time went by, I realized that wasn't going to happen. And please, don't make me out to be some kind of hero. I'm not. Believe me, if I'd ever caught the person who killed Brad, you'd have seen how much ugliness lies within me."

Dan rose and joined him. "I don't see *any* ugliness in you."

Gary grinned. "Yeah, but you're biased."

Dan stared at the photos, his heartbeat quickening. "You haven't asked me. Not once."

"Asked you what?"

"What I felt when I touched Brad's sweater. You were dying to, weren't you?"

Gary stilled. "You felt that?" Dan nodded, and Gary sighed. "I was frightened to, I guess. Plus, I didn't want you to think I was using you."

"I would never think that of you." Dan checked the door was closed, then took Gary's hand. "I like the lieutenant's idea. Solving murders or crimes that people have given up hope of *ever* having solved. That would be awesome. But you know what would be even more awesome?"

"What?"

Dan trailed his fingers along Gary's inner arm where the tattoo lay hidden. "Bringing you peace. Helping you to heal." *Now* the second vision made sense.

"Do I need healing?"

Dan lifted Gary's hand to his lips and kissed his fingers. "Yes, you do. And I think learning more about Brad's death is a big step in the right direction. Like I said to the lieutenant, I'm not making any promises, but… we can try."

Gary let out a long sigh. "It was twenty-three years ago."

Dan nodded. His face tingled. "And yet after all that time, I know something about his death that you don't."

Gary's breathing hitched, and for several seconds, he said nothing. Finally he croaked out the words. "What is it you know?"

Dan looked him in the eye. "I've been sitting on this for days, and I can't hold it in any longer. I don't know the name of the person who killed Brad, but one thing I *am* sure about—he knew them."

Keep Reading for an Exclusive Excerpt from
In Plain Sight
Book #2 in the Second Sight series
by K.C. Wells.

PROLOGUE

Boston, MA, Monday July 10, 2006
11.45 p.m.

FORENSIC PATHOLOGIST Del Maddox drove up to the barrier across the entrance to the Fort Point Channel Tunnel, where lights had been set up to illuminate the site. Judging by the amount of traffic he'd passed to get there, Boston was going to have more than its usual amount of pissed off motorists—the tunnel connected with the Ted Williams tunnel that headed out to Logan airport. On the other side of the barrier were fire trucks, police vehicles, and two ambulances, and from deeper within the tunnel came the sharp grind of cutting tools and raised voices.

Del sighed. *Welcome to Boston PD.* His first day, and it seemed he already had customers for his table.

An officer approached his car, armed with a flashlight, and Del wound his window down. He grabbed his badge from where he'd stowed it under the visor and held it open. Not that he needed it—Medical Examiner emblazoned on the car door was a bit of a giveaway.

The cop aimed the flashlight's beam at Del's credentials, then at Del's face, causing him to squint. He frowned as he lowered the flashlight. "Wait a minute. You're not Mike."

Del arched his eyebrows. "And who might Mike be?"

"Mike Harrison, the medical examiner."

"Then there can only be two possible explanations. Either I murdered Mike, stole his car, copied his ID, and added my own details to fool everyone into thinking I was a medical examiner—or I could actually be the *new* medical examiner, because the previous one retired last week." He smiled. "I'll leave you to work it out. In the meantime, can you move this barrier, please, and let me do my job?"

Way to go, Del. Ever heard the phrase, 'You never get a second chance to make a first impression'?

He blamed it on the job. His clients never told him if he was being rude.

The officer scowled but hoisted the barrier out of the way. "Mike was way more of a laugh," he murmured as Del drove past him.

"Good for him," Del muttered. He drove as far as he could into the mouth of the tunnel, then switched off the engine. He grabbed his bag from the passenger seat and got out. Then he opened his door again and rooted in the glove box for a flashlight. His safety hat was in the trunk.

The dark mouth of the tunnel sloped downward, and the site of the collapse was maybe fifty feet ahead of him, lit by emergency lamps. Del walked toward the yellow tape that marked off a portion of the road. Huge concrete panels had been moved by mechanical lifters, revealing the crushed form of a Honda Civic, surrounded by rubble. Above, a large hole gaped in the ceiling, the width of two panels. Men in safety hats and reflective jackets stood around talking in low voices, and Del counted about four police officers.

One officer approached him, flashlight in hand. "You the medical examiner?"

Del nodded. "How many casualties?"

The officer grimaced. "Two. One fatality and one guy badly injured. He was driving. He's on his way to the hospital already. The tiles completely crushed the passenger side of the vehicle. His partner was killed instantly, we think. We haven't removed her body from the wreckage yet, although the fire fighters have just cut through to take the roof off."

Del gave a nod of approval. He signaled to the paramedics waiting beside the wreckage, and together they walked solemnly to the crushed car. It didn't take long to lift and place her in a body bag. Del watched as they carried her away from the wreck to where the ambulance waited.

"Who is in charge of the scene?"

The officer pointed toward the fire truck. "Sergeant Michaels. He's over there."

Del glanced at the amount of debris. "How much concrete do they think fell?" He peered at the officer's badge. "Officer Mitchell."

"They estimate about twenty-four thousand pounds." He pointed up. "The tiles are reinforced concrete slabs, suspended from girders bolted to the ceiling roof. It seems the anchor bolts ripped loose." Officer Mitchell bit his lip. "Except they weren't the only things that fell." He crooked his finger. "This is where things get a little weird."

Del followed him. Officer Mitchell crouched beside another black body bag covering a heap on the ground. Del froze. "I thought you said there were only two casualties."

Mitchell's eyes sparkled in the strong emergency lights. "Strictly speaking, there were. But I have no idea what caused *this* casualty—well, apart from the obvious." He removed the bag, and Del's breathing hitched.

A skeleton lay on sheets of plastic, partially covered. Mitchell's remark about the possible cause of death suddenly made sense.

There was no head.

The remains had obviously been there a while, judging by the amount of decomposition. Del guessed at more than a decade. He studied the body, noting the pelvis.

"I don't suppose it's possible to tell right away if this person was male or female," Mitchell murmured. "Unless the Bible is correct and males have one less set of ribs than females."

"I hate to disillusion you, but we all have twelve pairs—though some people are born with eleven or thirteen. Doesn't appear to afford them any ill effects, however. But yes, it's possible to tell." Del pointed to the subpubic angle where the two bones met. "This was almost certainly male. The female pelvis tends to be wider." He straightened. "I can see why you'd think this a weird situation. Is the theory that the body had been stowed above us, placed there when the tunnel was constructed?"

"Yes. That was the early nineties. I checked."

Del hunkered down next to the remains. "The plastic didn't mummify the body. If anything, it created the ideal environment for bacteria—warm and moist." He took a closer look. "Interesting, though. Because of the air exchange, the initial decomposition went all the way to skeletonization."

"Even wrapped in plastic?"

Del arched his eyebrows. "As we all know, meat wrapped in plastic still goes bad." He stood, glancing up to the gaping hole in the ceiling. "A very weird situation indeed."

"But that's not the strangest part." Mitchell carefully drew back the two flaps of plastic that partially covered the skeleton.

Del blinked. "I see what you mean." Nestled within the wrapping were what resembled two vinyl pouches—very familiar pouches....

"Are they what I think they are?"

Del nodded. "Our unknown dead male had silicone breast implants."

His first day in Boston, and he already had a mystery to solve.

CHAPTER ONE

Monday July 9, 2018

"DO I LOOK nervous?" Detective Gary Mitchell fingered the collar of his dark blue shirt, then adjusted his tie knot for what had to be the fifteenth time that morning.

Dan Porter rolled his eyes. "Will you quit fidgeting? And seeing as you've asked, yes. The more you fidget, the more nervous you appear. It's only roll call, for God's sake."

It was way more than that, and they both knew it. Dan appeared calm. Actually he was immaculate, from his closely shaven square jawline to his characteristic quiff. His brown hair was swept up off his face, the warm brown tones matching his eyes, and his dark blue suit was impeccable with its matching shirt and purple brocade waistcoat.

As if he'd read Gary's thoughts, Dan speared him with a look. "And if anyone should be nervous, it's me. Right?"

Gary shoved aside his selfish qualms, his stomach clenching. "I'm sorry. You're right." Dan had nailed it. Lieutenant Travers's announcement at the end of May that a psychic would be consulting on the case of a serial killer had been met mostly with incredulity and ill-disguised skepticism. It didn't matter that Dan had subsequently helped them find the killer. Many of Gary's coworkers dismissed the role Dan had played in catching him, but paradoxically they wouldn't forget what Dan had revealed about one of their own.

Travers's about-to-be-revealed news was sure to be met with yet more incredulity and derision.

Dan's face glowed. "And that's what I love about you—you admit when you're at fault. Do you know what a rare trait that is?" He inched closer, his voice dropping to a whisper. "And if we weren't about to go out there, I'd show you exactly how much I love you."

Gary's chest tightened. "I'm not ready." It was still so new. Breathtaking, exciting, and stomach-churningly new. There were mornings when he woke to find Dan's arms wrapped around him and had to pinch himself in reassurance that this was no dream.

Hearing Dan say he loved him made it an awesome dream.

"Ready for what?"

"For everyone to… know about us. About me." Except he was pretty sure some people already knew.

Warm hands cupped his face. "You don't have to tell anyone *anything*, okay? It isn't a law, you know, that you have to come out as bisexual. It's *your* decision, no one else's."

"Riley knows." And in recent weeks, Gary had become increasingly aware of inquiring glances as he strolled through the precinct.

"But Riley won't say a word, and you know it. Hell, he said as much last month. That night you rode in on your white horse and rescued me, remember?" Dan placed his hands on Gary's shoulders. "And you *know* I won't do anything to make life awkward or uncomfortable for you. As far as I'm concerned, I'm here to do a job." His eyes gleamed. "Let's save everything else for when we're alone. And while we might be alone at the moment…." He removed his hands. "Just in case someone walks in unexpectedly."

"Good idea. Most of the people I work with don't believe in knocking." Then he added, "Except for Riley."

There was a knock at the door, and Detective Riley Watson stuck his head around it. "You guys ready?"

Despite the butterflies in his stomach, Gary laughed. "Your timing is amazing."

Riley entered the room and let out a low whistle as his gaze took in its contents. "I'm impressed. When you said Travers had found you an office, I expected something along the lines of the closet we were using." It wasn't huge by any means, but it had everything they needed—two desks with PCs, a printer-copier, a couple of filing cabinets, a free-standing whiteboard, and four chairs. No window, but Gary didn't mind that.

Gary snorted. "What a difference a month makes. Plus a lot of support from the chief."

And let's hope that support is enough. Gary expected opposition.

"We'd better get out there. I saw Travers on his way just now." Riley smirked. "I hope you two are prepared, because it looks as if the cat's out of the bag already."

"What do you mean?" Gary hadn't heard a whisper, at least not about his new role.

Riley opened the door and removed something from the outside. He handed the sheet of paper to Gary, who groaned.

"Great. Who talked?" Someone had drawn a cartoon of him and Dan seated at their desks, both frozen in blocks of ice. Below it they'd written Cold Cases Department.

Dan took it from him and chuckled. "This is really good. We should frame it." He scanned the office walls. "Did you keep the Cereal Killer one? That was great."

Gary knew better than to accept Dan's attempt at forced humor. "I guess we'd better go and let Travers make it official." He grabbed his jacket, putting it on as he strode out of the office, Dan and Riley behind him.

With every step he took, the churning in his stomach increased.

Gary didn't give a damn what his fellow detectives thought of him. But he sure as hell didn't want them giving Dan a hard time.

"THAT'S EVERYTHING." Sergeant Rob Michaels closed the folder on the lectern in front of him. He cleared his throat. "But before you all disappear, the lieutenant would like a word."

Murmurs rumbled through the assembled officers and detectives, and Gary's fears were confirmed.

They know what's coming.

Lieutenant Travers stepped up to the lectern, looking at them over his glasses. "I'm sure I don't need to remind you how valuable Mr. Porter's contribution was last month in helping us apprehend a serial killer, one who'd eluded us for some time." The rumbles increased, and Travers's eyes grew flinty. "Regardless of what you think about the aftermath of that arrest, justice was served. And that's why we're all here, isn't it? To see justice served?"

A hush fell over the room.

Travers nodded. "Well, the chief has decided we should be paying more attention to our cold cases. And there are a great many of them, some dating back decades. You know, in the days before you could send a sample off to a lab for DNA testing." He grinned. "And then complain about how long it takes to get the results." That raised a few chuckles. "So yes, times have changed. We have the gift of technology." He glanced toward Dan at the back of the room, seated next to Gary. "And now we have other gifts at our disposal." Travers squared his broad shoulders.

"Imagine if someone you loved had died or disappeared in unexplained circumstances. You'd want closure, even if it happened years ago. As I see it, a cold case is one where we had to admit defeat. Well, no one likes to do that. And with that in mind, as of today, Detective Gary Mitchell and Mr. Dan Porter will be working together exclusively on cold cases." That steel gaze was back. "I expect them to be given every cooperation."

"What makes you think they'll be able to turn up anything new?" That was Detective Will Freeman. Gary had figured he'd be the first voice of dissent.

He coughed, and chair legs scraped over the floor as the assembled officers and detectives turned to stare at him with expressions of both amusement and disbelief.

Gary met their gazes, his shoulders squared. "Mr. Porter's involvement may give us access to new information."

"You said 'may.'" Will stared at Gary. "That implies you have doubts about his abilities."

"He's not like one of those fortune-telling machines you find in arcades, all right?" Riley's face reddened. "You can't just put your money in the slot and out pops the bad guy. It doesn't work like that." Gary laid his hand on Riley's arm, and Riley expelled a breath. "Sorry." He glared at his coworkers. "But you guys haven't seen him at work—I have. And he's no fake. Ludlow started killing in 2014, and ten days after we brought Dan in on the case, we stopped him. Ten days."

Travers cleared his throat once more, and heads swiveled in his direction. "Do I have to repeat myself about offering cooperation?" Another silence fell, and he nodded. "Good. Because if you don't like this new initiative, I suggest you take it up with the chief. He loved the idea." And with that, he marched out of the room. As soon as he was out of sight, the murmurs began again, only louder.

Barely seconds later, Will Freeman marched over to where Gary, Dan, and Riley stood. That was all it took for others to follow.

Here we go.

Will came to a halt in front of them, his arms folded. "All that stuff in the media about the Ludlow case," he began, "it was all hype, right?"

Gary opened his mouth to tell Will where to get off, but Dan got there first. He held out his hand. "Give me your watch."

Will frowned. "Why do you want my watch?"

"Because you work with Gary, and he needs you to have his back. And the only way forward is to prove to you that what the media reported was the truth." He held his head high. "So give me your watch, and I can help you put all your doubts aside."

Will arched his eyebrows. "And what if you don't... *feel* anything?"

Around them the officers and detectives were all unusually quiet, their attention focused on the scene before them.

Dan has an audience. Gary hoped to God it wouldn't be a bust. He knew from experience Dan couldn't turn his visions on and off like a faucet.

Dan shrugged. "Then we'll try with something else until I do." His palm faced upward. "Your watch, please."

Will hesitated for a moment, then unclasped the stainless-steel bracelet and placed it in Dan's hand. Dan covered it with his other hand and closed his eyes. The room was silent, and Gary could hear nothing but the slow intake and exhalation of air.

Will refolded his arms. "Don't get excited, guys. Nothing's gonna happen."

Gary prayed Will was about to eat his words.

After a minute or two, Dan opened his eyes. He handed the watch back, and Will fastened the clasp. "So? What did you discover?" He stuck out his chin. "Gonna tell me what I had for breakfast?" He grinned at the audience surrounding them, raising a few chuckles.

Dan regarded him with a sympathetic gaze. "Your father gave you that watch for your twenty-first birthday."

Will blinked. "H-how did you know that?" Then he breathed easier, his usual brash demeanor returning. "You're good, I'll give you that. You saw the inscription on the back."

Dan shook his head. "Did you see me look at the back, even once? No, you didn't. So let me give you something else. He mentioned the watch the last time you saw him. Not that I'm about to mention where you were at the time. That's no one's business but yours."

Will's eyes widened, and his mouth fell open. "But... you couldn't...." He turned and pushed through the throng gathered around them, heading for the door, cries following his exit.

"Hey, Will, what's up?"

"Well? Did he get it right?"

"Aren't you going to tell us?"

"Show's over, guys." Rob Michaels called out from the front of the room. "You've all got work to do." Little by little the crowd dispersed, until only Gary, Dan, and Riley remained.

Dan glanced at Gary. "I don't think he'll give us any more trouble." His expression grew uneasy. "I didn't want to do that, but I've learned from experience that some people don't believe a word I say—until I show them. And then they're either fascinated, like Riley was when we first met, or scared shitless of what I'll see next."

"What *did* you see?" Riley asked.

Dan shook his head. "I'm sorry. It's not for me to say." He gestured toward the door. "Let's go to our office."

Riley patted him on the back. "Good luck. And in case I forgot to mention it…." His smile lit up his face. "Welcome aboard."

"Thanks."

They headed back to the office, and Gary closed the door.

"Okay, that was pretty much how I thought it would go down." He gave Dan an inquiring glance. "You okay?" He knew from experience that using his gift exhausted him.

"I'm fine, honest. That didn't take a lot out of me." Dan peered toward the door. "I think it took more out of Will." He looked at the pile of folders on one of the desks. "Are those cold cases?"

Gary nodded. "They're a real mix. Missing persons, kidnapping, death…. Travers sent them. To be honest, I'm not sure where to begin."

"Maybe we should spread them out, blindfold one of us, and stick a pin in one of them," Dan suggested. Then he stilled. "Is Brad's case going to be one of them?"

Gary's throat seized. He shook his head.

"That's probably a good thing. I can't see Travers being happy about us tackling that one. Talk about a conflict of interests. And especially with all the media interest following our recent success—and my involvement. The press would have a field day. I mean, can you imagine the headlines? 'Cop Uses Psychic to Investigate His Own Brother's Murder While Other Cases Go Unsolved. Your Tax Dollars at Work.'" His hand went to Gary's back. "I said I'd try, and I meant it. We don't need to involve Travers. We'll do whatever we have to on our own time."

Relief flooded through him. "Thank you."

A rap on the door had Dan dropping his hand quickly. An officer poked his head around the door. "Detective Mitchell? You have a visitor, a Mrs. Sebring. I've put her in Interview Room One."

"Thanks. I'll be there directly."

The officer hesitated. "But she's asking to see Mr. Porter too. She was very insistent about that."

Dan raised his eyebrows but said nothing.

"We'll *both* be there directly, then." The officer withdrew and Gary expelled a long breath. "I'm okay now. And this isn't the time or the place to discuss Brad. How about we go see our visitor?"

They left the office and walked through the crowded hallways filled with people and noise. Gary did his best to ignore the stares and murmurs, but he knew Dan would have a harder time doing that.

Maybe by the time we've got a few successes under our belt, they'll have warmed to the idea.

He wasn't going to hold his breath.

Mrs. Sebring stood as they entered the interview room, and Gary's first impression was of a very weary woman, maybe in her forties, pale, with shadows under her eyes. Her hair was scraped back and secured with a clip, and her face was devoid of makeup.

She headed straight for Dan. "You're the psychic, aren't you? The one I read about in the paper."

He smiled. "Yes, I'm Dan Porter."

"I'm here because of you. To be honest, you're my last hope." She didn't speak loudly, but Gary couldn't miss the note of desperation.

"What can we do for you, Mrs. Sebring?" He gestured to her chair. "Please, sit down." They sat facing her.

She lowered herself into the chair, studying their faces as if she was trying to reach a decision. Her forehead creased.

"First thing I need to know is… was it all true? Did you really find that serial killer?"

The edge of desperation in her voice grew more obvious.

Dan nodded. "I helped the police, yes."

Her expression hardened. "You never know these days. There's so much hype, disinformation… truth seems to have gone out of style."

"Mr. Porter provided valuable information that led us to the killer," Gary assured her. "So… why are you here?"

Mrs. Sebring's gaze flickered from Gary to Dan and back to Gary.

"Okay then." She shuddered out a breath. "My husband died in 2016. An accident, they said. But I know different. I *know* he was murdered." She met their stares. "And I want you to prove it."

K.C. Wells has an active imagination. Sometimes it produces rainbows and unicorns, but occasionally something darker emerges…

She lives on an island off the south coast of the UK where her favourite writing spot is the Lighthouse. The waves crash against the rocks, the wind howls, and she lets her imagination loose to follow its convoluted path, meeting diverse characters with stories to be told – and twists in the tale…

If you want to follow her exploits, you can sign up for her monthly newsletter: http://eepurl.com/cNKHlT

You can stalk – er, find – her in the following places:

Email: k.c.wells@btinternet.com
Facebook: www.facebook.com/KCWellsWorld
KC's men In Love (my readers group): http://bit.ly/2hXL6wJ
Amazon: https://www.amazon.com/K-C-Wells/e/B00AECQ1LQ
Twitter: @K_C_Wells
Website: www.kcwellswrites.com
Instagram: www.instagram.com/k.c.wells

Follow me on BookBub

K.C. WELLS

TRUTH WILL OUT

Merrychurch Mysteries: Book One

Jonathon de Mountford's visit to Merrychurch village to stay with his uncle Dominic gets off to a bad start when Dominic fails to appear at the railway station. But when Jonathon finds him dead in his study, apparently as the result of a fall, everything changes. For one thing, Jonathon is the next in line to inherit the manor house. For another, he's not so sure it was an accident, and with the help of Mike Tattersall, the owner of the village pub, Jonathon sets out to prove his theory—if he can concentrate long enough without getting distracted by the handsome Mike.

They discover an increasingly long list of people who had reason to want Dominic dead. And when events take an unexpected turn, the amateur sleuths are left bewildered. It doesn't help that the police inspector brought in to solve the case is the last person Mike wants to see, especially when they are told to keep their noses out of police business.

In Jonathon's case, that's like a red rag to a bull….

www.dreamspinnerpress.com

Merrychurch Mysteries: Book Two

Many consider Naomi Teedle the village witch. Most people avoid her except when they have need of her herbs and potions. She lives alone on the outskirts of Merrychurch, and that's fine by everyone—old Mrs. Teedle is not the most pleasant of people. But when she is found murdered, her mouth bulging with her own herbs and roots, suddenly no one has a bad word to say about her.

Jonathon de Mountford is adjusting to life up at the manor house, but it's not a solitary life: pub landlord Mike Tattersall sees to that. Jonathon is both horrified to learn of the recent murder and confused by the sudden reversal of public opinion. Surely someone in the village had reason to want her dead? He and Mike decide it's time for them to step in and "help" the local police with their investigation. Only problem is, their sleuthing uncovers more than one suspect—and the list is getting longer....

www.dreamspinnerpress.com

K.C. WELLS

A NOVEL MURDER

Merrychurch Mysteries: Book Three

Hosting the Merrychurch Literary Festival is just the distraction Jonathon de Mountford needs. Placating his father and keeping his boyfriend, Mike Tattersall, happy is proving an increasing struggle. But the small event takes on new proportions with the appearance of Teresa Malvain—former Merrychurch resident turned famous murder mystery novelist. But is something about the quaint village setting of her books a little too familiar?

Teresa's sudden death is certainly something right out of one of her stories, and Jonathan and Mike soon discover there are villagers who might not want the inspiration behind her books revealed.

When it emerges Teresa's severe allergic reaction was no accident, Jonathon and Mike are compelled to investigate, aided by a few people keen to help them discover the truth. But they're trying to work out what is fact and what is fiction, and the line between the two blurs constantly. And as for their relationship, Jonathon finally comes to a decision.....

www.dreamspinnerpress.com

MY FAIR BRADY

K.C. Wells

A spur-of-the-moment invitation
changes two lives.

A spur of the moment invitation changes two lives.

Jordan Wolf's company runs like a well-oiled machine. At least until his PA, Brady Donovan, comes down with the flu and takes sick leave. Then Jordan discovers what a treasure Brady is and who really keeps his business—and Jordan in particular—moving like clockwork. So when Jordan needs a plus-one, Brady seems the obvious choice to accompany him. After a major shopping trip to get Brady looking the part, however…. Wow.

Brady has a whole new wardrobe, and now his boss is whisking him away for a weekend party. Something is going on, something Brady never expected: Jordan is looking at him like he's never seen him before, electrifying Brady's long-hidden desires.

But can the romantic magic last when the weekend is over and it's back to reality?

www.dreamspinnerpress.com

BFF

K.C. WELLS

I'm about to do something huge, and it could change... everything.

I met Matt in second grade, and we've been inseparable ever since. We went to the same schools, studied at the same college. When we both got jobs in the same town, we shared an apartment. And when my life took an unexpected turn, Matt was there for me. Every milestone in my life, he was there to share it. And what's really amazing? After all these years, we're still the best of friends.

Which brings me to this fragile, heart-stopping moment: I want to tell him I love him, really love him, but I'm scared to death of what he'll say. If I've got this all wrong, I'll lose him—forever.